CHAOS

CHAOS

LANIE BROSS

DELACORTE PRESS

Text copyright © 2015 by Paper Lantern Lit, LLC
Jacket art copyright © 2015 by Mariesol Fumy/Trevillion Images

All rights reserved. Published in the United States by Delacorte Press, an imprint of Random House Children's Books, a division of Random House LLC, a Penguin Random House Company, New York.

Delacorte Press is a registered trademark and the colophon is a trademark of Random House LLC.

randomhouseteens.com

Educators and librarians, for a variety of teaching tools, visit us at RHTeachersLibrarians.com

Library of Congress Cataloging-in-Publication Data
Bross, Lanie.
   Chaos / Lanie Bross. — First edition.
      pages   cm
Summary: "Lucas must team up with a bank of Free Radicals to chip away at the plans of the Unseen Ones, attempting to unravel time and save Corinthe. New intrigue develops around Jasmine, as well as a compelling cast of Free Radicals"—Provided by publisher.
ISBN 978-0-385-74284-9 (hc : alk. paper) — ISBN 978-0-375-99080-9 (glb: alk. paper) — ISBN 978-0-307-97736-6 (ebook) [1. Fate and fatalism—Fiction. 2. Love—Fiction. 3. Supernatural—Fiction.] I. Title.
   PZ7.B7995178Ch 2015
   [Fic]—dc23
   2013041358

The text of this book is set in 12-point Cochin.
Book design by Stephanie Moss

Printed in the United States of America
10 9 8 7 6 5 4 3 2 1
First Edition

To my boys, who inspire and amaze me every day

1

"Close your eyes. Tell me what you see."

Luc scowled and crossed his arms. "How can we see anything with our eyes closed?"

"Just try."

Jasmine slipped her hand into her mother's and squeezed her eyes shut dutifully. It wasn't often that Mom took them out of the house anymore, and the trip to the Botanical Garden had been so spur-of-the-moment, so unexpected, that Mom had even forgotten to put Jasmine's shoes on. Jasmine was halfway to the car in socks before Luc had run after her, holding a pair of sneakers.

"Good girl." A soft hand rested on top of Jasmine's head, and fingers stroked her long dark hair. "Now take a deep breath. What do you see?"

Jasmine inhaled a breath as big as her lungs would

allow. A color came to her. Yellow. "Lemon?" she asked hesitantly.

"Yes. And what else?"

Luc snorted but Jasmine ignored him. He was going to ruin it. It felt so good to have Mom close, to feel her delicate fingers running through her hair again. She wanted to make her happy more than anything in the world.

"Strawberry," she said. "I see a strawberry."

Mom crouched down beside her. "That's good. What else?"

Jasmine took another deep breath and concentrated with every ounce of her being. She squeezed her eyes so tight, she saw little bursts of color. Bursts like fat fists. Fat fists like bright blooms. The heady aroma wrapped around Jasmine, filling her lungs, her veins with the throbbing scent.

"What do you see, Jas?" her mother prompted.

"I see . . . the flowers Daddy brought you for your birthday, only . . . brighter."

Her mother's delighted laughter sounded like music. "You can open your eyes now."

She did, feeling a rush of triumph. She had done it. She had made her mom laugh.

But when she opened her eyes, her mom was gone. Luc was gone. She was alone in a lush forest where the trees seemed to be whispering to each other. If she listened hard enough, she could make out what they said, except for an annoying whine coming from overhead.

"Mom?" The sharp bite of panic put an edge in her voice.

An ache started in her stomach, like she hadn't eaten for a week, and she doubled over from the pain.

Blood pounded in her ears, drowning out all other sounds.

Then a voice called to her out of the fog. Luc? She tried calling out, but her mouth wouldn't form words.

The whining returned, louder and filled with rage. It filled her head, pushed to get out until she thought her body would explode. In a moment of clarity, she knew what was happening.

She was dying.

"Jas, I'm coming. . . ." It was Luc.

But before he reached her, she fell.

Jasmine jolted awake, gasping for air. It took her a second to recognize that she was in her own bed, her own room. The heavy perfume that had haunted her dream clung to her sheets and her hair.

Outside her window, the sun had begun to rise, and the sky was alight with streaks of red and orange. Cracks in the plaster ceiling revealed intricate patterns, spidering outward into a twisted mass, like tree limbs in winter. Someone had made coffee and the aroma made her feel nauseated.

Jasmine sat up slowly, waiting for the usual fuzzy-headedness that followed getting high, but there was none. In fact, things were sharper than they'd ever been.

Except for her memory. Her memory was a blank. Had she partied too hard?

Carefully, she pushed the blanket aside and swung her legs over the side of the bed. Her muscles ached as she stretched her arms overhead. Jas waited for the room to tilt, for the bile to rise in her throat. But it didn't happen. She scanned her desk for her phone, but it was nowhere in sight. The clock on her nightstand read 8:42 a.m.

What the hell had happened? How had she ended up back in bed? What had she taken last night? She was hangover-free, at least. She felt clear, alert.

So why couldn't she remember?

Jasmine slipped on a pair of jeans that were slung over the chair. She looked at herself in the mirror on the back of her closet door. Her hair was a wild dark mess splayed out in a million directions, but her skin looked oddly glowing, as though she were standing in a patch of sunlight.

She shook her head. It was as if a curtain had been pulled over her memory. She could catch only glimpses, snippets of images, when the curtain fluttered.

T.J.

She was meeting him at the marina, but why?

Jasmine grabbed her favorite threadbare black sweater on her way out of the room. It was June in San Francisco and she was freezing. Maybe she'd been sick. Fever or flu or something. It would explain the whacked-out dreams she'd had.

Jasmine walked into the kitchen and found Luc sitting at their tiny table, absently looking out the window. There was an untouched piece of toast in front of him. Coffee was brewing, but it barely masked the scent of stale cigarette smoke.

"Hey," she said. He looked up, relief evident on his face.

"How are you feeling?" He pulled out the chair next to him and motioned for her to sit.

Uh-oh. Luc was in *serious mode*. His eyes were blood-shot and there were dark circles beneath them. It reminded her too much of when she'd woken up in the hospital after her overdose.

Oh God, had it happened again? Why couldn't she remember anything? Everything was a haze, and her last clear recollection was of Friday night. She'd gone to meet T.J. to break it off with him.

"Am I in trouble?" Her voice was hoarse, like it hadn't been used in awhile.

"What? No. Not at all." He shifted in the cracked plastic chair and looked at her. "I'm just . . . glad you're okay."

"What happened last night? I went to the marina, but after that . . ."

Luc shook his head. It put her on edge when he was quiet like this—like there was bad news he was trying to break to her. Like when he had to explain to her that their mom had died.

Wait. Had someone died?

Jasmine looked around the apartment. Dad wasn't on the couch, where he could usually be found sleeping off a hangover. Dread pooled in her stomach.

"Dad?" The word squeezed out through her tight throat. "Did something happen to Dad?"

"No, he's okay," Luc said. "He checked into some res-idential detox program."

"He *what*?"

"He decided he wanted to get sober," Luc said, pok-ing at the toast. "After you came home he said he wanted to get sober for us."

Jas couldn't understand how casually her brother was treating the news. Their dad was not the kind of man who asked for help, who admitted to an addiction.

"Which hospital? I need to see this for myself." She stood up and immediately felt dizzy, like the floor was drop-ping out from under her. She placed a hand on the table to steady herself.

"Whoa," Luc said, standing to ease her back into the chair. "We're not going anywhere. Not yet, at least. The roads are still a mess and you've been gone for two days—"

"Two days? It's *Saturday*," she interrupted. "What are you talking about? And why are the roads a mess?"

"Jas, it's Sunday," Luc said. "And there was an earth-quake . . ."

"That's impossible," she insisted. Nothing felt famil-iar. The single bulb over their heads flickered; she felt a sting of pain as if the light shot straight through her brain. This was worse than a hangover, she was sure. She rubbed her throbbing temple and tried to focus.

Why couldn't she remember what had happened after the marina? If she went to see T.J., it was possible she took something—but she hadn't *wanted* to take anything after the overdose. Not ever again.

"What happened to me, Luc? It wasn't drugs again, was it?" She had to be sure.

"No." He scrubbed his fingers through his hair, exhaled deeply. "I found you at the rotunda. There was this woman, Miranda . . ." He cut himself off. "You know what? It's not really important. The important thing is that you're home and that you're careful from now on."

"How can I be careful if I don't know what happened?"

"Jas, so much has happened in the last couple of days." He closed his eyes and took a ragged breath in. "Can we talk about this later?"

The last thing she wanted to do was talk about it later. He was keeping something from her and she wanted answers—now. But she could tell that Luc was upset. He'd done so much for her over the years, taken care of her when their dad hadn't. If he needed time, she would give it to him.

"Fine," she said as she leaned back in the chair. "But I need to get out of this apartment."

Luc had been more overprotective than ever, and it had taken a whole lot of convincing for him to stay home. He looked exhausted anyway, and Jasmine needed to be alone to think. She walked to the end of the street, where a large dump truck sat rumbling. Jasmine could smell the diesel in the air as men in yellow hardhats moved around the street, patching gaps in the sidewalk. A lamppost sagged close to the ground, and the fence of a parking lot bowed out toward the street.

California Pacific Medical Center was in walking distance, but she moved slowly, still recovering from the headache. She wondered about her dad's sudden change of heart. Why check himself into a program now? She could barely remember that warm, caring father — the one who threw her up in the air and called her his princess. Maybe deep down, she had always hoped he'd come back.

Jasmine passed a small café and could almost smell the roasted beans and buttery pastries. Her stomach churned, but she couldn't be sure if it was the smell of food or her own nerves. What if her dad wasn't really there? Or worse, what if he was sicker than Luc had suggested?

A deep pain returned to her temples, and Jasmine rubbed at the spots with her fingers. The light and noise drove tiny knives into her skull. The sounds of construction surrounded her — men drilling into the concrete and dump trucks collecting debris. It was too much. Every sound built on another until it reached a crescendo.

Jas walked faster, and she caught her breath when the hospital entrance came into sight. She had been brought here when she overdosed, and hoped to never come back. And now, here she was.

She needed to sit down for a minute, to tune everything out.

The doors whooshed open and Jasmine walked to the reception desk, leaning on it as she regained her senses. The smell of chemicals made her stomach flip.

"Are you okay?" the woman at the desk asked. She looked concerned.

"Yes—yes, of course," Jasmine stammered. "I'm here to see a patient. Jack Simmons?"

The woman nodded, then tapped on her keyboard. Jasmine looked around and realized how chaotic it was. Nurses and doctors hurried up and down the hallways, and the waiting room was overrun with people. A man was being treated in the hallway, a nurse in green scrubs wrapping a white bandage around his head. A doctor in a lab coat pushed along a woman in a wheelchair, barely missing Jasmine's foot.

Jas swallowed uncomfortably.

"Room one twenty-nine," the woman behind the desk said. "Down the hall, take the first right, and then push through the double doors and take a left."

"Thank you," Jasmine said. She willed her feet to move down the hallway. The deeper she went into the hospital, the stronger the smell of disinfectant was. It clawed at her throat, and she had to cover her mouth and put her head down.

The gray tiles under her feet didn't change as she walked, so she turned left and started to count them. When she got to twenty-two, she looked up and saw that she was only steps away from the room number the woman at the front desk had given her.

One twenty-nine.

Jasmine stood at the doorway. A soft *beep-beep* came from a machine at her father's bedside. The overwhelming scent of antiseptic filled her lungs.

This was a mistake. She turned and almost ran into a nurse.

"Hello. Are you a relative?" the nurse asked.

"His daughter," Jasmine managed to get out around her constricted throat. "Is he okay?"

"He's suffering from severe alcohol withdrawal. It's a good thing he checked himself into our detoxification program when he did."

"And how long will he be here?" She avoided looking in her father's direction. He looked small and sickly against the white sheets of the hospital bed.

"He'll need to meet with a mental-health professional. Then he'll begin a weeklong inpatient stay." The woman placed her tray down and checked his monitor. "He was given a sedative to help with the withdrawal symptoms for now, but you can say hello if you'd like."

"No, no, it's fine," Jas said, backing away from the bed.

"But there are no visitors allowed during the program. . . ."

"You said it was a week long?" Jas asked. "I can wait until he's out." She'd gone a week without seeing her dad before. At least he was here instead of passed out at O'Rourke's pub. She didn't want to say hello; she wanted to run away as fast as possible. The lights overhead made dots dance in her vision, and the sickly-sweet scent of hand sanitizer coated her tongue. She needed to get out, now.

She turned and ran.

At the end of the hall, she saw a bright red Exit sign and focused on it.

The doors exploded open under her hands.

Outside, she hesitated for just a second before turning left and running faster. Her only thought was to put distance between herself and the hospital as quickly as possible. She ran down Sacramento, turned right onto Fillmore, and then left, where a tilted sign indicated she was now on Clay Street.

She slowed to a walk, amazed that she didn't even feel winded. Luc always made fun of her for being a sloth, just because she didn't see the point of running up and down a field and kicking a ball into a net. And it was true she did fake illnesses a lot to get out of gym class. One time she'd even claimed she was coming down with whooping cough.

Since when could she run so fast?

She felt strangely alive, buzzing. Beneath the squealing of tires and occasional blaring of alarms and car horns, it was as though the air itself was speaking to her. She felt *connected* to everything—to the people lighting a fire in the alleyway as she passed by, to an old lady walking across the street, to the old lady's small dog. She could *feel* them, could feel what they were feeling. *Hunger. Loneliness. Curiosity.* She could suddenly sense all of it around her, as though the whole world's volume had been turned up.

Just across the street Jas saw Alta Plaza Park, which had not been damaged too badly by the earthquake. A longing rose up, fierce and fast, to run her fingers through the grass and inhale the moisture of the ground.

The wind whispered through the trees and she imagined it was saying *Jasmine*. She was halfway across the street before she even realized she had moved.

"You're supposed to block the ball, you shithead!" a voice shouted. The loud, familiar shout was followed by laughter.

Tyler, Justin, and Devon, all in their soccer uniforms, were kicking a soccer ball around the field just next to the trees. Jas ducked into the grove of trees. The last thing she wanted to do was explain to those guys what she was doing on this side of town on a Sunday.

She didn't trust them enough not to spread it around school that her dad was in the hospital, either.

She sat down and closed her eyes. The sounds she heard brought colors to mind—the bright blue *shush* of the ball through the grass, yellow explosions of voices, the deep purple of the wind. It made her feel a little dizzy.

She must have hit her head on something, *really* hard.

She didn't know how long she'd been sitting there, motionless, when she realized that Tyler and the others had gone. She peeked out from the trees and saw them, distantly, at the other side of the park, getting into a car she recognized as Tyler's.

She stood up, leaning against the trunk of a tree for support. There was a faint pulsing under her fingers, through the rough bark. The air shifted. She felt as if the tree was a hand, warm and inviting; she could feel its sap like blood. A high-pitched whine started in her head, just like in her dream, and it made her pulse leap. When she inhaled, there were new aromas, exotic ones that had no place in the middle of San Francisco.

She could hear everything: not just the wind through the leaves, but the clouds floating overhead, the trees inhaling and exhaling.

And . . . footsteps.

Two people were with her in the grove talking in hushed tones. A boy and a girl.

"I don't see him anywhere," the girl said.

"He is expendable. She's the one we're after." The boy sounded cold and determined.

Their whispers were as clear as if they were talking directly to Jasmine.

Jasmine felt uneasy, filled with a buzzing electricity that came from the air, from the wind, from the trees. She crouched in the cluster of trees, listening. She heard the wisp of metal against denim, knew instinctively that one had just pulled out a knife.

"There she is!" the girl shouted, pointing in Jasmine's direction.

A shock of red hair flashed between the branches as the girl fought her way toward Jasmine. The boy, a dark figure dressed in camo pants and a black hooded sweatshirt pulled low over his face, threw himself at the thick curtain of leaves between them, slicing through them with his blade.

The tree screamed—or maybe the screaming was just in her head. Jasmine felt hurt as though it were her own body that had been cut. She moved in the opposite direction. Her skin screamed in pain as she backed up against the trunk. The whine got louder, but the boy didn't appear to hear it at all.

He lunged again, and the noise grew deafening. Bloodlust ran through her veins like a fever. Without thinking, she grabbed the boy's wrist and twisted it forcefully, sending the knife to the ground. His eyes grew wide and he tried to get away, but he couldn't. Jasmine was stronger, and yet she felt completely wild—she had no control over this strength, no idea where it came from.

Her fingers slid around his throat and she started to squeeze.

The hood of his sweatshirt fell back.

A calm deadliness settled over the grove.

The scent of blood filled the small grove. Instinct took over.

The sharp points of her teeth felt unfamiliar against her tongue.

"Jas!" A voice pierced through the high-pitched sound at the edges of her mind.

Jasmine stopped to listen. Luc appeared several feet away, gasping for breath, and stopped when he saw her, his eyes wide with disbelief. Reality seeped into Jas, cooling the bloodlust, and her grip loosened.

What the hell was wrong with her? She let go of the boy and he stumbled back a few feet, where he fell onto his hands and knees, gasping for air.

Luc started toward Jasmine but then stopped and

picked something up off the ground. The boy's knife. He paled and spun around, facing the boy.

"What the hell are you doing here?" Luc demanded.

The boy just stared up at Luc with a mixture of pain and resolve on his face.

Luc stood over him with the knife clenched in his fist. Oh God, was he going to hurt the guy because of her? This was all so wrong. The whining had stopped, and now Jasmine heard the familiar sounds of the city. Her hands still shook, and she could still feel the faint beating of the boy's pulse under her fingertips. The lust for blood was gone too, and she felt sick, like she'd just ridden a mega roller coaster.

Something horrible had taken over inside her, and the worst part was that it felt so natural.

"Luc?"

He glanced over his shoulder at her.

She saw the hesitation on his face.

The fear.

Was he afraid for her or *of* her?

"We're only doing what we must." The girl stepped hesitantly from behind a tree. Her palms were turned up to show she wasn't armed. "You of all people must understand that."

Luc growled at the girl, "Haven't they taken enough already?"

Jasmine looked from Luc to the girl. Did they know each other?

"We don't make the rules," she said with a shrug.

Her casualness seemed to make Luc even madder. "*I* don't believe in your rules. That should be clear by now."

Jasmine watched the exchange, growing more confused by the second.

"You know how this has to end," the girl said. With a wary eye on Luc, she walked over to the boy and helped him stand.

They disappeared, and Jasmine sagged under the weight of what had happened. Luc wrapped his arm around her shoulder, pulling her against his chest.

"I don't understand." Jasmine felt as though she'd stepped out of a nightmare into that place where dreams and reality are still mixed together. "What just happened? Who were those people?"

"Shhh. It's okay." She couldn't help but notice how his voice shook.

Jas wanted to believe him, but it didn't feel like things were ever going to be okay.

How *was* this all supposed to end?

2

Luc paced in the kitchen. Jasmine was taking a shower. It was pure luck he'd seen Jasmine at that park. He saw the boy first, creeping around with what looked like a knife in his hand, and had reacted instinctively. Some loser, he'd thought, out to rob someone, or worse.

And then he'd seen Jas, and the real fear had kicked in. She'd looked too much like how he'd found her in the Forest of the Blood Nymphs: pale and feral and deadly.

But just as quickly, she was his little sister again, scared and confused.

They'd walked to the bus stop after Jasmine insisted she didn't need to go back to the hospital to have the cut on her arm looked at. The wound stopped bleeding almost immediately, but Luc couldn't relax. Dread was still a solid mass in his stomach.

Jasmine thought the attack was random, but he knew better. The knife he had found was achingly familiar.

Corinthe had had one exactly like it.

Just thinking Corinthe's name sent a pang through his chest. He missed her. He needed her.

She was his other. He knew it now, and he'd stop at nothing to get her back. He remembered sitting in the Great Gardens of Pyralis Terra. Corinthe lay dying, her head in his lap. They were surrounded by millions of stars.

"Please stay with me, Corinthe. Be with me. Choose me. I need you."

Her smile this time was the barest flicker, like a candle trying to stand up to a storm.

"I did choose you, Luc. Luc . . . I . . ."

That was the last thing she said before her eyes closed. He had promised her then that he'd find a way for them to be together again, and that promise fed the fire in his gut. He would never give up on her. But it appeared as though the Unseen Ones were trying to stop him already.

Luc would bet anything that the boy and girl who had attacked Jas were Executors, just like Corinthe had been: servants of order charged with making sure that what was fated came to pass.

It wasn't just the knife that proved it—it was what the girl had said about *only doing what they must.* Corinthe talked like that.

Corinthe *used* to talk like that.

But if they *were* Executors, why were they after Jasmine? He knew Executors faced severe penalties if they failed in their tasks. Hell. Corinthe had been tasked with his death—at least, that's what she believed—and she'd pursued him across worlds.

She was different, though. Corinthe questioned things. She was relentlessly fierce but also so vulnerable; he remembered being with her in the Land of the Two Suns, and how she had fallen asleep in his arms by the fire.

Ultimately, she'd sacrificed her life to save his.

Corinthe was dead. Pyralis had been saved. Order had been restored. So why had Jas been attacked? And why, then, had the Executors retreated? It didn't make sense.

Unless . . .

Unless the Executors hadn't been sent to kill Jas.

Was the attack a message to him? Did the Unseen Ones know what he intended to do?

Maybe the fact that Luc had found Jasmine mid-attack wasn't coincidence after all.

Earlier, Luc had gone looking for the Crossroad, but in a city as big as San Francisco, in the aftermath of the worst earthquake in two decades, it was an impossible task. Still, his instincts were different than they had been. Traveling across universes, seeing worlds where order ticked like a clock and places where shadows and people lived separately—it had changed him, somehow.

Losing Corinthe had changed him.

And he had the archer, the necklace Corinthe had given him, which would function as a compass to lead him to another world. He would use it to find the Crossroad that would lead him to Rhys, his friend from the Land of the Two Suns. Rhys had told him once that he turned back time. Luc would find him and have him do it again. They would rewind time and save Corinthe before any of this had happened.

In the bathroom, the water stopped running. A second later, Luc heard Jasmine begin to hum—some new indie song no one but fifteen people had ever listened to, he had no doubt. The sound made his chest ache. When Jas had disappeared, he'd been terrified he'd never have her home, and safe, again. How could he endanger her? If he continued looking for a way to save Corinthe, would the Executors go after Jasmine again? Would they succeed in hurting her?

He needed to make sure Jas stayed safe.

Then, if he could find the Crossroad, he could draw the Executors' attention to himself. Having Executors after him was old news. He could handle it. After he found Rhys and got the information he needed, he could save Corinthe and then things would be over for good.

Back to normal.

Happily ever after.

In the meantime, Jasmine couldn't know what was going on. Especially not how she had almost died in the Forest of the Blood Nymphs. If he tried to tell her— about Executors, and Crossroad, and other worlds, and Corinthe—she'd probably think the earthquake had shaken something loose in his brain.

He needed to protect her, and that meant she had to be protected from the truth.

The idea came to him at once: Aunt Hillary. As soon as the blow-dryer started going in the bathroom, Luc punched their aunt's number into his cell phone, praying she'd be at home and would agree to take care of Jasmine for a few days.

She was home, and she was as snippy as ever. Aunt Hillary had the personality of an ice pick. But she agreed to come pick Jasmine up in forty minutes.

Luc put down the phone, feeling slightly better. Aunt Hillary's house smelled like peppermint and lavender. She kept about a dozen cats around, too, and she had a way of making even comments about the weather sound like insults. Jasmine would be bored out of her mind.

Which was kind of the point.

Jas emerged from the bathroom in her familiar pink robe, her long hair, now dry, hanging loosely down to her waist. For a moment, Luc imagined it was a normal day—before the earthquake, before Jasmine's capture by Miranda, before the Land of the Two Suns and Rhys and the world of memory mists.

Before Corinthe.

But when Jas scooted past him and reached for a mug, the long red scratch on her arm proved the past few days hadn't been some kind of crazy, tangled dream.

He swallowed the lump in his throat. He would never be at peace until he found a way to save Corinthe. In a universe full of hundreds and thousands of worlds, there had to be a way to bring someone back from the dead. Giving up was not an option.

"That shower felt amazing." Jasmine smiled, and he

felt a surge of hope. His sister *was* okay. She was home safe.

Anything was possible and that proved it.

She filled the mug with water, stuck it in the microwave, and punched start. "Tea?"

"No thanks." He took pleasure in watching her stretch on her tiptoes to reach the tea, rustle through the cabinets for honey—familiar, everyday motions. But it couldn't last. Not yet. He cleared his throat. "Look, I need you to get dressed and pack a bag with some things."

She looked at him with her eyebrows drawn down. "Where are we going?"

"*You* are going to Aunt Hillary's for a few nights. I have something I need to do."

"Aunt Hillary?" Jasmine echoed. She shook her head and returned to spooning honey into the mug. "No way. I'll just hang out here. I've stayed alone a thousand times."

"I don't want you home alone," Luc said sharply. Jasmine looked at him. He took a deep breath. "Look, there are things going on that I can't explain right now. I need to know you're safe."

Jasmine turned to face him, crossing her arms. "Tell me," she said. "Whatever it is, I can handle it." She looked away. "Did I . . . was it something I took, Luc? Is that why I can't remember anything?"

Her voice trembled a little, and it made his heart ache. Jas had OD'd earlier in the spring. A combination of Ecstasy and alcohol. Since then, she had sworn she would stay off drugs, sworn she would stick with a psychiatrist. But Luc had spent months feeling like at any second, disaster would strike and he would lose her.

And then he *had* lost her—to Miranda, and the Forest of the Blood Nymphs.

He reached out and touched her shoulder. "You didn't do anything wrong. And when this is over, I'll tell you everything." Maybe.

Jasmine's dark eyes clicked back to his. "Promise on Mom?"

He made an X over his heart. "Promise on Mom. But for tonight, you go with Aunt Hillary. I already called her and she said it was okay. She's on her way."

Jasmine groaned. "What am I supposed to say when she starts asking about Dad?"

"You like fairy tales," Luc said, cracking a small smile. "Spin her a good one."

"Do I have to?" Jas asked as she sipped her tea.

Luc lifted his hands behind his neck and looked at the ceiling. After a long exhale, he let his hands fall to his sides and glanced at Jas. "It won't be for long. Just trust me, okay? Now please go get dressed and pack a bag so we don't keep her waiting."

Jasmine sighed exaggeratedly, but she didn't protest any more. She went down the hall to her room and closed the door. Luc glanced at the time. Ten o'clock. As soon as Jas was safely off, he'd use the archer to begin his search for the Crossroad.

He already knew where he would look first: the Land

of the Two Suns on the outskirts of the universe. Rhys knew secrets about the universe; he was the one who had told Corinthe and Luc about the flower needed to save Jasmine from the Forest of the Blood Nymphs.

Rhys would know how Luc could undo everything and save Corinthe.

Every time he closed his eyes, he saw her slipping from him, the sky lit up in oranges and reds as if a bomb had exploded the stars. He'd promised her that he would find a way to be with her.

He'd promised it to himself.

"I tore apart this apartment and I must've lost my phone last night—I mean, Friday night," Jasmine said, fifteen minutes later. She emerged from her room carrying a small backpack. Her dark hair was pulled into a ponytail, and without makeup on, she looked young and innocent. Like the sister he remembered. "What am I supposed to do without it? I still don't know why I can't stay *here*."

"The people who attacked you today might have followed us home." He debated whether to tell her more and finally settled for saying, "The truth is, I think I might know who they are."

"You know them?" Jasmine's eyes practically popped out of her head.

"I . . . recognized them," he said cautiously. "At least, I think I did. I'm going to find out for sure."

"They had knives, Luc," Jasmine said softly.

"Don't worry, I'm not going to do anything dumb. Not until I know for sure, anyway." He grinned at her, hoping she'd return the smile. But she just stood there, staring, looking troubled.

A loud car horn sounded outside and Luc went to the window. An old Buick was parked downstairs. Definitely Aunt Hillary. When he turned, Jasmine's chin was trembling.

"This just feels wrong," she said.

He crossed the room and gave her a big hug. "Everything will be okay, I swear it, Jas." He'd been making that promise a lot lately.

She pulled away and made a face. "You are going to owe me so big."

He smiled. He nudged her shoulder with his and picked up her bag. "You used to tell me that Aunt Hillary reminded you of the Wicked Witch of the West."

"I think it's the wart on her chin," Jasmine said, and they both laughed. Then she got serious again. "You be careful, okay?"

"I will," he said, and mentally added, *I hope.*

They walked down the two flights of stairs to the main door. Outside, the air was cool, and still layered with a fine white dust kicked up from the earthquake. It shimmered almost like snow in the air.

Aunt Hillary blasted her horn again. Luc rolled his eyes. Didn't she see them right there? He jogged down the porch steps and yanked open the door to the dinosaur-era Buick. A blast of peppermint-lavender scent hit him right in the face.

Aunt Hillary hadn't changed at all. Her hair was twisted into a tight knot, and she had on the brightest orange lipstick he'd ever seen. The wart on her chin trembled as if it, too, were impatient. Her fingers, which tapped impatiently on the steering wheel, were covered in gaudy rings.

"Well, look at you two." The tone of her voice made it clear she didn't think they looked good. "*He* couldn't even bother to come down and see you off. Or is he keeping a barstool warm already?"

Luc ignored her and stood back to let Jasmine climb in.

"Big-time," Jasmine whispered, and then plastered on a smile. "Hi, Aunt Hillary."

"Don't you look just like your mother with your hair like that. Everyone always said she was a beauty, but I never saw it myself."

Let the insults begin.

"I won't be long," Luc said, ducking his head to address the words to Jasmine.

"Let's get moving, then," Aunt Hillary said. "Do you have any idea what the roads are like? You'd think a city this size, on the West Coast, would be able to recover from an earthquake faster than this."

Jasmine gave him a look that begged *please let me stay and I'll join a convent and never say a bad word again,* but he just leaned in and kissed her cheek. The sooner he got started, the sooner it would all be over. He hoped.

"This neighborhood certainly looks *interest*—" Aunt Hillary's voice cut off when he shut the door.

Jasmine glared at him out the window as the car crept down the block. Luc watched until it turned and disappeared, then ran back upstairs to grab his backpack and a jacket. The Land of the Two Suns got very cold at night, and this time, he'd be ready.

Luc stepped outside their apartment and pulled the archer from his pocket. It popped open and the tiny figure began to spin. It slowed and nearly came to a stop, pointing east.

Luc moved in that direction, his instincts sharper than they had been. Traveling across the universe, seeing worlds where order ticked like a clock or oceans were composed of shadows—it had changed him, somehow.

The archer, the necklace he had taken from Rhys, would function as a compass and lead him to another world. It pointed toward Market Square.

When he reached Third Street, the archer's bow quivered right and left.

Luc's heartbeat stuttered with it.

The Crossroad had to be close.

The sun had already dipped below the tops of the buildings around him. Power had not been restored to this part of the city yet, so dusk sat heavy; the buildings were dark brushstrokes against the faded-denim-blue sky. With most of the shops in this area closed, the streets were largely quiet and empty of people, except for the sounds of work crews close by.

It was a long shot, but he didn't have anywhere else to start.

The archer had stopped with its tiny arrow pointed toward the Market Square angel.

Luc circled the angel statue, the same way he had that

morning. The archer swung safely on the chain around his neck. He hoped this was an entrance to the Crossroad.

Corinthe had told him to look for something out of place, something not quite right; inconsistencies, flaws in the logical tapestry of the world, were a sign of an entrance. He stared up at the angel, its pose strikingly similar to the enormous, blank-faced statues that had come alive and granted him passage to the Great Gardens in Pyralis.

He did a double take. The angel's wings had been raised toward the sky earlier, he'd swear it. Now they were folded together, lowered.

The back of his neck prickled and his breathing sped up. Luc looked around to be sure no one was watching, then reached under his shirt to pull out the archer.

It leads you to your heart's desire.

Rhys.

Luc closed his eyes and chanted the man's name over and over in his head. He pictured the Land of the Two Suns.

The tiny archer spun around in circles and Luc held his breath. *Come on.*

For what seemed like an eternity, the archer simply continued to spin. Luc's chest was tight with impatience. After several long seconds, disappointment numbed his hands. The archer was still turning, as fast as ever. Maybe he'd misremembered the position of the statue's wings. Maybe he'd wanted to find the Crossroad so badly, he'd invented one.

But just then, the archer stopped, its arrow pointing directly at the statue's stone wings.

Just like that, Luc was flooded with excitement. His hands shook slightly as he circled the statue. The wings seemed to shimmer in front of his eyes, and when he reached up to touch them, they spread upward in a graceful arch and a flash of blinding light took his breath away.

The force of the sudden winds blew him backward, and Luc found himself falling through darkness and shrieking noise. For a moment, he panicked, and he felt a hundred thousand invisible fingers ripping at his body. He had to focus or he'd be lost in the Crossroad forever.

He gripped the archer and pictured Rhys surrounded by red sand and a black ocean.

Take me to Rhys.

3

Miranda paced back and forth inside her cell. The constant pulse of this living world, in the walls, the ground, the air, reminded her that her time was limited. Each thump a moment closer to her death.

What did it matter now? Corinthe was dead and Pyralis was intact.

The Unseen Ones had won again.

Miranda hadn't even fought the Tribunal when they sent several Radicals to bring her back to Vita to await trial. Once, the idea of the Tribunal would have been inconceivable. Once, the Radicals had lived up to their name: full of passion and energy and war. But no more. The Unseen Ones had squeezed them slowly into submission, had turned the Free Radicals into slaves.

The world the Tribunal called home was unlike any

in the universe, and though she was being held there as a prisoner, Miranda had to admit that it was a strangely beautiful place.

Strange, to be imprisoned inside a vast living creature.

The bars of her cell resembled twisting strings of DNA, forever moving, undulating, unbreakable. They shone like polished silver, catching bits of light as they moved, and were razor sharp. Each time she stepped close, bits of bright light sizzled along the thread of living molecules, electrifying the bars. Miranda knew that one touch would send a deadly shock through her body.

Her cell hung suspended above the tissuey floor of the main chamber, and a thin membrane resembling skin stretched above and below her, making the floor of her cell sink slightly when she moved.

Outside her cell rose great white spires of bone, curving like ribs around a cavernous space that housed the pulsing life center of Vita. Here is where the Tribunal handed down punishments.

There had been no sign of the council members in the days—or was it weeks?—since she'd been dragged here. But now, as Miranda watched, flickers of light began appearing all around the dais. Steam rose from the ground and, one by one, the members of the Tribunal slowly assumed corporeal form.

Dread spread through Miranda. This was it. They were assembling for her trial.

Tess's familiar form materialized and Miranda felt the

dull ache of her loss—they shared the same matter, but Tess had made it clear Miranda was now on her own.

One chair remained empty: Rhys's. Secretly she had been hoping that despite everything, he might come to her defense. Stupid. The last time they talked, he made it clear that there was nothing left between them. Rhys had chosen to die an outcast. It was the reality of those who chose to live free. It was also why Miranda had tried to change things. One force should not rule the universe in its entirety. Fate must learn to bow to chance.

But Rhys had refused to fight with her.

The great love they had shared was gone.

He would not come to her rescue.

There was no one to speak on her behalf, which would make the Tribunal's job that much easier. Sirius sat in the center, the spot reserved for the oldest star in the universe, and waved his hand. The swirling bars in front of Miranda fell away, leaving one side of her prison open.

"Miranda, you have been charged with treason against the Tribunal. Your actions nearly caused our ruination. You behaved recklessly and without consideration of the Tribunal's wishes. What have you to say to this?"

A fire-haired woman had stood and was addressing Miranda. Councilwoman Basia. One of the first Radicals, and much too conservative for Miranda's taste. Of course she would be the one to pass judgment.

Rebellion flared inside Miranda like a flame. This was the source of her power, the true source of all the Radicals' power—the desire to be free. The resistance to following rules. "You are content to sit and do nothing while the Unseen Ones treat you like caged dogs. You, our *leaders*, have suppressed us to the point of extinction. So why shouldn't we fight for our lives? We are Radicals. Once whole worlds bowed before us, and any one of us was strong enough to split the fabric of the universe in two."

Murmurs ran among the Tribunal. Some members looked angry, while others looked scared.

"You say you have a grand plan," Miranda continued, "but in the meantime we are dying. By the time you realize you were wrong, it will be too late." She wanted to shriek, to reach through the bars of her cage and shake every one of them, but even if she could reach them, they would never understand. They had grown too content. They had forgotten their true purpose. "We weaken each time a Radical dies. Our power is in our numbers, can't you see that?"

"Excuse me, Tribunal, may I speak?" Tess stepped up before the council and Miranda stared. She had not expected this.

Several council members protested, but the man in the middle silenced them with his hand. "You may."

"Miranda has always been hotheaded." Tess had taken a form Miranda had seen her use quite often, a human body with long brown dreadlocks. But her image flickered; she was obviously very tired. "Surely you can see that what she does is out of love for the Radicals."

This was certainly an unexpected twist. Here Tess

was, defending her against the Tribunal. Miranda's chest swelled with admiration and something deeper than that. Yes. With love. Tess was the closest thing Miranda had to a daughter. She was not alone after all.

"If you would extend mercy this one time, I'm sure she will abandon her idea of a revolution." Tess stared directly at Miranda, as though trying to communicate a warning to her. Miranda looked away. Tess might have been trying to help. But believing that Miranda would agree to bow to the wishes of the Tribunal proved that Tess really did not know her anymore.

"Tell us, Miranda. If we agree to leniency, will you stop this destructive path and abide by our rules?" The head council member stared directly at her.

"There can be no other answer but her death," a second councilman said. "*He* has escaped. If they should manage to join forces . . ." Though he spoke in a soft whisper, Miranda overheard.

They could only be talking about one person. Ford.

He was a Radical who believed, like her, that no one should dictate how others lived or died. And he would not let her rot here forever. Not when power was within his grasp.

The head council member ignored the objection. "If you accept our terms, you will remain imprisoned here at Vita for the rest of your days. But you will be allowed to live."

"What kind of life is that?" Miranda's hands shook with barely controlled rage and she clenched them into fists at her sides. How dare they insult her with such an offer? "You must all be mad. I'm a *true* Radical. I will have freedom or I will have nothing."

There were several explosions of light and sound as various Radicals temporarily lost control of their bodily forms.

"So you decline our offer of leniency?" the head council member asked.

"I *decline* to admit that I'm wrong. I choose to go down fighting, and you should, too." Miranda stood tall, her chin up in defiance. No matter what happened, she would never bow to their demands.

"Then as head council of the Tribunal, I sentence you, Miranda, to death, at the hour the sands of time have determined."

An enormous hourglass rose from the podium. Red sand immediately began to sift down into the bottom of the hourglass.

Miranda stared at her death sentence.

When the last grains of sand had passed through the hourglass, she would die.

4

The wind abruptly fell away. Luc found solid ground under his feet and staggered forward, off balance, doubled over by the heat. His sneakers sank into sand. When he opened his eyes, he saw the great red cliffs extending in a line as far as he could see. To his left was an ink-black ocean, washing silently against the sand.

He'd made it.

He turned slowly. Two suns burned brightly in an ash-white sky. In a weird way, it was good to be back. It made Corinthe feel closer. She had found him once, in this world, had wrestled him to the ground on top of the cliffs. He remembered how he'd pinned her to the ground, had seen himself reflected in her violet eyes, the color of a sunset sky. . . .

As if the world itself wanted to help him, a quick gust of wind burst across the sand and revealed a tiny crystal at his feet. It glittered in the suns and he bent to pick it up, sifting through the sand. He sucked in his breath.

In his palm he held Corinthe's crystal earring. She was wearing the pair when he first met her on Karen's houseboat, and had eventually given them to Rhys. Luc balled his fingers into a fist to try to crush the searing jolt of pain the memory caused.

Had Rhys left it here for Luc to find?

Luc covered his eyes and scanned the ocean of shadows, looking for the familiar silhouette of Rhys's sailboat. Nothing but black, all the way to the horizon.

Then something moved. Luc squinted. The horizon seemed to shift. Then it rose, as if a great wave were building out at sea. The tide of shadows drew back, so more and more of the red beach was exposed. It reminded Luc of pictures he'd seen of a tsunami; before the wave came, the tide abruptly went out, leaving a litter of seaweed and trash and driftwood behind.

What the hell was going on?

At the horizon, the wave was growing taller. Luc was standing on a vast stretch of flat desert where, only an instant before, the ocean had been. His throat was dry.

The wave began to move.

Shit.

It was surging toward him: a vast black shadow, tall as a mountain. Luc took a step back, then another, nearly tripping in the sand, until he felt the flat stone of the cliffs behind him. The wave was so tall it blocked out the sun. For a second, Luc was plunged into darkness.

Then the wave simply broke apart. Figments, shadow

people, poured out of the wave like foam surging off-shore. They crawled up the beach; they streamed past Luc without acknowledging him.

They were leaving. The Figments were leaving the Ocean of Shadows. Where was Rhys?

"Excuse me." He tried to grab at the nearest Figment; it was insubstantial as mist, and didn't look at him. He addressed another Figment. "Hey. I need to find Rhys. Do you know where I can find him? The chemist?"

Rhys was known for sailing the Ocean of Shadows, mixing potions to help the Figments survive their exile.

The Figments ignored him.

But then one turned its blank, dark face in his direction. "Come," it whispered, its voice gentle, soft. A girl's voice.

She merged with the group, and Luc followed, desperately trying to distinguish his guide from the thousands of other Figments flowing down the beach, moving parallel to the cliffs. He was sweating freely now. He took off his jacket and tied it around his waist as he slogged across the shifting sands. His throat was parched, and he was acutely aware of time passing.

At least Jas was safe.

Just when he feared he'd made a mistake, he saw the Figments ahead of him slipping through a thin fissure in the side of the cliff face, sucked like dark beads of liquid into a vertical mouth. It was so narrow, Luc could barely make it through sideways. After a few feet, the tunnel widened, and Luc could walk normally again. The ground sloped steeply upward, and rough-hewn stairs

were carved in the stone. A dim light shone from somewhere up ahead, illuminating just enough of the darkness
that Luc could follow the Figments.

It was hot and damp. The stairs were so steep Luc
walked practically doubled over, using the rock walls for
support. He felt dizzy with heat and closeness. Surely it
had been hours since they'd started walking. But he had
to keep going. He had to find Rhys.

After what seemed like an eternity, the slope leveled
off. In front of Luc was a makeshift door, a curtain made
from some kind of hide; the Figments passed through it
without so much as a rustle. Luc shoved aside the curtain and felt a rush of relief so strong he could have cried
out.

He had made it. This was the room where Rhys had
taken Corinthe to recover; this was where Rhys had told
Luc about the Flower of Life.

It was even warmer in here. A fire crackled in the
corner.

There was a dark shape lying in the bed.

Luc swallowed hard.

No.

The blind chemist lay tucked under the same quilt
Corinthe had used. Mags, his pet raven, sat perched on
the headboard, cawing softly.

"Ahhh, my boy. Welcome back. Welcome back."
Rhys's glazed eyes were fixed on the ceiling. But of
course, he had recognized Luc. Luc had stopped wondering how Rhys's sight worked.

Luc couldn't form words. It was obvious that Rhys

was dying. His face had lost almost all its color, and his cheeks were as sunken as those of a skeleton. The skin of his hands was paper thin, as if he'd aged a thousand years since Luc had last seen him.

Luc took the archer from around his neck and pressed it into Rhys's hand. It seemed the only thing he could do. "I'm sorry," he said. His voice broke and he cleared his throat. "I stole it from you."

Rhys shook his head, and returned the archer to Luc. "I won't need it again." A smile flickered across his face. "My time is done."

"But . . ." Luc shook his head. It was impossible. Rhys had been fine—strong, happy—when Luc had left him. "Only a few days ago—"

Rhys cut him off. "Time moves differently in every world, my boy. Time moves differently for everyone." Rhys gripped his blanket. "I went in quest of my one true love. I knew what I was risking. I am too weak, too old, too foolish. So I die an old fool. *I'm sorry, Miranda.*"

Rhys had his head turned away, so Luc didn't know if he'd heard the man correctly. Before he could ask, Rhys's sightless gaze was back on him. "What about you, my boy? Did you find your one true love?"

"Yes." It hurt too much to think about, much less talk about. He hadn't been able to share his grief. "But I lost her again. Corinthe died in Pyralis. She said it was how it had to be, but it can't be." He swallowed back the tightness in his throat. He could hardly breathe. "This can't be the end."

"I am sorry," Rhys said softly.

Luc looked down, blinking back tears. He'd come hoping that Rhys would help him; he was the Radical who had once turned back time. There had to be a way. Luc hadn't cried since Corinthe died. He wouldn't start now. Anger replaced his sorrow. "Her death was supposed to put everything right again. That's what she said. But just this morning, Executors attacked my sister. It was all supposed to stop. Why hasn't it all stopped?" Luc's voice cracked and he took a deep breath.

"The Unseen Ones work in mysterious ways," Rhys said, and Mags cawed in agreement.

"Bullshit." Luc was tired and desperate; he hadn't expected Rhys to stand up for the Unseen Ones. "You know that's bullshit. You warred against them once. You told me that you turned back time. Tell me how."

Rhys shook his head. "I may have misspoken that night. The drink, the celebration . . ."

Despair welled up inside Luc, causing his chest to tighten like a vise. "No. You said time and space flowed like water. You said that love was eternal. Now you're telling me it's a lie?"

Rhys sighed. "No, my boy, it's not a lie."

"Then help me. Please."

"Even if I wanted to, I can't. I'm not long for this world, or any other, for that matter." And it was true; Rhys seemed to be shrinking in front of Luc's eyes. "Remember, Luc. The path to righteousness goes straight through the heart."

"Riddles?" Luc was suffocating in the heat. He had crossed worlds to be here, and now Rhys was refusing to help. "I ask for an answer, and you give me riddles?"

"Life and death are the greatest riddles we must solve, aren't they?"

"Goddamn it, Rhys." Luc sank down on the edge of the bed and dropped his face into his hands. He had not thought about failure, because the thought of never seeing Corinthe again hurt too much. "No more riddles."

Now, Rhys, his last chance, was dying, and there was nothing else to do. Corinthe was lost to him forever. It *had* all been for nothing. She was wrong.

Agony burned inside Luc. He lifted his head, stared down at his friend through watery vision. "She was my Other. . . ." He trailed off. "I just want her back."

The bed shifted as Rhys, wincing in pain, pushed himself up onto his elbow. Luc heard his labored breath and thought how unfair it all was. Everyone was leaving him.

"What you want is not impossible." Rhys's voice was very soft. So soft that Luc thought he had misheard the man.

"What?" Luc's heart beat fast. He was afraid to breathe, in case Rhys would take it back.

"*Almost* impossible, maybe," Rhys said. His unseeing gaze drifted across the room as if he was remembering. A faint smile danced over his lips before his strength gave out and he sank back onto the bed.

Luc leaned over Rhys, holding the man's callused hand between his.

"Almost impossible, I can work with," Luc said desperately. *Almost* meant that there was a chance, however small.

Rhys smiled again, back in the present moment. "You are so like me. You are the way I once was. A passionate idiot." His smile faded. "There is only one person I know of who has the kind of power you need. But she might refuse to help you. Be prepared for disappointment."

"She?"

"Her name is Tess, and she is a Radical, like me." Rhys seemed about to say more, but then he shook his head and continued in a stronger voice: "She is strong-willed. There may be no swaying her to your side."

"What do I tell her?" Luc asked. "How can she help me?"

"She'll take you to the place—" Rhys wheezed, unable to finish his sentence. "She'll take you where you need to go. The Figments can help you find her. They will lead you to her." Rhys made a weak gesture with one hand; several Figments materialized from the flickering shadows in the cave.

Luc was desperate to leave, but the sudden sickly pallor of Rhys's skin made him hesitate. He couldn't let Rhys die alone.

As usual, it was as if the chemist could read his mind. "I told you. Time moves differently for everyone; but for everyone, time does run out. Such is the way of things. To die here, at home, is enough for me."

Emotion burned in Luc's throat. This would be the last time he would see his friend.

"My boy, don't be sorry. Death is a part of life." Rhys closed his eyes and for a wretched moment, Luc thought the man had died there next to him. But he opened his eyes once again. "You must go now. Time also does not stand still, waiting for us to act. Good luck, my boy. May you find what you seek."

"Thank you." The words seemed pathetic and insufficient, but Luc didn't know what else to say. "Thank you for everything. I will never forget you, I promise." He swallowed. His last words to Rhys were so thick they stuck in his throat. "Goodbye, Rhys."

"Goodbye, my boy," Rhys said, withdrawing his hand. He had a faint smile on his face, as if he could see something Luc couldn't.

When Luc and the Figments reached the mouth of the cave, the suns' light was brutal. He stood for a second, blinking, dazed, filled with grief that felt like an animal clawing in his chest. If he quit now and went home, back to Jasmine, there was a chance the Unseen Ones would leave him alone.

But he knew he couldn't give up on Corinthe. Finding her was like coming home to warmth after a long, brutal night in the cold. Finding her was what he had been waiting for, without knowing he had been waiting for it. Without her, he was only half a person.

He would never give up.

Something his mom used to say, some AA quote, probably, came back to him as he stood there, hesitating.

You can't go back, Luc, you just have to keep going forward. One step at a time.

The Figments had paused, too. They were waiting for him to decide.

"Take me to Tess," Luc said.

5

The sand was halfway through the hourglass now. How long did Miranda have left?

The members of the Tribunal had long since vanished. She was alone in Vita, at least for the moment.

Could she find a way to free herself before they returned? If she could get out and find Ford, he would help her. Together they could take down the Tribunal. He must hate them as much as she did; he, too, had been imprisoned for treason.

A thrill raced through her. She remembered how young they had once been, how powerful. She remembered how they had once made a vast sun go dark; she remembered the sudden cold, and planets dying, shriveling to dust, until they looked like the ruined, puckered surface of Humana's moon.

It had been intoxicating.

But she knew that it was hopeless. She was weak now—too weak even to cast off her human form, assumed so long ago, when she had first tried to ensnare Corinthe in her plot to ruin the Unseen Ones. There was no chance of escape. Her powers were diminished here, eaten up by Vita's vast hunger. It was part of her punishment, she knew.

A fissure of steam began under her cell, and for a moment, Miranda wondered if the Tribunal had decided not to wait after all. If this was it, she would fight bitterly to the end. But it wasn't a council member who appeared.

It was Tess.

"Come to gloat?" Miranda fought back the ache in her chest. She should have been beyond feelings now. Everyone had turned against her.

Still, Tess had once been hers. Born from a star Miranda and Rhys had created. A child of their power.

"I don't have much time." Tess gripped a small vial in her hand. Before Miranda could ask what she was doing, Tess opened it and overturned its contents.

Immediately, there was a horrible sound from the pulsing walls, from the very membrane of her cage—as if Vita were screaming. The potion hissed and steamed, and as Miranda watched, it began to eat through the floors, through the twisting strands that enclosed her, creating wisps of black smoke.

The air smelled like burning flesh, and the sound—the scream—continued to build.

"You gave life to me and I can't let you die," Tess said simply. "Now go, or the Tribunal will find you."

Miranda fought another wave of feeling. This was the difficulty of all the time she had spent in Humana. She had become too sensitive. Too prone to emotion. "I meant what I said, Tess. I will try to find a way to destroy the Unseen Ones."

"I know." Tess took a step back. "I meant what I said as well. I will do everything in my power to stop you. I won't have your blood on my hands. But we are still enemies."

The potion, which could only be the blood of a Blood Nymph, burrowed through the living tissue, eating holes in Vita's flesh, creating a tunnel in its wake. As Miranda slipped inside, the screaming crested, becoming a high, constant howl, the frantic wail of a dying animal.

The rib spires shook. The pulse of Vita quickened. This living world screamed in pain.

"Go!" Tess shouted at her, and then she wasn't Tess anymore, but light.

Miranda wasted no time.

She followed the poison to her freedom.

6

All night, Luc followed the Figments across a landscape of rock and red sand, fighting back exhaustion, shivering in his jacket now that the suns had gone down. It was pitch-black—there was no moon in the Land of the Two Suns—and he had to follow the Figments by their whispers as they instructed him to *turn left, go forward, watch your step.*

It wasn't until dawn that the Figments stopped. They had stopped, seemingly, in the middle of a desert, with nothing but red sand for miles in any direction. Several dozen feet away Luc saw a small pool—a puddle really—of silvery water. At first he took it for a mirage, a shimmering trick of the suns. But as he approached, the liquid rose into the air, until he could see himself reflected in the surface like a huge mirror.

He looked to the Figments, but they remained where they were. This was it. He was on his own again. Before he could change his mind, Luc took a deep breath and stepped through the mirror.

Even though he had braced himself for it, the swirling winds and howling noise of the Crossroad knocked him off his feet, and he was falling, once again, into darkness.

Stay calm. He gripped the archer in his hand. He thought the name: *Tess, Tess, Tess.*

As abruptly as ever, the ground appeared. He landed on his feet, but the momentum of his fall propelled him forward, straight into a collapsed lamppost. He banged his shins against hard metal and tumbled to the broken pavement. His palms skidded across the ground, and he felt the bite of tiny pebbles in his skin.

"Shit." Only after he spoke out loud did Luc realize how quiet it was. His voice echoed faintly. He picked himself up, wincing, wiping his palms on his jeans. The archer had fallen from his grip and lay sideways in the dirt.

For one dizzying second, he thought he'd somehow landed back in San Francisco after the earthquake. The blue sky, the wispy clouds, the high, round sun, and the lampposts and billboards—it looked like his world, but a world destroyed by some awful event. Piles of rubble, half-collapsed buildings, overturned cars coated with white dust—the destruction stretched as far as he could see.

The impression that he was back on Earth passed quickly. The streets were wrong, and the buildings, too.

And the people. There were no people. He *felt* it, as though the air itself were lonely.

"Hello?" Luc called out. Nothing. Just a light breeze that sent dust skittering across the street.

In front of him loomed a vast building with an ornately carved facade. Like everything else in this world, it was stained with age and seemed in danger of collapsing. The whole world felt abandoned. Why had the archer led him here?

Tess. She must be here somewhere.

Luc picked up the archer and tucked it back into his pocket. He climbed the splintered stone steps and pushed open a door hanging loosely on its hinges. Inside, it was very dark and smelled like mildew and old paper. He was in a long hallway; he kept his hands on the walls and felt plaster flake away beneath his fingers.

The darkness lessened as he made his way down the hallway, which ended abruptly in a vast room, at least four stories high and as long as a city block. Several crumbling stone staircases spiraled up the walls like ancient serpents, and behind the coiling staircases were hundreds and hundreds of shelves with thousands and thousands of books. No wonder he'd smelled paper. Luc had never seen so many books in one place before. Not even the San Francisco Public Library came close.

The place was abandoned. That was obvious. Portions of the ceiling had crumbled at some point, littering the floor with debris. Trees grew up from between long cracks in the floor, and the largest one, which stood in the middle of the room, stretched all the way to the open air. A weak stream of gray sunlight filtered into the room from the hole in the ceiling.

Then Luc noticed ornate, heavy-looking candelabra lining the walls, their tiny flames dancing and winking at him. Who had lit them? Who kept them burning?

Tess?

"Hello?" Luc called out.

This time, there was no echo, only a whispery sound, like pages of a book blowing in the breeze.

"Is anyone here?"

When no one answered, he moved cautiously around the room, peering into dark alcoves and stepping over toppled furniture thickly layered with dust. It looked like the place had been ransacked at some point long ago. Dust was heavy on the floor and muffled his footsteps.

In one shadowed alcove, he noticed a brass plaque. It was coated with grime, and Luc used a corner of his shirt to wipe it clean.

LIBRARY OF THE DEAD

A chill went through him.

What the hell?

Stepping closer to the lowest shelves, he quickly saw that the books weren't organized by any numerical system. Instead, categories were marked on small, rust-spotted placards at the top of each shelf.

FORGOTTEN ORPHANS

Luc pulled a thin brown book from the shelf and flipped the cover open.

WILLIAM HENRY FERNIVUS
17 MAY 1195–12 FEBRUARY 1200

He felt sucked into the book by some invisible force and couldn't look away. As he skimmed the pages, the heaviness, the ache that Luc had felt outside gripped him again. The pages of the book were brittle, and Luc wondered whether they had ever been touched. He worried that they might crumble into dust.

A thin, sad book, for a thin, sad life.

And then, as he reached the end of the book, he heard it: a sigh, a *human* sigh that came from the pages, from the spine.

He let the book drop. He took a quick step backward, as if the book were a snake that might bite him. He hadn't imagined it. He was sure. The book had sighed.

He stooped, retrieved the book, and quickly shoved it back onto the shelf.

He moved down the row. More names. More dates. In Scorned Rulers, Luc pulled out a book titled *Napoléon Bonaparte 15 August 1769–5 May 1821*. This book, too, had a mesmerizing quality. In it, he scanned the dictator's early childhood, his military training in France, his exile to Elba. Then, his death while under British confinement.

It was all of Napoléon's life in the book, from birth to death. Not just his major historical accomplishments, but

his secret longings also. His humiliations and disappoint-
ments. His shame. Things only the man himself could
have known. It filled Luc with an eerie feeling, like he
was prying into a version of the past he wasn't meant to
see, a version meant to be buried forever.

He knew he should be looking for Tess. He knew
that's what had brought him to this world in the first
place.

But he had to see more.

All around Luc were towers of books, each volume a
person's life. *Library of the Dead.* How had these records
gotten here? A kind of magic that translated a person's
life into book form? He felt humbled, in awe of all the
histories that surrounded him. Blood hammered in his
ears as he climbed one of the rickety staircases to the
second level, transfixed.

CHANGED THE WORLD

GREAT INVENTORS

MISSING MOTHERS

He almost skipped right past it before his mind registered what he'd found. Missing Mothers. The section was
large—larger than it should have been. His finger was
shaking as he moved it carefully along the spines, trying to decipher each faded name. There were more than
a dozen Daphne Simmonses, and he had to pull down
several books before he found the one he was looking for.

Luc swallowed. He wasn't sure he wanted to know

any other version of his mother—of the woman who had tucked him into bed, had taught him about the stars and which constellations were the best for making wishes, and had let him and Jasmine eat brownies for dinner on their birthdays.

He couldn't *not* open it.

She had been happy once. At least, he *thought* she'd been happy. The need to know for sure sent his fingers flying over the pages.

The book was written in the first person, as though every thought, every breath, had found its way onto these pages. The pages were organized by date, and Luc looked up the day he was born and read about his mother's joy, greater than she had ever thought possible. The day Jasmine was born, and how their mother had looked at her children and wanted to give them the world, the sky, and the stars.

Luc took a shaky breath and closed his eyes. He already knew what happened next. It would always end the same way, no matter what corner of the universe he had found, what world he had stumbled into.

> *Today I saw a little dark-haired girl that reminded me of Jasmine. I almost went up to her, but I couldn't. I don't deserve to.*

Luc didn't just read the words; he heard them, a regretful exhale, like his mom was whispering to him from far away. He quickly thumbed ahead a few pages.

I called today. Luc answered the phone but I couldn't bring myself to say anything. Hearing his voice made it hurt so bad. My babies. It's too hard to think of them. Too hard to do much of anything lately.

He flipped to the last entry as his heart thundered in his chest. This was it. The day she died. His stomach rolled and he took a deep breath. He knew the details already.

Heart failure due to acute drug overdose.

But it was different reading about it in his mother's words—like being inside her mind. The slow slur of images as she lay in a dirty alley, just steps from the ocean, bruises covering her thin arms, too tired to go any farther.

But he reread her last thought over and over.

I love you. I love you both so much. Maybe I'll sleep for a while, and then I'll come and see you in the morning.

He didn't know how long he stood there, staring at the words, reading them over and over. Corinthe had believed in fate. She believed that everyone's destiny was already determined. Had that been his mom's destiny all along? To die alone, exhausted, a stranger to her family?

It wasn't fair.

He closed the book with sudden fierceness. He put it back on the shelf, then stood, staring at it, feeling anger build and crest inside of him, coursing into his arms and fists. It was too much. He slammed his fist into the bookcase. Wood splintered and books fell at his feet, but he didn't care. Voices, murmurs, whispers seemed to rise and then float away in the quiet. Fire burned in his stomach. He wanted to rip the library apart with his bare hands.

Some memories should go unrecorded. Maybe it was best to forget.

But almost as soon as he thought it, he had another thought: Corinthe.

Her book would be here. Had to be.

Maybe there was a way to undo it, to rewrite the end. Maybe that was why the Crossroad had brought him here, to this horrible place. But books lined the walls; there were multiple floors above him. He'd never find Corinthe's book without a card catalog or something to point him in the right direction.

The archer!

Luc pulled it out and opened it. It began to spin slowly, and Luc ran in the direction it pointed. He followed the archer like a compass until it stopped completely. When he looked up, he saw it.

FATES AND EXECUTORS

There was a single shelf. Fates were immortal; Executors were not, but could be killed only with difficulty. But Corinthe's book was missing.

He felt a flicker of hope. Maybe she wasn't really dead. Maybe he was fated to bring her back, somehow. If only he could figure out how Rhys had . . .

He stood, stunned, struck by an idea.

Rhys. Rhys had been dying when Luc left him. That meant his book should be in the library. His life. Everything he'd done in his life. How he'd turned back time to save the woman he loved.

The secret that allowed him to use the tunnels to turn back time.

Luc again held up the archer, focusing on Rhys's kind voice.

Luc ran through the stacks, guided by the archer's tiny arrow. He was terrified he wouldn't find Rhys's book. Radicals were anomalies of the universe, created by chaos, not born in the traditional way. Would their life be chronicled among all the rest?

Then, the archer slowed to point at a far, dark corner of the library. Luc saw a small plaque that said FREE RADICALS. The stacks were shrouded in darkness, hidden away from the rest.

When he turned the corner, his steps faltered. A girl stood there, holding a book. He hadn't considered that other people might be in the library.

She slowly closed the book and turned her head. She did not seem surprised to see him. Her hair was twisted into dreadlocks tied with canvas strips. There was a wild energy simmering just under the surface of her skin. The look in her eyes reminded him of Miranda, and he instinctively reached for the knife that was no longer there.

"Tess," he said. It wasn't a question.

She came toward him. When she stopped, they were practically nose to nose. She looked human, but he could tell, he felt, that she wasn't. It was like watching a really convincing movie in 3-D—you could tell it wasn't real.

"And you are?" she said. Even her voice was a very convincing imitation. He knew, instinctively, that she was more powerful than either Miranda or Rhys. He forced himself to not be afraid.

"I'm Luc," he said. "I'm a friend of Rhys's."

The black of her pupils swallowed all the color at the mention of his name. "Rhys sent you?"

"Yes."

"Why?"

It was strange looking in her eyes—like staring down two dark tunnels. But Luc refused to look away first. "Rhys changed time once. He went back to save someone. I need to do the same thing."

Tess stared at him for a second longer. Then she turned away, shaking her head. "He was a fool for doing it," she said quietly. "What he did nearly cost him everything. He died in exile."

"He saved someone he loved," Luc said.

"She didn't deserve it." Tess turned back to him, eyes momentarily flashing white, and in that second, he had a fraction of an idea of who she really was, what kind of power she controlled, and he lost his breath. Then the impression passed, and her eyes returned to normal.

"He said you could help me. That you were the only person who could."

"He was wrong."

Tess tucked the book into her belt. Luc glanced at the binding. Rhys's book. She started to turn away, and Luc grabbed her arm. She froze, staring at his hand, as if unused to being touched.

"Please," he said. "Please. Just tell me how."

She was still staring at his hand, as if she had never seen one before. "Time is not a single place," she said quietly, almost as if she were talking to herself. "Time *is* space. It's a tunnel that moves in infinite directions. It carries more energy, more possibility, than the force that created the universe itself."

Luc seized on the only words he'd understood. "A tunnel," he said. "Okay. So how do I get there?"

She lifted her eyes. Now they were violet and reminded him of Corinthe's. "I already told you. I can't help you." She sounded sorry. "This is much bigger than you can understand. Go back to your world and forget."

"I'll never forget," Luc said fiercely.

Tess smiled sadly. "Everybody forgets," she said. "Everybody, in every world, is forgotten. All libraries go to dust, and all books will someday be unread." She gestured to the thousands of shelves extending toward the ruined ceiling. "That is the rule of the universe." She detached herself gently from his grip. "Go home. Before it's too late."

She turned away from him. Could he grab the book from her belt? He doubted it. She was stronger, much stronger than him. But he wouldn't need her if he had Rhys's book. The risk was worth it.

But before he could move, two flashes of light blinded him. He stumbled backward, blinking. When his vision cleared, he saw that two more people had materialized in the gray light.

Except they weren't people, not really. They looked like abstract watercolor paintings, their features sketched improperly, as if the painter had been too lazy to do it right. Luc knew that this was closer to how Tess must look when she wasn't trying to assume a human form, and he felt awed and also afraid.

"I'm being followed now?" Tess said. She sounded unconcerned.

"You helped Miranda escape." The person—or thing—that spoke had no discernable mouth. But Luc heard the words perfectly.

Miranda had kidnapped Jasmine. Miranda had raised Corinthe and then betrayed her.

It was Miranda's fault Corinthe was dead.

And Rhys had sent him to beg for help from someone who was on Miranda's side?

"Miranda was right about one thing," Tess snapped. "We *have* become just as bad as the Unseen Ones."

The shapes lunged for Tess, and Luc saw his chance. Just as he grabbed the book from her belt, her belt, her body, her face—all of it evaporated. It was as if she just *exploded*. Suddenly, the room was full of sparks. Flames leapt across shelves like eager fingers, and columns of smoke spiraled toward the ceiling, but Luc had the book. Now he just had to get out before the whole place went up and took him with it.

He covered his mouth with his sleeve, fighting the urge to gag.

The smoke was so thick, so instantaneous, he couldn't tell which way was out. He stumbled toward what he thought was the hallway, only to find himself in yet another recessed portion of the library, an alcove with no exit.

The fire had eaten up almost a whole wall. The air was thick with heat, with the roar of the flames. Luc's lungs were burning. He knelt, trying to catch his breath. Through the smoke, he saw a huge table, the same one he'd passed when he first came into the library. The exit. It had to be there.

Crawling on his hands and knees, Luc made his way to the far side of the room. Heat weighed down on him like a thick, wet hand. The dry wood of the rafters snapped; showers of bright sparks rained down on him. He dove under the table, panting, but each breath felt like a burn. He huddled under the table, unable to see more than a few inches in front of him. His breath rasped in his throat.

He crammed the book into his backpack, then tried to figure out which way was out. Thick smoke filled the room and Luc fought to take a breath. He stumbled toward the exit, doubled over to avoid the thickest of the smoke. His eyes were watering.

All around him, the library was full of screaming. Howling, shrieking voices crying out in agony: the screams of millions and millions of pages, of souls, shriveling to dust.

The noise was like an ice pick to his brain. It sent him to his knees. He crawled the last few feet to the door. Once outside, he pushed to his feet and ran, his chest burning, his backpack slamming against his back.

Even blocks away, he could still hear the books screaming.

It wasn't until he threw himself into the shimmering Crossroad that he'd come through earlier that the voices finally stopped.

7

When Jasmine opened her eyes the next morning, sunlight streamed through the filmy white curtains, bathing the small room in brightness. For a second, she couldn't remember where she was. Then she took in the old desk, the lace doilies that covered her bedside table, the collection of small, stiff teddy bears on the wooden bookshelves, and the smell of cats. Of course. Aunt Hillary's house. She rolled over to check the clock.

11:24.

She'd slept for more than twelve hours?

Jas had never found her cell phone, but Aunt Hillary had a vintage rotary phone on the table—everything Aunt Hillary had was old-fashioned—so Jasmine sat up and dialed Luc's number. After several rings, it went to voicemail. Again. She'd tried him a dozen times last night, but never got through.

"Just me again. Call me so I know everything's okay."

After she placed the receiver back in the cradle, she pulled her knees to her chest and leaned against the iron headboard. The bed squeaked every time she moved, and the sound echoed in her head. She tried to sit as still as possible.

Somewhere outside, a bicycle bell rang; then Jasmine heard a thump. A newspaper, she thought. The bell came closer. Curiosity sent her to the window, and when she pushed back the curtain, she saw a kid riding his bicycle, occasionally tossing a paper onto a porch.

At the end of the block, a man stood outside his house talking on his phone. *Baby, I'll get there as soon as I can. Don't be like that. I miss you, too, and can't wait to* . . .

A woman stood at the window of the same house, watching the man. A sudden wave of suffering washed over Jas, and she stumbled away from the window.

What was happening to her?

She dropped her head into her hands. Though she wasn't trying, she could still hear them, feel them, and more. Pipes popped and creaked inside the walls of Aunt Hillary's house, like gunshots echoing in her head. Even her own pulse sounded overly loud. The *thump thump thump* of her heart was like being in a front-row seat during a rock concert drum solo.

The smell of lavender and black tea filled her nose. Aunt Hillary had made toast earlier, too.

Jas heard Aunt Hillary's footsteps long before she got to the door. Then the door squeaked open and her aunt poked her head into the room. "Oh, you're awake.

I thought you might sleep all day. Saw on the news that your school is closed today, some kind of water main problem, so you can help me do some gardening."

Aunt Hillary knew where she went to school?

"Are you hungry?" her aunt asked.

Jasmine shook her head. She really wasn't. They had had turkey and bacon clubs last night for dinner, and apple pie for dessert. Despite her meanness, Aunt Hillary could bake amazingly sweet pies.

Maybe, after all these years, there was a chance she wasn't so bad after all.

"Brush your hair. You're a wreck," her aunt said, and shut the door.

So much for fresh starts. Jasmine stood and slipped out of the T-shirt she always slept in, then pulled on her jeans and favorite sweatshirt. Luc hadn't called yet, but there was no way in hell she was staying there a second longer.

She pulled her hair into a loose ponytail and stood in front of the gilt-framed mirror. Dark circles ringed her eyes, and she looked paler than usual. A faint bruise shadowed the right side of her face, and she ran her fingers over it, willing herself to remember.

Nothing.

What was Luc trying to protect her from?

"Sorry, Luc," she whispered to the mirror. She wanted answers. She stuffed a few things into her messenger bag and tiptoed into the hall.

"Aunt Hillary?" she called out experimentally. No

answer. She moved to the window that overlooked the backyard and saw Aunt Hillary bent over her bed of pansies, up to her wrists in dirt. Perfect.

Jasmine went into her aunt's room, wrinkling her nose at the overpowering smell of mothballs and lavender-scented candles. She pulled her notebook from her bag and scribbled a short note.

Went out for a bit.

Short and sweet.

She went down the stairs and out the front door. For a second, the noises of outside—the *whoosh* of cars on the road, the flushing of toilets, someone warbling in the shower—threw her off. She fumbled in her bag for her earbuds and shoved them in her ears. Better.

It was a quick two-block walk to the bus station. They'd passed it on the way in last night and Jas had made a mental note exactly where it was in relation to her aunt's house. Without her cell, she felt exposed, naked. What if Luc called their aunt's house and she wasn't there? He'd be worried and mad.

Jasmine almost turned around and went back.

But what if Luc had really done what he'd said—had tried to track down Jasmine's attackers? Luc could be super overprotective—she didn't trust him not to do something stupid. What if he was in trouble? A chill ran down her spine, despite the sun. She had to find him.

She had a few twenties and her metro pass in her

wallet. The bus ride to Richmond would give her time to think. When the 44 pulled up, she swiped her card and made her way to the middle, where she could sit alone, leaning up against a window. She tried not to gag; there were only a dozen people on the bus, but they were producing a thick, cloying aroma of perfume mixed with sweat and soap and coffee. She switched to breathing only through her mouth. But then she could almost *taste* the odor, which was a hundred times worse. Her stomach flipped over and she swallowed, then gave up and just breathed normally.

Maybe she had some kind of neurological condition? She'd read about that once—epileptics who smelled funny things just before they had seizures. Or maybe she was pregnant.

Except she wasn't having sex. And pregnancy wouldn't explain why she could hear better, and why she could *feel* things, too.

She closed her eyes. Friday. What was the last thing she remembered?

She followed the thread down.

Four o'clock. She'd gone to the marina to meet T.J. around four. He was stoned already, offered her a joint. It took at least three tries before he understood that she was breaking things off. She was sick of the fact that he screened her calls when he was out, that he flaked on plans, that he always said he'd drive up the coast with her and never did. She was sick of how much he smoked, and she was sick of getting messed up with him.

The doctors said she could have died. And T.J. just blew the whole thing off, like she was making a big deal out of nothing, like getting your stomach pumped was no big deal.

Still, she'd felt crappy after she dumped him. T.J. was the first guy who'd ever really paid attention to her—Luc's friends were scared to even look in her direction. She'd taken the long way home that night. Luc was at Karen's stupid boat party, and Jasmine wasn't in the mood to be at home by herself.

What else did she remember? Her ring. She had realized her ring was missing when she got home. So she'd left a note for Luc, because she couldn't reach him on his cell. Service by the harbor was crap, she knew. Then she'd returned to the marina. She remembered: black water glittering in the moonlight, boats silhouetted against a sky sprinkled with stars.

The *next* thing she remembered was waking up in her bed Sunday morning.

How could an entire weekend just . . . disappear like that?

She felt someone approach. When she opened her eyes, she saw that a middle-aged woman had sat down next to her. Her hair was long and black. She looked vaguely familiar, but Jas couldn't place her. When the woman caught Jasmine staring, she smiled. There was a gap between her front teeth.

"It's going to take awhile to clean up this time," she said, nodding toward the streets outside the window.

Jasmine glanced out and saw a crew with a bulldozer pushing a pile of brick and concrete out of the intersection. The building at the corner was missing its entire facade. Twisted wires and metal stuck out at odd angles from where the bricks had been.

"You probably weren't even born yet when the last big one hit in '89 . . . ," the woman said.

When she stared a little too long, like a peddler waiting for a handout, Jasmine gestured to the earbuds in her ears, universal sign for *sorry, I can't hear you*—even though she could hear perfectly. The woman smiled and made a gesture of understanding. The feeling was still there, and the déjà vu of the situation unnerved her. It was important, but why? There was something there, behind the woman's eyes, that reminded Jas of someone. But the association remained out of reach.

When the bus stopped at the Richmond playground, Jas disembarked. She was still wondering about the woman, trying to place her. She turned left and started across the street. She'd stop at home. Maybe Luc had finished his mysterious business and decided to crash.

The noise of the city closed in around her: construction trucks lifting and moving big chunks of fallen buildings, jackhammers, sirens wailing in the distance. She turned up her old MP3 player, despite the fact that she hadn't used it since a horrible pop phase when she was twelve. Since then, she'd gotten into live music and old records. But the music drowned out the noise, and her sunglasses helped with the glare.

Too bad there was nothing she could do about the

smells. She'd never noticed how much the city reeked: scorched wires from a partially burnt storefront, the sharp bite of gasoline, and fresh-baked bread. At least it felt good to be walking. Her body felt lighter, full of energy, like she'd gulped down multiple cups of coffee.

She turned up Lake Street and climbed the steep hill, practically without feeling it. Luc left in pursuit of her attackers. That meant he knew them, or at least why they'd gone after Jasmine.

We're only doing what we must.

Haven't they taken enough already?

The exchange made no sense to her. Okay, so if they were doing what they must, it meant they were acting on someone's orders. Had someone set up a hit or something on her?

She shook her head reflexively. That kind of thing happened in Mafia movies, not in real life. Besides, she hadn't hurt anyone and didn't owe anyone money.

Then she thought of T.J., but she quickly dismissed that thought. Yeah, he'd been a little pissed when she dumped him. But he wasn't dangerous, even if he was kind of a dick.

There was something she was missing. And she was sure it had to do with what had happened over the weekend, the huge black fog in her memory.

She jogged up the stairs to their apartment building and looked around once before she slipped inside, in case she was being followed. Then she scolded herself for being melodramatic. There had to be a rational explanation for everything that had happened. The holes in her memory. Luc's urgent mission. The change in her mind, the sharpness of her hearing.

Because if there wasn't a rational explanation, it probably meant she was going crazy.

"Luc?" Inside the apartment, she took out her earbuds. It was very quiet. She could tell immediately he wasn't home.

But *someone* had been here. The certainty swept over her like a wave. Things looked out of place, rearranged. But maybe that was another aftereffect of the earthquake? She hadn't paid too much attention yesterday.

Still, she double-checked that the door was locked behind her and all the windows were secured. The door to her room was open, and she peeked her head in before pushing it all the way open, as though she expected someone to jump out at her.

On the floor next to her bed was a picture frame. When she picked it up, she saw that the glass had been shattered. This, surely, had not been on the ground yesterday. It was a picture of her, Luc, Mom, and Dad in front of a mountain. One of the few family pictures she had. Her mom was giving a thumbs-up to the camera. Luc had Jasmine hefted in his arms. And their father was wearing a floppy hat so big it shaded his face.

Carefully, she took the picture out of the frame and flipped it over.

On the back, in her mother's neat handwriting, read: *Luc, 5, Jasmine, 3. Yosemite National Park.*

Her throat squeezed and she felt a sudden ache in

her chest. They'd been happy then. She didn't remember much about their mother, or about the years before she relapsed and disappeared. But her dad had told her they'd been happy, and she believed him.

A tiny flickering noise by the window caught her attention and her body reacted instantly. She tensed up. Had the attackers returned? She grabbed a Disneyland snow globe, one of the last things her mom ever gave her, and crept closer to the window.

But instead of someone trying to get in, she saw a small firefly batting against the window, trying to get out.

"Where did you come from?" she said, setting the snow globe on the floor.

It was dim in the bedroom and the firefly flickered in the half dark. Jasmine couldn't help but laugh. It pinged against the window and went dark, then lit up and tried again to escape.

"Okay, hold on." She flipped the window lock and raised the window to let the bug escape. As she stepped back, her shoe kicked something and it hit the wall with a clunk.

She stooped down. A marble. Why the hell was there a marble in her room? It was beautifully colored and reminded her of the handblown Venetian glass her friend Susan's parents had in their dining room.

No. Not colors. Pictures. Moving images, swirling and dissipating and re-forming. What kind of marble was this? She saw a long, dark tunnel, then when she turned the marble a little, shadowy figures appeared, and then it changed yet again, into a structure that looked exactly like the rotunda at the Palace of Fine Arts.

The rotunda. Luc had said he found her at the rotunda Sunday night.

An idea struck her: if she wanted to remember what had happened this weekend, she had to retrace her steps. She'd start at the Palace of Fine Arts. Maybe something would click.

She didn't know where the marble had come from, but she knew it was a sign. She slipped it in her pocket, scribbled a quick note to Luc in case he came looking for her, then left the apartment for the bus stop. This time, she didn't bother with the earbuds.

By the time the bus stopped near the Palace of Fine Arts, an undercurrent of excitement ran through Jasmine. She felt sure she would remember something here, and could start stitching together the hole in her memory.

The smells coming off the bay were sharp: salt and algae, dried seaweed, old driftwood. She'd never noticed how heavy the air was this close to the ocean. Thick with energy and life. She had to push down the urge to change direction and walk toward the shoreline. It was cooler here. A fine mist covered her skin, and when she looked up, she noticed that the sky had turned gray and gloomy. She'd been so wrapped up in her thoughts, she'd missed the rain clouds moving in.

She moved faster, jogging across the nearly empty street to the entrance of the Palace of Fine Arts.

The area had been badly damaged in the earthquake.

Yellow police tape hung across the pathway, presumably to keep people away from the debris. Jas looked around. When she saw no one, she slipped under the tape and hurried down the path—now fissured with cracks, some as wide as her finger—toward the rotunda. Awareness sizzled along her spine. There was something here, she could feel it, dancing just out of her consciousness.

Familiar.

Instinctively, she reached to twirl her ring, a nervous habit. Of course, it wasn't there. She'd gone to look for it at the marina on Friday night . . .

In a flash, a memory resurfaced:

She knew Luc would kill her for going out again, but she needed that ring. Luc had won it for her at a carnival. One of the best nights of her life. So she'd retraced her steps, ending up back at the place where she and T.J. had argued. She scoured the boardwalk on her hands and knees, hoping more than anything the ring hadn't fallen through the planks into the water.

Then: footsteps behind her.

A woman appeared where moments earlier there were only shadows. She looked vaguely familiar, like maybe someone Jas had seen in a magazine. She was beautiful enough to be a model, with long black hair and dark eyes. But the way she watched Jas put Jas on edge. No one came to the marina at night except to party or score or use or hook up.

"Well, it looks like fate does exist," was what the woman said.

Jas remembered that she had one strange-looking tooth, almost like a fang. The woman held something out, and Jasmine remembered feeling so relieved, so happy that the woman had found her ring, but before Jasmine could ask how the woman had known what she was looking for, there was a brilliant flash of light. . . .

Jasmine came out of the memory like a swimmer coughed up from a riptide. She gulped in air, suddenly aware that she was standing, motionless, halfway down the path. The memory had hit her forcefully and just as forcefully faded once again into the mist of her mind. What had happened after that? Who the hell was that woman? Had she drugged Jas or something? You read about that sort of thing all the time. Crazy people. Like women who stole people's babies.

Pain pounded in Jas's head. Each new thought, every unanswered question and doubt was like a spike in her brain. The only thing she could do was to keep going forward. Maybe seeing the rotunda would unlock another memory.

The rotunda had suffered massive damage; almost the entire top had collapsed. Three columns on the far side had crumbled completely. It was just a pile of broken concrete now.

Police tape was strung along the entire outside of the rotunda, and a No Trespassing sign was attached to one of the fallen columns. Jas ignored it and ducked under the bright yellow ribbon.

She hadn't taken two steps when a boy stepped out from behind a half-collapsed column on the left.

They both froze. He wasn't much older than she was, but he was almost a whole foot taller, with unruly dark hair and a pale face that looked like it belonged in an old painting. His eyes were such a bright shade of blue they almost looked fake. She could smell leather and pine and something else, something wild that she couldn't put her finger on. Like the air before a huge storm. It made her pulse race faster. Heat crept into her cheeks.

"What are you doing here?" the boy asked.

"I'm looking for something." It was the first thing she thought to say. The way he was staring made her instantly aware of the fact that she'd barely brushed her hair this morning and had not bothered with a speck of makeup.

"Aren't you just full of demands," he said. He casually slipped something into his pocket. The yellow T-shirt he was wearing said CATHEDRAL STREET, and she couldn't help but notice how well it fit him. She looked away.

"I don't know why you're here. Like I said, we're on different sides—"

"We've never met," she said.

He shook his head. "Last night. You followed me. . . ."

"You're getting me mixed up with someone else." Despite herself, the thought made Jas angry. What did she care? "Who are you, anyway? What are you doing here?"

"Same as you," he said. "Looking for something."

He was still staring at her, almost *into* her, in a way no guy ever had before. She felt exposed and excited all at once. Her breath hitched in her throat. Normally, guys talked to her chest. This guy made her feel like they were alone in the world.

"Then we're both looking for something," she said, deliberately breaking eye contact. She picked her way over one of the collapsed columns, and the buzzing sense that she was close, that she had been here, grew stronger. There was something here—something that would unlock the mystery of the past few days. All of this seemed so familiar, but why? Of course she'd been to the rotunda before, but this was different; something had happened to Jasmine here. Something important. The certainty was like an itch just under the skin that got worse the more you ignored it.

She started moving pieces of concrete almost automatically, digging through the debris from the base of the toppled column with the toe of her shoe. Then she bent down and pushed aside a large chunk of plaster.

"Really—what are you doing?" the boy asked. He had come up right behind her.

"I *said* I lost something here," she insisted. "Right before the earthquake. It's kind of important—like a family heirloom." It wasn't a total lie. She *had* lost her ring, which felt like a family heirloom, even if it was worth two bucks.

He squatted and began to help her clear away large chunks of plaster.

She spotted it after only a minute: a dark hole, and

a set of crumbling stairs. Her heart leapt, and the sense that she was on the verge of a great discovery—on the verge of piecing it all together—intensified.

"Whoa," the boy said. "Is that like a secret entrance or something?"

"Or something," Jasmine said. She hopped onto the fallen column, then carefully lowered her legs into darkness until her feet touched the stairs. Inside, the air felt thick and damp. The sense of déjà vu grew stronger. Had she been here this weekend? At the bottom of the stairs, dull light was shining from some invisible source.

"This is definitely not safe," the boy said. But he lowered himself after her, through the opening.

"Who's following who now?" she said. "Shouldn't you be out, you know, helping people and saving puppies?"

To her surprise, he grinned. God, he was hot when he smiled.

"I am helping people. I'm helping you." He was looking at her again, the same way as before, like it was just the two of them in the world.

She cleared her throat. "Look . . . about the thing I lost."

"The heirloom." He kept a straight face, but she had a feeling he was making fun of her. She glared at him.

"It was a ring," she said haughtily. "But I didn't lose it. It was . . . stolen. And I got a tip that it might be stashed around here."

"A tip?" he repeated.

"Yeah." She forced herself not to blink. She had a feeling, though, that he could read the lie on her face.

"We've met."

"I'm positive we haven't." And she was. She would remember someone like him.

They shared a silence; then he shook his head and said, "Let's go look for it, then." He moved past her and his body brushed against hers in the tight space. Tiny jolts of electricity rushed through Jasmine. That had never happened when T.J. touched her. "Careful," he said. "Looks like part of the wall has collapsed."

He held out his hand and she took it reluctantly. Not because she didn't want to, but because she was afraid of what his touch might do to her concentration. His grip was firm but gentle, and his palms were totally dry. Their hands fit together perfectly. Heat roared through her body as they moved carefully down the stairs, avoiding the places that had crumbled away.

When they reached the bottom of the stairs, Jasmine saw the source of the light. The ceiling had partially caved in, and light filtering in from above illuminated some kind of living space. Most if it lay in rubble, except for a claw-foot tub in one corner that looked ridiculously out of place.

Had someone really lived here? Broken teacups were scattered on the ground near a sink that was partially detached from the wall, revealing rusted pipes. Multicolored glass crunched underfoot; Jasmine saw that a shelf with dozens of colored bottles had been upended.

A faded rug was just barely visible under the dust, and the corner of a picture frame stuck out from beneath a pile of loose plaster. Jasmine bent and removed the frame, carefully brushing the dust from the glass. It was a painting, a boy and a girl holding hands and staring off toward mountains in the distance.

Yearning rose out of nowhere, thick in her throat.

She set the picture down.

The boy craned his neck to squint up at the sky. "So what now?"

"Look for a ring." Jasmine needed to buy time. She kept waiting for another memory to rise like a wave. She made her way across chunks of concrete and earth to a second doorway. "I'll check in here."

Inside the second room—a bedroom, she guessed—one whole wall had caved in. Behind the bed, a torn poster hung from one side, and a chest lay broken, spilling its contents like guts across the floor.

She stooped and picked up a silk skirt. It was about her size. Maybe some runaway had squatted down here? Maybe even one of the attackers? It seemed plausible. Now if only she knew why, and how the skirt related to her and Luc. Jasmine made her way to the nightstand beside the bed, surprisingly intact given the destruction of the rest of the room.

There was a piece of paper there, taped neatly to the wood. In handwriting eerily similar to her own, was written:

Find Ford.
He'll know what to do.

Again, she had a wave of intuition that was almost like certainty. "Ford?" she called out, then held her breath.

Immediately, he responded. "Yeah? Find something?" Then, a second later, he appeared in the doorway. His face was very serious. "How do you know my name?" He was looking at her, eyebrows drawn down and suspicion in his eyes.

Jasmine's head was spinning. She felt as if the room were getting smaller. Who had left this note? How had they known that Ford would be poking around?

She moved to conceal the note from view. "I . . . I think you told me. Outside. Remember?" She swallowed. She could tell he didn't buy it.

He held up a hand, cutting her off. She'd been distracted by the strange note, the pounding rhythm of her heart, but then she heard it: footsteps coming down the stairs, whispered voices. She recognized the voices.

It was the boy and girl who had attacked her.

Panic slid down her spine. How had they found her again so quickly? Were they stalking her?

Ford turned, as though to go investigate, but Jas grabbed his arm and pulled him behind the bed, forcing him down into a squat. She ignored the way her skin tingled when touching his.

"What — ?" Ford started to ask, but Jas shook her head.

The voices were louder now. The boy and girl had reached the bottom of the stairs; she could hear them moving through the main room, feet crunching on the glass, breathing heavily, as though they'd been running. But she could *feel* them, too. Their determination. Their ruthlessness.

Her thighs ached and her legs were shaking. She and Ford were trapped. They would find her any second now. They must have heard the frantic pounding of her heart. To Jasmine, it was as loud as a marching band.

"We're going to have to run." She leaned in so close to Ford, she could practically taste him. For a second, the smell of his skin—like pine trees and fire and rain, all mixed up—made her dizzy.

Luckily, he didn't ask questions. "Follow me," he whispered.

She couldn't stop the slight tremble in her limbs when his breath washed over her ear.

Ford stood up, keeping his hand wrapped around hers. It made her feel slightly better. They inched toward the doorway that led to the main room, sticking close to the wall, moving in complete silence. Jasmine was extra careful about where she placed her feet.

They flattened themselves against the wall next to the doorway. Ford peeked around the corner, then made a complicated gesture to Jasmine with his hands.

In the other room, the boy said, "Are you sure this was the place?"

"I'm sure," the girl answered.

"Real craphole," the boy said.

"Just find her."

Ford bent down and picked up a piece of copper pipe

that had become dislodged during the earthquake. Jasmine thought he must be arming himself for a fight, and her throat seized up. She'd never hit anyone, never gotten violent at all except in some stupid self-defense program she'd taken instead of gym class freshman year.

But then Ford tossed the pipe so it landed with a clatter in the far corner of the bedroom, and Jas understood. As the boy and girl came rushing into the room, their attention fixed on the other side of the room, Ford and Jasmine moved. They made it only two steps into the main room before the stalkers pivoted, shouting, and leapt after them.

But a two-foot advantage was better than nothing, and Jasmine was fast now.

Unfortunately, they were fast, too. The girl's fingertips grazed Jasmine's hair as she reached the staircase. Jas twisted her head away and the girl growled in frustration. Ford was taking the steps two at a time, and Jasmine sprang after him.

Jasmine's heart was bursting through her throat.

Once they were outside, Jas would scream for help. Once they were outside, they'd be okay. . . .

Just a few more steps . . .

Then Jasmine felt a hand wrap around her ankle. She fell hard and fast, slamming headfirst into the concrete lip at the top of the staircase. Pain spiked out at the impact, and stars danced in her vision. She tried to cry out, but shadows were advancing along the edges of her vision too quickly.

"Wait!" Ford called out, and she felt the electric brush of his fingers against hers before they were wrenched away.

Help me. That was the last thought she had before everything went black.

8

This time, Luc was able to keep his footing in the Crossroad, but barely. It was like trying to stay afloat in a river flowing simultaneously in different directions, or trying to score a goal from inside a tornado. He fought to keep control over his body. Openings, vivid and multi-colored, bloomed like huge flowers on either side of him. He knew they must have been openings into different worlds.

Panic overtook him. The universe was much too big to contemplate, and there were hundreds of thousands of worlds. What if he ended up in the Forest of the Blood Nymphs? Or somewhere even deadlier?

Thinking that made him think about Jasmine, waiting for him at Aunt Hillary's house. The great flower had brought her back from death after the Blood Nymphs had nearly killed her, but it hadn't cured her entirely. She was different now. The way she'd fought off the Executors proved it.

He wondered how long it would be before she noticed the change.

He wondered if she was safe, and if she was worried about him.

Luc tried to fight his way to an exit, any exit, but it was no use. The winds were too strong. He staggered on, borne forward like a piece of driftwood at sea. All around him, shimmering colors twisted together to form new colors, a continuously changing canvas that was both breathtaking and terrifying. He found himself driven forward by a strong current the color of Corinthe's eyes.

Corinthe.

Even her name brought a fresh wash of pain. This was all for her. He couldn't forget that. If he didn't do everything in his power to find a way to alter time, he would be lost. Rhys had known how, but his friend was gone.

Another life lost.

He wished the chemist was there now, to guide him, to tell him what to do.

The swirling colors ebbed, slowly, to a thick gray mist, and Luc knew he was washing up onto the shore of a new world. Outside the Crossroad, the air was much colder. A sudden chill overcame Luc. He shivered and rubbed his arms for warmth. Maybe he had gone back to the world of possibilities? But no. It was too cold.

His teeth chattered. He jogged in place, trying to stay warm. A mountain rose in the distance, tall and capped with snow. Icy air swept down from its peak, bathing everything in subzero temperatures. Luc could feel it deep in his bones. It was worse, far worse, than the Land of the Two Suns at night.

He needed to find shelter before he froze to death.

Up ahead, Luc saw a small grove of trees, which would at least provide protection from the wind. He needed somewhere he could sit and look over Rhys's book. He trudged through the snow toward the woods. His sneakers were little protection against the cold and the wet.

He pulled his hood up and over his head and drove his hands into his pockets. In the silence of this new world, Luc's muffled footsteps seemed to echo off the mountain itself. Other than the trees, he saw nothing alive, nothing growing—nothing but snow and ice.

Finally, he reached the trees and stepped between two medium-sized trunks. Their boughs were covered in heavy snow and, burdened by the extra weight, drooped toward the ground. But it was slightly warmer away from the wind.

Luc slid his backpack from his shoulders and set it down in the snow. While Jasmine had showered, Luc had grabbed an old army surplus backpack and thrown in a pair of thick gloves, a new lighter, and five protein bars.

The last time he traveled the Crossroad, he'd been unprepared. Not this time.

Unfortunately, the lighter would be of no use. There was nothing dry to burn. He wrestled on the gloves, still shivering, and pulled out the book he'd taken from Tess in the library.

Rhys's book. Rhys's *life*.

Luc sat down on his backpack and leaned against one of the tree trunks. A dull ache throbbed inside his chest, and he closed his eyes, imagining Rhys was there with him as he read the words.

> *There is a coldness inside me that I can't fight off. I've been cast out. Exiled. I knew the risks when I embarked on this course. I thought it was worth it. What is life without love? But now, I fear that the sacrifice might have been for nothing. There is a vast nothingness inside me. Who am I if not a Radical?*

Luc closed the book and the voice fell abruptly into silence. The longing, the pain in Rhys's voice was too much. Rhys spoke about cold—was that why Luc had been driven to this freezing world? Had Rhys's book somehow guided him here, to this vast and empty place?

What is life without love? A good question. Luc thought of the bittersweet kiss he and Corinthe had shared, their first and last. How her eyes had lit up like two suns. How finally, at last, he'd felt a sense of belonging.

Failure was not an option. A popular mantra that Coach had them repeat before every game.

Luc flipped through the pages, hoping there was something about the tunnels of time, about how to go back.

Time does not move forward. It moves in different directions and can be created, manipulated, and altered. A single change can ripple across the whole universe, generating change in every world.

It is power like nothing I've ever felt. I've succeeded where even the Unseen Ones have no control.

Controlling these combinations however, is next to impossible. I did it, but it cost dearly. I am only a shadow now, cast out, weak.

My love lives on, but each day I grow weaker, closer to death.

Luc swallowed against the wedge of emotion lodged in his throat. Rhys had seemed happy when they met, sailing the Ocean of Shadows, tending to the needs of the Figments—but it had been only a mask.

Did everyone have secrets? Luc wondered. Corinthe had hidden behind an idea of Fate. His mom had hidden within the comfort that drugs could give her. His father had chosen the bottle.

Luc flipped through the pages. He knew that going back in time was possible—the book proved that Rhys had done it—but it didn't say *how.*

Blank pages rustled in the quiet, but Rhys's voice had stopped speaking.

"Come on," Luc muttered.

"That doesn't belong to you."

The voice came out of nowhere. For a split second, Luc thought the book had spoken in a voice that was not

Rhys's. Then Tess moved out of the shadows, becoming solid as she approached him. He could tell she was tired. Her form seemed more fluid than it had earlier, as if she couldn't bother to keep it together.

But her eyes were dark. Wild. Urgent. Wounded, too. Maybe she'd been hurt in the fight with whatever those *things* were—those shadow figures who'd attacked in the library.

"It's not yours, either." Luc slowly pushed to his feet, never taking his eyes off Tess. He shut the book and tucked it under his arm. Wind howled through the trees, picking up snow and swirling it around them. It was as if Tess's presence had attracted the wind.

"It's mine more than anyone's," Tess said. "Rhys gave me life. His energy created me, and now that energy is all that's left of him and it's in that book. I want it back."

Now Luc understood the wounded look. She was grieving, like he was. "If you'd just help me, I wouldn't need it," he said. His breath condensed in the air. Slowly, he tucked the book back into his backpack and zipped it closed. The only way she'd get the book was by agreeing to help him or taking it by force. Tess watched him like a predator, her muscles tense like she was waiting for him to try to escape. Like she would pounce and tear him to shreds at the slightest movement.

But she didn't move. She only said, "I can't help you, because you don't understand what you're trying to do. This isn't a game. Time is not a toy to be played with. By changing one small thing, it could ripple outward and disrupt the universe. Are you willing to take that chance? And what do you think will happen to your world? The safety of everyone you know would be gone, because you think you're in love."

"I *am* in love," Luc corrected her. "And yes, it's worth the risk. I'm not scared." Luc hoped he was doing a good job of bluffing. He was deathly afraid. But he wouldn't screw up. Failure was not an option. He would bring the universe back, restore it to what it had been before Corinthe died, in balance and intact.

Everyone wins.

Tess shook her head as if she could read his thoughts. "She was fated to die. She accepted it, so why can't you?"

"Fate isn't everything," Luc said. "You're a Radical. You should know that better than me." Luc was quiet for a second, fighting for the right words. "I made her a promise. I have to keep it."

Tess sighed. For a second, she looked so tired, he almost felt bad for her.

Almost.

"I'm sorry," Tess said. "Your journey must end here."

She moved across the small clearing, her movements graceful but slow. Did the cold affect her, too? After all, he had learned from Rhys that a Radical was born in the fiery explosion of a star.

Luc twisted sharply to one side, then ducked between the trees and began to run.

He risked a glance over his shoulder. She was almost on top of him again. Shit. She was too fast. Just as she reached for him, he faked left, then spun off to the right. Tess grunted in frustration and he took off again, cold burning his lungs, blood pounding in his head.

The mountain was closer than it looked, and all too soon he was approaching a wall of rock. Should he try to climb? A few feet ahead of him, he spotted a small overhang, like the entrance to a cave. Maybe he could take shelter there and fend her off—but no, then he'd be trapped. Before he could make a decision, Tess slammed into his back, sending them both sprawling into the snow. He felt her grab for his backpack and used the last of his strength to buck her off, sending her toppling over onto her back.

She was on her feet immediately, but so was he.

They squared off, neither giving an inch.

"Give me the book and I won't hurt you," Tess said.

Luc wiped his mouth and his hand came away red. A rock must have cut his face. He was too cold to feel it. There was nowhere to run. The slope behind him was steep and covered with heavy snow. He'd never be able to outrun her.

"I won't."

"I'm giving you one last chance—" Tess said, but the rest of her words were drowned out by a dull roaring, like an ocean crashing on a beach. She stiffened; a look of terror passed over her face.

Luc turned around. A hundred feet above them, an enormous sheet of snow was breaking free from the mountain. With a tremendous *crack*, it raced toward them, a surging wave of snow, devouring everything in its path, snapping whole trees as if they were matchsticks.

The earth shook like no earthquake Luc has ever experienced. The sound was deafening.

Luc made a split-second decision. The overhang, and the small cave, was his only hope.

He dove forward, throwing himself into the small gap underneath the overhang. The cave was shallow but wide, plenty big enough for two people.

"Take my hand!" he shouted at Tess. But she didn't move. She was frozen, her mouth open.

Snow began pouring over the ledge, rapidly blocking his vision. Luc protected his head. Thunder exploded around him. This had to be what the inside of hell sounded like. It went on for only half a minute, but it felt like hours before the ground stopped shaking and the air grew silent once again.

A thick layer of snow had piled in front of the ledge, leaving only a small gap through which Luc could see the sky. But it was enough. The stone ledge had kept him from being buried completely. He punched through the snow with his elbows until the opening was large enough to accommodate him, secured the backpack, then slithered out of the cave on his stomach.

Tess had disappeared.

"Tess?" Luc shouted. His voice echoed across the vast landscape. He trudged a little farther up the slope, then turned around, shielding his eyes, to see if he could spot her. But there was nothing but white.

Had she been buried alive? Even though she'd been trying to steal Rhys's book, and probably would have killed him to get it, the idea made him feel queasy.

The entire upper quarter of the mountain had come off during the avalanche, just sloughed away. Instead of a peak, there was now a crater, open to the sky like a vast wound.

So. Not a mountain. A volcano.

Steam hissed from the opening at the top, unlike anything he'd ever seen. Colors, almost like those of the aurora borealis, twinkled above the crater. Could it be the opening to the Crossroad?

After taking one last look for Tess, Luc started trudging through the snow toward the summit. It wasn't more than a football field's length to the top, but his sneakers sank into the heavy drifts of snow, making each step difficult, and biting wind whipped down the slope, making it hard to take a breath. The wind battered his body, as if it were a conscious force, as if it were trying to prevent him from reaching the top. He forced himself to keep going, even though he could no longer feel his fingers and his ears ached from the cold. He refused to die in this bleak, lifeless world.

Near the summit, the wind changed. Warm, humid air rolled up from the crater, creating waves of white steam that hissed as they cooled and condensed abruptly into more snow.

Luc pushed the hood off his head. In front of him, colors swirled and danced in the steam. He ventured closer to the crater's edge, and saw that the colors emerged from a wide gap at the bottom of the depression. They looked stuck, almost, like streamers bound to something solid.

Could he be looking at some kind of tear in the Crossroad, maybe caused by the avalanche? It was as if the gap had created a path into the Crossroad where no path was supposed to be. But the crater was deep, and he didn't know whether he could safely climb down its steep ledge and make it to the opening. Even if he could, he didn't know if he would *fit*.

He remembered, suddenly, the first time he had ever ventured into the Crossroad. He'd been standing at the edge of a roof, terrified. Corinthe had been threatening him with a knife. Even then, she'd been the most beautiful girl he'd ever seen. It seemed like an entire lifetime ago.

He was going to have to jump again—straight into the colors flashing toward the sky. He checked the straps of his backpack, then backed up several feet from the rim. He took a deep breath and felt the air burn his lungs. Now.

He started sprinting. But just before he sprang from the edge, his foot broke through a layer of ice and he tripped. Momentum propelled him forward. He slid over the edge of the crater and plummeted.

Instinctively, Luc covered his head and braced for impact. Except there was none. At the moment of collision, Luc simply passed *through* the ground as if it were no more than air.

He fell into a vast nothingness where wind howled and voices whispered, yet he couldn't feel his own limbs. When he tried to move his arms, there was a disconnect between his mind and his body. He existed, but not in this reality.

A sound began, whether in his mind or somewhere around him, he couldn't be sure. It shook the air, shook him all the way to the bone. Wind came up out of nowhere, and he was sucked into a vacuum that felt like it was tearing him apart.

It was the same as when he and Corinthe crossed through worlds: the unbearable howling winds, the relentless tearing at his body until he thought he would shatter. But under it all was the sense of familiarity. If he could make it through, there *was* something at the end of the pain.

Just when he thought he'd be ripped from limb to limb he was thrown into the Crossroad. Colors spun around him, twisting upward like a tornado, leaving him standing on trembling legs.

Luc regained solid footing. He stood. The voices, usually so loud, seemed like faint whispers now. He wondered, briefly, whether this meant he was getting less human. Mortals weren't supposed to wander the Crossroad.

But he was tired of rules.

The archer was in the small flap pocket of his backpack. He gripped it in his hand and watched the figure spin. He needed guidance. Would it work this time? He focused on Corinthe, her face, her eyes, the fiery yearning in his gut.

Time, he thought. Show me to the tunnels of time.

Instead, the tides around him swirled faster, more violently. It felt as though the universe was fighting him, and Luc struggled to keep his balance, to keep from panicking. He barely kept his grip on the archer. He clenched his teeth against the pain. Winds buffeted him sideways, turned him around in circles.

The tiny archer continued to spin wildly. There was no doorway, no ripple that might indicate a new world. It was all just colors and winds, an endless stream flowing in multiple directions.

The trinket was useless.

The Crossroad was useless.

Anger rose in him, swift and hot. He wouldn't let the Unseen Ones win. All he wanted to do was save Corinthe. Why was the universe fighting him so hard? Love was supposed to triumph over everything. Wasn't that what everyone always said?

So why the hell wasn't it working for him?

The archer was still spinning. Enraged, Luc threw it.

And watched as, instead of disappearing, the tiny arrow *pierced* the shifting wall of color and hung there, trembling.

All at once, the winds quieted.

The colors stopped spinning.

It was silent.

The archer was stuck as if buried in bubble gum.

When Luc reached out and pulled it, long strands of fibrous color dripped from the tip of the tiny arrow. Black, inklike shadows dripped from the spot where the arrow had been embedded, as if the Crossroad were weeping.

Luc tucked the archer into his backpack and examined the tear. It was barely the size of a pinprick, but behind it, he could hear sounds—not whispers, but a faint humming, like the noise of some enormous generator. He stuck a finger through the hole and tugged, and the rip grew longer. Luc was repelled by the slow ooze of black liquid from the opening, but he didn't stop.

The Crossroad, Corinthe had told him, ran everywhere, between all worlds.

So what ran behind the Crossroad?

When the opening was the width of his shoulders, Luc carefully maneuvered his head through it. Bright blue lights sizzled along tracks that reminded him of the sparks that rained down continuously in Kinesthesia.

The last time he and Corinthe had been there, the world had started to collapse around them. Luc wondered if it was even there anymore. Could the universe survive without its center?

Luc shook his head. This was not Kinesthesia; there was no gigantic clock, no grid, no river of metal.

There were just . . . wires. That was what they looked like, wires. Everywhere. They ran as far as he could see in both directions. Bursts of bright color zipped along them in rapid intervals.

The air was charged with electricity and the hair on

his arms stood all the way up. It was like the time he'd gone to the science museum in seventh grade and put his hands on a glowing static ball, but a thousand times that. Ten thousand. The pressure grew. It felt like his skin was crawling with a thousand bugs.

He wanted out.

But when he went to retreat, the opening gripped him, like a mouth closing. The Crossroad was *healing* itself, he realized with a sense of nausea; fibrous strands of color were weaving around him like skin regenerating, trapping him in place.

In the world beyond the Crossroad, the world of wires, Luc noticed thick cables knotted only a foot or so away. He plunged an arm through the hole and reached out to grab the nearest cable. It was as thick as his wrist. He checked his grip and heaved.

The cable snapped, sending off a waterfall of sparks. Luc smelled burning flesh and wondered, briefly, whether he was on fire. Then he realized he was smelling the Crossroad, the stink of the hole widening to release him, opening its jaw.

A million pinpricks of light pierced Luc's body, until the pain became too much, and he simply let go.

9

Jasmine slowly sat up. She was in the middle of the rotunda, surrounded by debris: tumbled columns, mounds of plaster and Sheetrock. The last thing she remembered was falling. She knew she'd hit her head, but when she felt around for a bump, she found nothing. She didn't even have a headache.

Ford was gone. Her attackers were gone, too. Maybe Ford had chased them off?

"Are you okay?"

Jasmine looked up at the figure that spoke. An older woman with graying hair looked down at her, her face filled with concern. On her jacket was a tag that said RED CROSS VOLUNTEER.

The woman moved to help her, but Jas scrambled to her feet.

"I'm fine," she said quickly. She noticed that the

entrance to the underground room had been covered over again. Was Ford responsible for that, too?

Had she blacked out again?

Panic crashed over her in a wave. Jesus. There was something really wrong with her.

"There's an ambulance in the parking lot," the woman was saying. "Maybe we should check you out."

"I really am fine," Jasmine insisted, backing away. At the edge of the rotunda, she turned and staggered down the path. The woman called out to her, but she kept going.

Jasmine's vision was blurry, uneven. Her hands shook and her knees felt like Jell-O.

She sank down onto a bench, remarkably still intact, at the end of the pathway. Was this why Mom started using drugs, to stop an endless loop of craziness? Had she gone through this too? Did she forget things, find herself places she never remembered going to?

But Jas did remember.

Jas remembered discovering the strange room; she remembered meeting Ford. She remembered, too, a note on the table, a message scrawled in her own handwriting. More craziness. And then she'd been attacked again. She'd been *followed*.

But it all came back to the same question: why?

A prickly feeling on her neck grew stronger and she turned. A man with piercing blue eyes stood on the other side of the pond watching her. Or was he watching the swan swimming among the fallen trees along the water's edge?

Jasmine stood up. She suddenly felt exposed, and she unconsciously tugged down her shirt. What if she was being observed, even now? She hurried down the path to the street. A siren started wailing and soon a fire truck zoomed past, disappearing around the corner. She clamped her hands over her ears. Still, sounds penetrated: hissing from a broken pipe; people crying, calling out names; all punctuated by the constant wail of sirens, near and far.

What was happening to her? She staggered along the sidewalk, her hands still covering her ears to block out some of the sounds. They crashed into her, added to the chaos in her head. She couldn't think straight.

Where was she going now?

She had to find Luc.

She fumbled in her pocket for her cell, then remembered that she'd lost it somewhere after she blacked out Friday night.

There had to be some place around where she could make a quick call. She needed to hear his voice, to tell him what had happened. She needed him to tell her she wasn't going crazy.

She hurried south down Baker, toward the bus stop that would take her home. It wasn't until she got there that she realized her bag was gone. She had no money, no metro card. Had she been robbed, too?

She took a deep breath. She had to focus. She searched her pockets and found a couple of crumpled dollar bills — enough to pay her fare to the next connect, anyway.

The ride down Divisadero was bumpy, and after the second time her forehead slammed into the window, Jas had to stop leaning against it. The coolness had felt good;

without it, the noise around her crept back in, loud and overbearing. The stale air made her feel like she was suffocating.

She tried covering her ears, tried humming, counting backward, but nothing helped. It was the enclosed space, the confinement that made it worse. She staggered to her feet and toward the front of the bus and climbed off at the very next stop.

It didn't matter where she was, it only mattered that she could breathe fresh air again. When she did, the faint undercurrent of something familiar tickled her nose.

She tilted her head and closed her eyes, trying to pinpoint what it was. Then, over the scent of smoke and oil from the machines sending black smoke into the air, she found it.

Her pulse leapt with excitement. She could smell pine and leather, a strange combination, for sure. There was something else, too, something harder to pick up on, but it was there.

She moved without realizing it, led only by her senses and a vague memory. It wasn't fear that had her skirting a pile of bricks covering the sidewalk, that kept her going forward despite the destruction around her; it was something else. Something that made her skin tighten and her breath catch in her throat.

Anticipation.

Like she stood perched on the edge of a cliff with nothing below her.

There was no reason to trust that she was heading in

the right direction, but it felt right, connected to everything else. At the corner of Jackson she stopped. The aroma was stronger there, and she slowly looked around to find the source.

A small sign in hand-painted yellow letters hung over a nondescript wooden door. It read CATHEDRAL STREET. Ford had been wearing a shirt with the same name. It hit her with startling clarity. The scent. It was his.

And whatever this place was, it had to be connected to him, too.

She opened the door and stepped into a dimly lit hallway. From inside she could hear grunts and voices and the muffled sound of something—or someone—being hit. She thought of the two people who'd attacked her. Had Ford brought them here? Was he in trouble?

Were they?

At the end of the hallway, a smudged door opened onto a boxing ring. Two people were circling the ring, sparring, occasionally throwing punches, while a man leaned on the ropes, yelling instructions. Heavy bags hung from the rafters, and a tiny older woman was pummeling the hell out of one of them.

A kid Jasmine's age was sitting behind a huge desk next to the door, and he waved her in with indifference, his gaze barely lifting from the magazine he was reading. She stepped farther into the room and saw, painted on the floor, a large circle with two crossed boxing gloves and the words CATHEDRAL STREET across them, just like on the T-shirt Ford had been wearing.

As if thinking about him made him materialize, Ford emerged from the locker rooms. He was wearing athletic shorts and sneakers and no shirt. She hadn't realized before how in shape he was; he had the body of a serious athlete. She noticed he wasn't bruised at all—obviously, he had escaped Jas's attackers fairly easily. He was walking next to a big guy with the face of a bulldog.

Jasmine dropped to her knees in front of the welcome desk, pretending to tie her shoe. Though she had come hoping to find him, now she felt as if she was spying on him. Had he seen her? She didn't think so. When she peeked up, his back was to her.

"So this is the main floor," the bulldog-looking guy was saying. "You can see that we're pretty straightforward here. No treadmills or fancy equipment. Old-school, you could call it. Our clients are pretty hard-core, too. Even the earthquake yesterday didn't stop us for more than a few hours." The guy pointed to the ring, where the trainer was demonstrating a right-hook technique. "Since this is your first time training here, you get a free T-shirt."

Bulldog gestured to the guy behind the desk, and, barely looking up from his magazine, the guy tossed Ford a yellow Cathedral Street T-shirt from a stack. "You can start on the basic bag today, loosen up, test it out. We have pay-as-you-go pricing, but if you decide to commit, we can put you on a monthly training schedule. Just depends on what you're looking to do."

Jas moved onto her second shoe, untying and retying it as slowly as humanly possible. It didn't make sense;

the trainer was obviously confused. The earthquake had happened two days ago, on Saturday.

"I'll just start with the day option for now," Ford replied. "Not sure how long I'll be here."

"You just move to town?"

"Just this morning, yeah. Hell of a welcome."

Jasmine's face was burning. Was Ford lying to the trainer? He couldn't have gotten into town this morning, because she had run into him at the rotunda last night. And what about the T-shirt? He'd been wearing it at the rotunda. Hadn't he?

She didn't understand. Her head was spinning and the smell of sweat and varnish was making her nauseous. And there were only so many times you could tie and untie your laces.

She straightened up. Now Ford was on a bag, running through moves that the trainer called out. The muscles in his back rippled with every punch.

"You've done this before," the trainer commented. "Nice form."

She knew she had to make a choice: approach Ford and ask him what had happened at the rotunda, or leave. She couldn't just stand there. But she found she couldn't take her eyes off him. He moved lightly, almost as if he were dancing. He wasn't even breaking a sweat.

The guys in the ring watched him, too, while they wrestled out of their gloves and scrubbed their faces with towels. Soon they ducked out of the ring and headed to the locker room, and the woman stopped pummeling her bag and turned, wiping her face with her forearm.

"Hey, Nick, I need to square up with you today," the woman called out.

"Keep working on the uppercut," the trainer told Ford. Then he and the woman headed straight for Jasmine. Crap. When the trainer spotted her, he stopped short. "Can I help you?" he grunted.

Jas gave him her best I'm-innocent smile. "Oh, sorry. I was looking for Dave?" She pulled a name out of the air. "He said he was coming to meet me here?"

"No trainers named Dave here," the guy said. "We got a Steve, but he's not on schedule today."

"That's it. Steve." She pouted. "I was sure he was going to be here."

"Give me a second. Gotta take care of some housekeeping, then I can call him."

"Thanks so much," she said. As soon as the trainer and the older woman moved into the office, Jas started moving toward Ford. He must have answers for her. He was her only hope.

They were alone in the gym now, except for the guy behind the desk. Ford started pummeling the bag, his hands moving so fast they were practically a blur. Jas had never seen anything like it. Her breath caught in her throat. He ducked and dodged and twisted. Still, he wasn't sweating.

She felt strangely frightened of him. When he stopped moving, it took her a second to find her voice.

In that second, he threw one more punch.

The bag exploded. Sand went everywhere. Jasmine covered her mouth to keep from crying out. Impossible.

"Shit," Ford muttered. Jasmine ducked behind a row of kettlebells. Earlier, at the rotunda, he'd seemed harmless. Helpful, even. But what if he wasn't harmless? What if he was in league with the people who'd attacked her, somehow? Maybe the whole thing had been a setup.

"What the hell happened here?" The trainer burst out of the office and charged over to Ford.

"I—I'm sorry," Ford stammered. He did look sorry. "I can pay you back."

Jas backed up slowly; as soon as she reached the hallway, she turned and ran, hurtling herself out the door. The desk guy was talking on his cell phone outside and barely looked at her. She crossed the street quickly and took up a spot behind a parked car. She felt like a creep, but she also felt, in the same intuitive way she'd been feeling things since she woke up, that Ford had something to do with her attackers.

And Miranda. How did Miranda fit in?

She watched Ford push open the door. For a moment he hesitated, and his gaze swung in her direction. She ducked, concealing herself behind the car. When she straightened up again, Ford was halfway down the street.

She tugged up her hood and followed him at a distance. She didn't know what she was hoping to find, but Ford must be connected to the attack at the rotunda. How else could she explain the note, and the fact that he'd abandoned her there and chased off her pursuers?

She was so intent on keeping him in her sights—he moved quickly, head down, hands stuffed in his pockets— she barely noticed they were passing close to the hospital where her dad was staying. Just ahead was Alta Plaza Park and the thick grove of trees where she'd been attacked. She sped up, as if she could outrun the memory.

"You're supposed to block the ball, you shithead!" a voice shouted. There was a loud explosion of laughter.

Jasmine felt a flickering sense of unease. Familiar. Everything was very familiar.

She turned and saw Tyler, Justin, and Devon, Luc's friends, kicking a ball. They were wearing the same clothes they'd had on yesterday, when she'd also seen them kicking a ball, in the very same park, at the very same time of day.

This time, though, they spotted her.

"Jas. What's up?" Tyler called out. He tossed the ball to Justin and jogged over to her. She glanced down Jackson and saw a yellow shirt—Ford—duck into a building at the corner. She couldn't lose him.

"Hi, Tyler." She waved and tried to keep moving, but he caught up with her this time.

"Hey, wait up. I've been trying to call Luc all weekend. Is he okay?"

She narrowed her eyes. "Why wouldn't he be okay?" she asked cautiously. Did Tyler know that Luc had gone looking for her attackers?

"Well, you know." Tyler looked uncomfortable. "Because of everything that happened at Karen's party."

Jasmine didn't know whether to feel relieved or disappointed. He didn't know anything. She shrugged. "He didn't say anything to me about it."

Tyler looked down at his shoes. "Yeah, well, I probably wouldn't want to talk about it either, if I caught my girlfriend—" He broke off suddenly.

"Caught my girlfriend what?" Jasmine said. She was curious, even though it shouldn't have mattered; she had never liked Karen and had never understood how Luc could date someone whose idea of a deep conversation was a ninety-minute discussion about which bikini to take on vacation.

Tyler blew out a long breath. "Cheating," he said. "Luc caught Karen cheating."

Jasmine felt her mouth drop open. Why hadn't he told her? She felt a flicker of guilt. Maybe he hadn't wanted to worry her, or maybe he didn't think she could handle it.

Luc always took care of her. But there was no one to take care of him.

She made a silent promise: She was going to do better. She was going to be better. For Luc.

"I'll let him know you've been trying to reach him," she told Tyler. "Look, I gotta go. I'm supposed to be meeting someone."

At the corner was a small coffee shop: Tully's Coffee. Damage to the block looked minimal, although the green awning had partially detached from the building and hung limply next to the door. Inside, Jas was assaulted by the smell of roasting coffee—so strong she could practically taste it.

The coffee shop wasn't large, and only a few people

were clustered around the small bistro tables—Jasmine registered their individual conversations without actually listening. Ford was gone. How had he disappeared so fast? Had he left the coffee shop while she was distracted by Tyler? She cursed softly. She should have just walked up to him at the gym and demanded answers. Now she had no way of finding him.

"Why are you following me?"

She spun around. Ford.

She hadn't even heard him approach.

Jasmine took a deep breath. "Because I need answers. You disappeared on me."

"I wish I had some. . . ." Ford raised his eyebrows. "And I hate to break it to you, but we've never met. I most definitely would remember you."

Heat climbed up Jasmine's neck. He had the sexiest smile, and a small freckle, like a tiny star next to his left eye. She hadn't noticed that before. "At the rotunda," she said impatiently. He was messing with her. "What happened to the people who were chasing me?"

The playful smile disappeared. "Look," he said, and frowned. "I don't know who you think I am, but you've got the wrong guy."

She stared at him. "But—"

"I don't know you," he said, raising both hands apologetically. "I don't know what you're talking about. Sorry." He scanned her face one more time, like he was trying to decide whether she was crazy. He tried to sidestep her, but she grabbed his arm and a shock ran through her body.

Ford took a quick step back and a flash of recognition passed over his face. When he looked into her eyes again, he seemed afraid. "Look," he said, lowering his voice, "I don't know what kind of game you're playing. We both know we're on different sides, so stop following me. I won't help you."

"What?" Jasmine was more confused than ever. "I'm not on anyone's *side*. I don't know what the hell is going on. All I know is we were at the rotunda together. Then you disappeared. Now you're pretending that you don't even know me." She crossed her arms.

"*Miranda,*" Ford muttered, so quietly Jasmine almost didn't hear him. The name sent a jolt through her.

"What about Miranda?" Jasmine asked quickly. She still had no idea who Miranda was, but it couldn't be a coincidence that her name kept coming up.

"I knew she must have had something to do with this," he said. He didn't look afraid now. He looked tired. "Time was always an obsession of hers."

"I need to talk to her." As soon as Jasmine said the words, she knew they were true. "Do you know where I can find her?"

His expression changed again. This time, she didn't know how to read it. "You really don't know what you are, do you?"

Before she could answer, a woman pushing a baby stroller nearly knocked her off her feet. "*Excuse* me," the woman said. "You're blocking the counter."

"Sorry," Jas said. By the time she turned back around, Ford was out the door. She would follow him for as long as it took to get the answers she needed. He obviously knew more than he was saying. And Jas could be very persistent.

She started to push out the door when a stack of newspapers caught her eye. A huge headline was plastered across the front page: EARTHQUAKE ROCKS SAN FRANCISCO. LIVES LOST, INFRASTRUCTURE CRUMBLES.

The date on the top of the paper was Sunday, October 14.

Sunday. That wasn't possible.

"Are these yesterday's paper?" she asked a girl with a skunk stripe in her hair who was cleaning off a table nearby.

The girl shook her head. "Nope. We restocked this morning."

It felt as if the ground were tilting. For a second, Jasmine thought maybe they were in the middle of an aftershock. "Today is Monday."

The girl gave her a puzzled look. "It's Sunday."

Jasmine pushed blindly out the doors.

A sharp, stabbing pain drove through her temples. The earth seemed to blink, and suddenly the ground dropped away.

10

Luc couldn't be sure how long he was in darkness.

It could have been a few seconds, a day, or even longer.

But then he was aware again: of his heartbeat, of the dryness of his throat, of the ache in his palms and shoulders.

He opened his eyes. He was inside a tunnel, staring up at a web of wires and tangled cables. It reminded him of a subway, deep under the earth, shadowed and empty. Then he remembered how he'd pierced the membrane of the Crossroad and fought his way through to the other side.

Carefully, he pushed onto his knees, then stood on shaky legs. Invisible weight pressed in all around him, making it an effort to move. Even breathing was a struggle. With each inhale, the air seemed to take minutes to seep down into his lungs. Like everything was traveling through syrup.

The cable he had grabbed—the one that had snapped—was hissing on the ground, emitting sparks and the stench of acrid smoke.

The tunnel extended in both directions as far as he could see. And everywhere, wires: threaded like spiderwebs, looped and coiled like snakes, hanging like tree branches above and behind and on every side of him. None of the wires seemed to end; he couldn't see where they were connected or what they connected to.

And the place he'd fallen through—the tear in the wall of the Crossroad—was gone.

He began walking, picking a direction at random. He was trying to quell a sense of rising panic. How long had it been since he'd said goodbye to Jasmine? It seemed like weeks. She would be worried about him.

And he was no closer to saving Corinthe.

There had to be another way out. There was always a way out.

This world looked almost liquid. It seemed to shimmer when he moved; the cables swayed lightly, as though disturbed by the tiniest air currents. Each time he took a step, dark ripples extended outward, like waves on the ocean, though his feet met with solid ground. It made him feel off-balance, as though he might plunge into darkness at any second.

Then, ahead of him, Luc saw something out of place: a shadow, a momentary disturbance, as though someone else was slipping through the darkness ahead of him, weaving between the cables. His heart sped up. Could someone else be in this vast tunnel with him?

He moved more quickly, fighting through the syrupy air, breathing hard. He wasn't alone. The person was sticking to the shadows, ducking underneath the webs and loops of the cables, moving nimbly, as if familiar with the landscape. Maybe Luc could learn the way to an exit.

He was close enough to call out. He stepped on a wire and sparks sizzled under his foot. The person spun around, temporarily illuminated by the flashing light.

Black hair, wide eyes, a face like a predator. Miranda.

Instant rage ignited in his gut. Luc launched himself at her before she could react.

Surprise gave him a momentary advantage. He pinned her against a nest of cables, his forearm across her throat. The air around them filled with static. Miranda twisted out of his grasp. She moved more slowly than he remembered. Maybe the tunnels were affecting her, too.

Or maybe she was sick. The thought filled him with joy.

She lunged at him, but he sidestepped, then grabbed her arm and twisted it behind her back. He needed to restrain her. He knew what she was capable of. Even in her weakened state, she was much stronger than he was.

Luc grabbed blindly for one of the cables above him. It burned his palm, but he barely felt the pain. Miranda was trying to buck him off, snarling, twisting from side to side. He wrapped the cable around Miranda's throat. She coughed, and clawed at the cables with her fingers.

Just one tug and it would tighten. Suffocate her. It would be so simple.

She had killed Corinthe, or might as well have. She deserved to die.

"Give me one reason I shouldn't kill you right here," he spat out. But he knew he wouldn't do it. He couldn't.

"Because you need me," she rasped. "We're on the same side now."

Luc snorted. "You tried to kill me. You almost killed my sister. You betrayed Corinthe." His throat was tight with rage. He could barely force the words out. "We'll never be on the same side."

Miranda's eyes rolled toward him, like those of a frightened horse. But she wasn't afraid. He knew that she knew that he wouldn't kill her. "You can't manipulate the tunnels without me. You don't know how. I do. Rhys told me."

"What are you talking about?" Luc tightened the cable enough to make Miranda go still.

"The tunnels of time," she gasped. "I'm impressed. No human has ever found them."

"Don't lie to me," Luc growled.

The look in her eyes changed. She barked out a laugh. "Don't tell me you're here by *mistake*."

He pulled the cable even tighter and her laughter turned into a wheeze. She tried to pry the cable from her throat. Luc saw that she still wore Jasmine's ring.

The anger was like a curtain; he couldn't think anymore. He wanted her to die.

"Together we can bring the Unseen Ones down," she choked out. Now she did look scared. "They can restore life to Corinthe. They can do anything. We're on the same side, Luc. Don't you see that?"

"No." His arms were shaking from the effort of restraining her, and his lungs felt like they were being flattened. If he killed her, he might never find his way out of the tunnels. But he couldn't let her live. She had imprisoned Jasmine among the Blood Nymphs. She had manipulated Corinthe, lied to her, used her.

Killed her.

Miranda's hands dropped from her neck. Her eyes fluttered. "The tunnels of time will kill you . . . ," she whispered.

Now or never.

Luc stepped back, releasing her. The cable slipped from his numb fingers. Miranda gagged, sucked in a deep breath, and stood heaving and coughing with her hands wrapped around her injured throat.

"Good choice," she rasped.

Luc surged forward and grabbed her hand. Her slender fingers made a fist, but he pried them open. "This," Luc growled as he slipped the ring off, "does not belong to you." It was only a cheap carnival ring he'd won years ago, but it was Jasmine's—and he was determined to give it back to her. He squeezed it tightly in his hand before slipping it into his pocket. "Now tell me how the tunnels work before I decide to take my chances without your help."

Rhys had said that time was infinite: forward, backward, past, present, future. All of these loops and coils around them, all of the liquid shimmer: it had to be time itself, flowing by.

Miranda lifted her head. She pulled her lips back, baring her teeth. "Can't you feel it? The tunnels are trying to kill you. Your blood will turn to lead. Your lungs will turn to stone. The tunnels will destroy anything that does not belong."

"There has to be a way." He had made it this far. But now what? There were millions of cables and wires—probably billions of them. How was he supposed to know how to bring back Corinthe?

"You can't help Corinthe if you're dead," Miranda said, as though she had read his mind. But she must know there was only one reason he would risk traveling the Crossroad again. "There's another way. If we work together, we can both get what we want."

Miranda was right about one thing: the atmosphere of the tunnels was oppressive. Luc didn't know how much longer he could withstand it. The fight had taken almost all of his energy, and what was left barely kept his heart beating. He was having trouble staying on his feet.

"Promise me you'll stay away from my sister." He didn't know whether Miranda had something to do with the attack on Jasmine, but he couldn't rule it out. Not after Miranda had kidnapped her and used her to bait Luc into the Crossroad.

Miranda frowned. "I have no interest in your sister.

If she's in trouble, it's not my doing. She drank from the garden, from the Flower of Life, which *you* cut down."

"She was dying," Luc said, his voice shaking.

"And you returned her to life. The Unseen Ones will not be happy. Their only concern is balance, and they are not happy. She drank the nectar, and now there are consequences. There must be balance. Action and reaction. Chaos and order. Death and life."

Icy shivers ran down Luc's spine, even though sweat ran down his forehead. "What are you talking about?"

"Only blood can feed the Flower of Life. Death to life, life to death." Miranda's black eyes glowed in the unnatural light. "It's all connected."

"More riddles," Luc spat out.

Miranda ignored him. She was moving her hands along the blackness between the cables, as though feeling an invisible wall for a crack. "I'm your only hope, Luc." Beneath her fingers, the darkness began to sizzle and spark. Her face was tight with concentration. A small hole appeared and started to grow larger; beyond it, Luc could see the flashing colors of the Crossroad. It was as if her touch were acid, eating away at the blackness. A vein pulsed in Miranda's forehead; she gritted her teeth and slowly parted her hands. As she did, the hole in the darkness grew larger. "Go. Quickly. The tunnels will heal themselves. I won't have the strength to save us a second time."

Luc hesitated for a second. She was his only hope of getting out of this place. She had said there was a way to save Corinthe. Once it was all over, he could still make her pay for what she'd done.

Miranda's arms were trembling. "Go!" she shouted.

Luc threw himself into the Crossroad, into the blur of colors and winds and whispered voices, staggering, disoriented by the brightness after the darkness of the tunnels. But he could breathe again. The crushing weight he'd felt in the tunnels was released. He felt his lungs expand in his chest, could practically feel the blood in his veins start flowing again. He could have cried out with joy.

Miranda followed him. Almost immediately, the hole behind them healed, webbed back together.

She had kept her first promise.

"Now what?" he asked.

"Come," she said, without looking at him.

Even though she was obviously tired, Miranda controlled the Crossroad with little effort. As she walked, the colors ebbed and split, like currents parting around an obstacle. The shrieking winds and voices withered into silence. Luc had never seen anything like it in all the times he'd gone through the Crossroad. Not even Corinthe had been able to control the Crossroad this way.

Luc followed behind Miranda, fighting through the crashing waves of color and sound in her wake. It was like trying to swim behind a speedboat. He staggered forward as quickly as he could. If they were separated, he would never find her again, he knew.

"Where are we going?" he asked.

"You'll see."

"Why should I trust you?" He reached out and grabbed her arm, spinning her around to face him. Her eyes flashed. But then she smiled, revealing the familiar pointy tooth, sharp as a fang, next to her incisors. It reminded him of what she was, what she had done. He needed to be careful around her.

"Because I need you, just like you need me," she answered.

"Why?" The short time he'd spent in the tunnels of time had exhausted him. How long had it been since he'd left San Francisco, since he'd seen Jasmine off, since he'd eaten? "Why do you need me?"

"We both want something back that was taken from us. We share a common enemy. That's a very strong bond." Her smile faded. "No more questions now. We must go very, very quietly."

Before he could ask what she was talking about, the winds released them; the colors shifted, ebbed away, until all that was left was a dull blue light. Mist swirled around them and Luc knew that they had reached another world.

Just as suddenly, the mist released them. Luc was standing on a surface as smooth as glass.

No. A surface *made* of glass.

Everything was made of glass. Light reflected off the surfaces like prisms, creating brilliant colors that danced all around them, much like being in the Crossroad. It reminded Luc of a contemporary sculpture, all sharp-edged glass that appeared delicate and deadly at the same time.

Steep shards of glass punctuated the ground, extending toward the sky, creating a sort of maze leading off into the indistinguishable distance.

It was deafeningly quiet, so silent it hurt his ears.

Miranda leaned close so she could speak directly into his ear. "Welcome to Aetern," she whispered. "Place of the eternal fire."

11

Jasmine caught herself just before she fell.

The pain in her head faded. She stood, gasping for breath, fighting the urge to throw up. Had there been another aftershock? But the few people she saw on the street seemed unfazed; whatever had happened had obviously happened only to her.

She shivered. The air was full of mist. Overhead, dark, stormy clouds were knitted together in the sky.

Only moments earlier, it had been clear and sunny.

She ducked back into the coffee shop as the sky opened up and rain began to drum on the sidewalk. The red-haired girl was still behind the counter, but she was wearing a different shirt. There were more people now, some standing in line, others crowding the tables. The windows were fogged up from the heat of their bodies.

It was wrong. All wrong.

Intuitively, she glanced at the stack of newspapers by the door again.

Cleanup Efforts Continue. Search For
Survivors Continues, Day Two.
Monday, October 15.

She froze. Was this a joke?

Hysterical laughter bubbled up in her throat. She looked over her shoulder to see if the girl was watching her. It *had* to be a trick — some hidden-camera, practical-joke kind of thing. Maybe it was a new reality TV show. But the girl didn't even glance her way.

A man in a dark suit started to push past her, a large to-go cup in his hand.

"Excuse me." Jasmine licked her lips nervously. Her throat felt parched. "Could you tell me what day it is?"

The man looked at her curiously. "Monday."

"Are you sure?" she blurted out.

"I had to go back to work today. So yeah, I'm pretty sure." He pushed out the door and jogged to a car double-parked at the curb, using a newspaper as a makeshift umbrella. Jasmine followed him out onto the sidewalk, mindless of the rain. She barely even felt it.

She breathed in deeply, like the school counselor, Mrs. Cole, had instructed her to do when she felt over-whelmed. If she wasn't caught up in an enormous con-spiracy of practical jokers, that left only a couple of possibilities:

She was crazy.

She was jumping back and forth in time.

Time. Ford had said something about time. He was talking about Miranda. *Time was always an obsession of hers.*

And the note she'd found in the hidden room: *Find Ford. He'll know what to do.*

Luc had mentioned that Miranda was responsible for what had happened to Jasmine on Friday night.

It all kept coming back to the same woman. Maybe Miranda was the crazy one.

Maybe Jasmine would be okay. She had to believe that.

Jasmine stepped back from the curb as a bus rumbled by. If it was truly Monday—*again*—then Ford would be at the rotunda. Maybe she could get him to take her to Miranda.

Jasmine ran down Jackson—noticing, again, how easily she took the hills, despite the fact that it had been hours (days?) since she'd last eaten—past the park and the gym where she'd seen Ford boxing. She caught the bus at the next stop and slipped loose change from her pocket into the slot where the driver sat.

She made her way to an empty seat.

The voices of the passengers around her slugged through her mind, distorted and deep. The constant lurching of the bus, the starting and stopping, sent spikes shooting into her head. She felt sick to her stomach. Time travel. Christ. It was something out of a science-fiction book. It was impossible.

Wasn't it?

When the bus shuddered to a stop near the Palace of Fine Arts, she exited quickly, staring at the ground. She couldn't have been on the bus that long, but with so many streets still without electricity and the sky filled with deep gray clouds, it looked darker than before. She estimated it must be around four p.m., about twenty minutes later than the first time she'd met Ford at the rotunda. She hoped he would still be there.

Jasmine walked in the direction the bus had gone, her head down and hands in her pockets. Divisadero was familiar enough to her that she knew where the rotunda was.

Rain ran under her collar, soaked her shirt, and made her long hair stick to her face. But it felt true, and real. It convinced her *she* was real.

The debris had been cleared away from in front of the hidden staircase. What did that mean? Had Ford discovered the hideout himself? A strong feeling of dread washed over her. The attack. It was here she'd felt a hand grab her ankle; it was here she'd blacked out.

Suddenly, she realized that if it really was Monday again, that meant her attackers would pursue her here, to this very spot, *again*. She was an idiot to have come.

She froze when she heard footsteps. A familiar figure moved into the light. Ford.

"What are you doing here?" he said.

She came down the stairs toward him. His face was in shadow. "Leaving," she said. She seized his hand. "And you're coming with me."

"I thought I told you yesterday—" he started, but Jas cut him off.

"Yeah, I know. Different sides and all that. But you have to trust me on this one."

Ford wrenched his hand away from hers. "How did you know where to find me? Were you following me again?"

"Not exactly." How much time did they have before her attackers appeared again? "Look, there's no time to explain everything. But we need to go. *Now.*"

He hesitated for a second longer. Then he sighed and shrugged. "Lead the way."

They made it only halfway up the stairs before the boy appeared above them, blocking their way.

"Run!" Jasmine shouted, but it was too late; there was nowhere to go. The boy launched himself at her and drove her backward, into Ford. All of them fell. The air whooshed out of Jas's lungs when she landed on the concrete floor, catching Ford's elbow in her side.

Quickly, she rolled free and stood up, ignoring the shooting pain in her knee. The faint light from the main room barely illuminated the stairway. Ford scrambled to his feet, but the boy from the park was on his feet just as quickly. The knife glinted in his hand.

He didn't look like a deranged stalker or a hired killer. He looked like any other guy Jasmine might know. He wore jeans, a dark T-shirt, and a worn brown leather jacket. His hair was a little too long, and it curled over his eyes.

"What the hell?" Ford said.

"Stay out of it," the boy said. He kept his eyes on Jasmine, even as he addressed Ford.

Ford growled. "Like hell I will. You have a knife in your hands."

For just one second, the boy glanced at Ford. "This isn't about you."

In that second, Jasmine struck. She drove her knee straight into the boy's groin. He howled in pain. His gaze swung around and met hers. Then he doubled over, falling to his knees. Jasmine had to step over him to reach the staircase, but he barely seemed to notice.

"Come on," she said to Ford.

Jas burst into the open air and collided with the female attacker on the other side of the door. The girl was obviously startled; Jasmine reacted first and grabbed the girl's arm, yanking her into the stairwell. Ford flattened himself against the wall as the girl stumbled, her arms swinging wildly for balance. Before the girl could right herself, Jasmine pushed her and sent her rolling down the stairs.

"Remind me to stay on your good side," Ford said.

They ran past the fallen columns and the chunks of fissured concrete and debris. At the street, she stopped. She blinked rain out of her eyes. Which way now? Her attackers would find her again. They had done it twice already.

As if on cue, raised voices came from the direction of the rotunda. Jas's heart was wild with panic; she could feel it pounding in her throat.

Ford grabbed her hand. As always, a jolt of electricity went through her when he touched her. "This way," he said, pulling her toward the bay instead of inland.

"Where are we going?" Jasmine looked over her shoulder as they ran. When they were a hundred yards away, she saw the boy and girl burst into the street. The boy still looked a little green, but he was moving *fast*.

Ford led her to the parking lot and yanked her over to the nearest motorcycle. He pulled a helmet off the handlebars and tossed it to her. She barely managed to catch it.

"Put it on," he said, already climbing onto the bike.

As Jasmine was fumbling with the clasp, she saw the ignition spark, and the bike rumbled to life.

"How'd you do that?" she asked.

Ford revved the throttle a few times. "Are you going to keep asking questions or are you going to get on?"

He was right. Jas had ridden with T.J. enough to know how to fasten the chin strap and swing her leg over the bike, behind Ford. From the corner of her eye she saw someone running toward them shouting. She threw her arms around Ford's waist, clasped her hands, and held on tight, and the bike jumped forward.

Ford drove across Lyon and wove around a pile of debris, then crossed Marina and turned left onto Mason. A car swerved around them, horn blaring, but Jas barely heard it over the frantic beating of her own heart. The girl and boy were still chasing them on foot, unnervingly close.

How could they run so fast?

Not human. The words, the idea, suddenly broke into Jasmine's consciousness, and she knew it was true. They weren't human. They couldn't be.

She remembered how she'd watched Ford split a bag apart at the boxing gym. Was he something other than human, too?

They shot down Mason, the throttle wide open and the engine loud. The storefronts sent back a watery reflection of their headlights. Jas peeked over Ford's shoulder and couldn't hold back a shriek of surprise. Someone had run into the middle of the road and stopped, right in their way.

The girl. She held the knife waist high, waiting for them. Waiting for Jasmine.

"Hold on!" Ford shouted. He didn't stop; he aimed straight for the girl. He leaned forward and Jasmine gripped his waist. His coat was slick with rain. Jasmine's chest was tight with terror. He was going to run the girl down.

He was going to kill her.

Ford. She tried to shout his name, but she couldn't get the word out of her throat. It was too late anyway. They were almost on top of the girl, so close Jas could see her mouth open in surprise, the small dimple between her eyebrows as she frowned. Jas squeezed her eyes closed and braced for impact.

But the bike kept purring along. They didn't even swerve.

When Jas looked back, she saw the girl picking herself up off the pavement. She must have jumped out of the way just in time. Jasmine exhaled. The girl was quickly swallowed up by the distance and the dark. Jas wondered what had happened to the boy with the long hair.

She knew that both of them would be back. They wanted her dead. That much was obvious.

She still had no idea why. . . .

On their left, lit windows streamed past and buildings danced in and out of sight.

On their right, the wide mouth of the bay was open to the dark gray sky. The salty smell of the bay mixed with newly cut grass and dew.

Several more minutes went by before Ford slowed the bike and they veered right, onto a boardwalk along the beach. The bike trail. The normally packed trail was empty as Ford guided the motorcycle with ease along the boardwalk.

Jas was cold. Salt spray from the bay mingled with the rain. She leaned in closer to Ford, feeling the heat radiating through his back. He smelled good. As she pressed close to him, she remembered what he had looked like without a shirt on, the muscles, the jacked-up strength.

Not human. She quickly pushed the thought aside. She was too tired for questions and doubts.

Maybe they would just keep riding forever. That would be okay with her.

Ford weaved expertly around the pitted spots on the trail and places where the earthquake had punched a fist skyward, leaving broken piles of wood in its wake. They jumped back onto the road. Ford slowed the bike and pulled into a parking spot at Fort Point. When he cut the engine, Jas pulled off the helmet and swung her leg over the seat, surprised at how solid the ground felt under her feet. The crash of the waves against the rocks was thunderous, and the sky was still bleeding rain. Jasmine realized she had no idea what time it was—the clouds had turned everything a uniform gray.

Ford climbed off after her and put a hand on her back.

"We'll be safe here for a while!" he shouted, leaning close so she could hear him.

Jas was so surprised by how nice it felt to hear him say *we* that she couldn't even ask where *here* was. He started toward the chain-link fence put up to keep people out of the section of the fort under the Golden Gate Bridge, which rose above them, a vast steel giant with fingers pointing to the sky. A big No Trespassing sign was visible in the half dark. Ford ignored it. He shoved at the gate, exposing a narrow gap just large enough to slip through.

He motioned for Jasmine to enter. She hesitated. Jas had sworn to Luc to stay out of trouble. Even thinking about her brother, and where he could possibly be, made her chest feel heavy. What if something had happened to him? What if those crazy assassins, or whatever they were, had gotten him?

Thinking about the boy and the girl and the possibility of their return made her decide. She slipped through the gate, and Ford followed. She could still hear the slurring of the waves against the shore and the drumming

of the rain on the damp sand, loud as a march. She realized with a start that although Ford was walking next to
her, she couldn't read anything off him—no feelings. No
wants. Nothing.

"What are we doing here?" They had arrived at the
base of an enormous cement footer that served as one of
the bridge's supports. Here the noise of the waves was
even louder, amplified by the arched steel beams.

"Hiding." Ford stopped in front of a narrow door.
There was a lock but no visible handle. The door was
barely distinguishable from the gray cement all around
it. Ford fumbled in his pocket, and Jas watched him
shove a thin file into the lock. She glanced around to
make sure no one was watching. But they were alone.
Just the beach and the bay and the endless rain.

The lock gave with a click, and Ford held the door
open and motioned for her to go inside. It was pitch-
black. The air that reached her from inside was warm
and dry and smelled musty. Again, she hesitated. *This is
where the dumb girl in every horror movie walks right into her
own death.*

"Now it's your turn to trust me," Ford said with a
small smile. Her stomach jumped. He was right. Jas
stepped into the darkness. When Ford stepped in and
shut the door behind them, the noise of the waves was
suddenly silenced. Jasmine found the unexpected quiet
deafening.

"Just ahead, to the right, there's a small room," Ford
said. He rested a hand on her hip to guide her; warmth
radiated from his touch. This close, she could smell the

cinnamon scent of his skin. It was comforting. Familiar, somehow, even though he was a stranger.

And he was obviously keeping secrets.

But she was glad to be out of the rain and the cold.

Ford nudged her forward. She stepped carefully, her hand on the rough wall. She could feel slight vibrations coming from the floor—impact from the waves, maybe, and the wind—and smell something sweet, honeylike.

"Here we are," Ford said. He moved around her. There was that delicious word again—*we*. A light flickered and Ford raised a hurricane lantern to eye level. "It's not much. But we should be able to hide here for a while."

The small space looked like some kind of mechanics' room that had long ago been stripped of its contents. A couple of blankets were folded neatly on the floor, and a camp stove sat in a corner. The ceiling was so high it was lost in the vast darkness beyond the small circle that the lantern could illuminate. The air smelled tangy, like salt—but there was that second, deeper layer of sweetness as well, almost as if there had been flowers growing here at some point.

"Is this where you live?" She hugged herself, trying to get warm. It was warmer here, but not by much, and her clothes were heavy and water-soaked from the rain.

Ford set the lantern down and grabbed one of the blankets, shaking it out before he wrapped it around her shoulders. She buried her nose in the soft fleece. It smelled like him.

"I'm staying here for a bit," he answered cryptically.

Jasmine realized she didn't know how old he was. He quickly changed the subject. "How about something hot to drink?"

Jasmine sank down onto the other blanket and watched as he lit the small, one-burner camp stove, then set a teapot to boil. His movements were relaxed, easy, as if the two of them hadn't just gone on a wild motorcycle ride through the rain to escape a couple of homicidal maniacs. Jasmine's hands were still shaking, and her mind was spinning around and around—she couldn't make it land on any logical explanation. Maybe she was in shock.

"Are you all right?" he asked, looking up at her as if he could read her thoughts.

"Been better," she said. She hugged her knees to her chest. "It's not every day someone tries to kill me." She didn't even know how to talk about the other part—how she had left her aunt's house on a Tuesday and wound up in Monday again.

There was a mug sitting next to a glass jar full of tea bags on a wooden shelf. Ford added a tea bag to the mug, poured in water, then sloshed in liquid from a bottle he wrestled out of his pocket. She raised an eyebrow.

"You trying to poison me?"

He half smiled. "You don't like whiskey?"

She took the mug from him. It was hot, and felt good in her hands.

"Go ahead," Ford said. "It's best when it's hot."

It did smell amazing, with hints of vanilla and wild-flower. The tea was delicious and the whiskey added just enough of a good burn. It lit a fire in her stomach and, after a few sips, made her swirling thoughts begin to settle. She closed her eyes for a second, savoring the taste and the silence.

"So. Do you have any idea why?"

Ford's question surprised her. She opened her eyes and saw that he was staring at her.

"Why what?" she asked.

His dark eyes drilled into her. "Why someone is trying to kill you."

"None." She set the steaming tea on the ground. "I have no idea who those people are, or why they're following me."

"Following you?" Ford repeated. "You've seen them before?"

It occurred to her that he didn't know about the attack in the park. *Or* that she'd already lived through the attack at the pavilion twice. Would he think she was insane if she told him that time was skipping around?

Probably. But somehow, confined in this little room and feeling safe for the first time in days, she felt she could truly trust him.

She took a deep breath. "This isn't the first time they've attacked me. Actually, this isn't the first time they've attacked us, either." Ford frowned. Jas rushed on. "Look, this is going to sound crazy. But I knew they'd be there today because they attacked us in the same spot . . . not yesterday, really, I guess today, but *before. . . .*" She knew she wasn't making any sense. She glanced up at Ford. His expression hadn't lost its neutrality.

"Time shifted, then?" he asked, as if it was a regular occurrence.

Relief broke in her chest. "Yeah. Exactly. Time *shifted*." He still didn't react. "I don't know how else to explain it. I get this horrible headache and everything gets bright. Then, when I open my eyes, I'm somewhere else. A different day."

"Go on," Ford said.

She wrapped her fingers around the mug again. The tea—or maybe it was the whiskey—was making her limbs feel heavy, and a cozy warmth spread through her veins.

"The last day I really remember clearly is Friday. Then there's this chunk of time just . . . missing. My . . . brother won't tell me what happened." Jasmine stumbled over the word *brother*. Luc was in trouble—she could sense it—and it was all her fault. "And there's more. I can smell and hear and, like, sense things a thousand times better than before—sense people, even, and what they're feeling. Except for you. Not you." Her face was burning. She looked away from him. "I don't understand any of it," she finished. "I don't know why those people are trying to hurt me."

Ford was quiet for a minute. Then, abruptly, he stood up. "They're Executors," he said, taking her empty cup. "It's what they do."

Laughter bubbled up from deep inside Jas. What had he put in her tea? She felt light, giddy, and not quite solid. "Executors? Like 'off with your head' type of people?"

When he turned back to her, he was frowning. "You

really don't know, do you. About *anything*." He shoved a hand through his hair.

The way he said *anything* sent goose bumps up her arms. Suddenly, she didn't feel giddy anymore. "I—I don't know what you're talking about," Jas said quietly.

He sat down across from her with a deep sigh. His eyes searched her face, as if he was debating how much to tell her. Finally, he said, "There are forces out there charged with keeping order in the universe. They obey their laws blindly, without care or thought for others. And they don't stop. They never stop." His voice held such bitterness that Jas wanted to reach out and hug him. But she had too many questions.

"What do you mean, *forces*?" she asked. "Like . . . physics and stuff?" She had never been any good at math and science. Except astronomy. She knew the positions of all the stars, had memorized them with Luc when she was a little girl.

Ford shook his head impatiently. "Not forces. People. People like the girl and boy who attacked us today."

"Executors," Jasmine said. Ford nodded.

She inhaled sharply. It was insane. But so was everything that had happened to her. "How do you know all this?"

Ford shrugged. "The universe is big, and complicated," he said. His eyes were like starry skies: points of light dancing in the middle of darkness. "I've seen many parts of it."

She bit her lip. *Not human.* The words were impossible to ignore this time. "So . . . you don't think I'm crazy?"

His lips turned up at the corners and he looked at her sideways. "I think you're *a little* crazy. You did knee an Executor in the groin."

"He didn't leave me much choice." Jas couldn't remember the last time she'd smiled. It felt good. She scooted back so that she could lean against the cement wall. Ford was still watching her with that intense look in his eyes. She looked down. "What about all the other stuff? Like . . . like about the Executors." Her heart was beating fast—it was being here, in the half dark, next to him, and trying to understand. "You're saying they're after me, right?" She tugged at the blanket still draped around her shoulders. "But why? It doesn't make sense. You said they keep order. It's not like I'm some great threat to the universe."

She waited for him to agree with her, but he merely shrugged. "I don't know. But you're not safe. You won't be, until they're dead."

"So . . ." Jasmine tried to work up the courage to ask the questions she needed to. "Are you an Executor, too?"

Ford snorted. "Not likely. I don't follow orders from anyone." Then his voice got quiet. "But I knew an Executor once, a very, very long time ago."

"Are you saying you're older than you look?" He nodded. Jas squeezed her hands into fists. "Like thousand-year-vampire old? Or old-man old? I think old-man old is creepier."

He smiled, just barely. "Older than that."

Jas swallowed. "So, what . . . what are you?"

She thought he might not tell her, but after he reached

over to turn the camp stove off, he grabbed the lantern and moved to sit next to her. He, too, leaned back, tilting his head so it rested against the wall. "I'm . . . different, like you."

His face was only a few inches from hers. She could feel the energy flowing between them, liquid and warm. "You're saying we're the same?"

"Sort of," he said. "I can't really explain it, though; it's complicated. We're . . ."

"On different sides, yeah, I know, you said that already." Jas pulled her knees to her chest and hugged the blanket tighter around herself.

"I don't want to hurt you." A muscle twitched in his jaw. He looked almost angry. "I *won't* ever hurt you. You can trust me." He started to reach for her, then seemed to think better of it.

Jasmine hesitated. Then she found his hand in the dark and squeezed it. "I do trust you," she said.

Ford turned to her and smiled. It changed his face. He became so beautiful it was almost hard to look at him. Jasmine pulled her hand away.

"You're tired," he said softly.

She nodded. She was tired—drowsy and warm and safe. She didn't understand everything he had told her, but she didn't care. She wanted to forget about the Executors and where Ford had come from. He was here, and he was protecting her.

How long had it been since she had slept? The storm was muffled by the thick walls. From here, the rain was no more than a hum. Humming . . . her mother was humming in the kitchen. . . .

"Come on," Ford whispered. "You're falling asleep."

He guided Jas onto a mattress lying in the corner and tucked the blanket around her shoulders, as if she were a child.

"Would you hold me? Just until I fall asleep?" She barely knew what she was saying. She was cold and he was warm. She was swaying, rocking on a dark ocean. He lay down and slid one arm carefully under her head and the other around her waist.

The contact was electric. She could feel his breath in her hair. . . . She wanted to kiss him. . . . She pressed against him and he held her tight.

Please don't wake up yesterday. She wanted to be right there, with Ford, when she opened her eyes again.

In the safety of his arms, for the first time in days, she slept.

She woke up sometime in the middle of the night and saw Ford standing in the shadows on the far side of the room. The lamp had been extinguished. It was almost completely dark, except for the silvery light of the moon, which shone faintly through a small window set high in the wall. It had stopped raining, but water was still dripping rhythmically to the ground next to Ford's bare feet, leaking from some invisible spot above him.

Jasmine watched him twist and jab, almost as if he were shadowboxing. But his palms were flat, and as he moved, the water simply rose from the pool at his feet; it stopped dripping and hung suspended. Drops of water, dark as ink, began spinning when Ford closed his fingers into a fist.

Jasmine was suddenly awake, and terrified.

Then, just as quickly, he stopped moving. All the water fell, splashing down onto the concrete, and the steady dripping resumed. He turned and Jasmine quickly shut her eyes so he wouldn't know she'd been watching him.

She heard his footsteps approaching the mattress. She kept her eyes squeezed shut, willing her heart to slow down. He tucked himself back behind her, draping an arm over her waist. Soon she heard the even rhythm of his breathing.

Slowly, she began to calm down.

She was probably imagining things.

She was probably dreaming.

She would ask Ford about it in the morning.

12

They went in silence through the world of glass.

Each step was agonizingly slow; each time Luc stepped down, he feared that all the glass would shatter and he would plummet into nothingness. Miranda didn't speak. When he had tried to question her further, she had merely placed a finger to her lips.

The terrain changed gradually. They moved into a vast network of glass stalagmites that reached for the sky. The glass spires were dazzling in the setting sun: red and gold fires seemed to smolder in their surfaces, and Luc had to shield his eyes to keep from being blinded. It was like being inside a many-faceted crystal, or at the bottom of a cavernous maze built entirely of ice.

Luc was aching for sound, for motion, for anything alive. This place was even worse than the world of snow—even quieter, the air vibrating with things unsaid and sounds begging for release.

They broke free, at last, of the maze, only to find themselves at the base of a towering mountain of glass. Writhing wisps of what looked like steam curled upward from the top and stretched to the sky. Overhead, colors twisted into each other, creating the most amazing blown-glass effect.

It reminded Luc of watching a glass blower at the art center last year. How the glass had turned molten, pliable enough for puffs of air to be blown into the center. The man had dipped and blown and shaped the glass until it became a multicolored orb that looked almost otherworldly.

Molten glass was rolling down from the top of the mountain, giant tear-shaped beads that then hardened and formed ridges that made the side of the slope look like the back of an enormous glass reptile. The ground beneath them vibrated with a low and constant hum, and another sound, fainter but still discernible. A steady beating rhythm.

Thump. Thump. Thump.

Then came a crackling noise, like massive bones being roused from a deep sleep. The entire mountain seemed to move, and Luc took a step back.

"You see, Luc, how the guardian of fire hungers." Miranda whispered so quietly, he was forced to lean in to hear her, even though being close to her made his skin crawl. "He needs souls to feed the flame."

"What are you talk . . ."

The question died in his throat. Because as he spoke, as he watched, the mountain *moved*. It was slight, but Luc was sure of it.

And Luc saw it wasn't a mountain at all, but an enormous monster—with teeth as sharp and glittering as icicles, and a dark cave of a mouth, and a tail spiked with glass as sharp as a razor.

Each of its legs was as wide as a house. As it rose, a huge shadow fell over Luc, a darkness that blotted out the sun smoldering on the horizon. It had no eyes that Luc could see, but that didn't matter. The monster knew where he was. It swung its vast head, that enormous surface of planes and angles and pitted shadows, toward him. Its mouth gaped, large as a tunnel.

He needs souls to feed the flame.

The monster reared back. Luc scrambled out of the way before a giant glass foot came down inches from where he stood. Luc glanced at Miranda. The monster was ignoring her, almost as if he couldn't sense her at all.

Of course. She was a Radical. She had no soul.

Now Luc understood: She had led him here to be bait. She had led him here to be killed.

Next time—if he ever got a next time—he would slit her throat.

The monster's foot came down again, this time barely missing his head. He couldn't save Corinthe if he was dead. With one last murderous glare at Miranda, he started to run toward the forest of stalagmites.

Luc ran. Every time his feet pounded on the ground, cracks webbed out from under his sneakers. It was like running over a pond that hasn't had enough time to freeze. Luc risked a glance behind him and crashed straight into a giant glass stalagmite. As it toppled, Luc felt a quick pressure, almost like the touch of the wind. The glass at his feet was stained a bright red. It took him a second to realize he was bleeding.

The monster was already on top of him again. It had caught up without having to try.

Luc spun around. He couldn't outrun this thing; he'd have to figure out a way to fight it. Behind it, Luc could see Miranda moving across the now-empty landscape, the large blank sweep of space where the monster had been perched. In the distance, a small glowing orb the size of a football sat in a spun-glass nest. The eternal flame—it had to be.

And Luc knew: Miranda would win. Corinthe would be lost. Jasmine would be alone.

The monster lowered its head, razor-sharp glass teeth glinting in the dying light, the vast cavern of its mouth open to swallow him.

Luc took off his backpack, the only weapon he had. As the monster lunged for him, Luc swung, shattering a large chunk of glass from its jaw. He swung again, feeling a surge of hope, aiming for one of its teeth. But the teeth were too sharp; the monster sliced the backpack easily in half, scattering its contents—the protein bars, his phone, Rhys's book—just out of reach over the glassy ground.

Rhys's book.

Whispers came from the pages—secrets, snippets of Rhys's whole life, disappearing in the thin air. The monster opened its huge jaws again. This time Luc had nothing left—nowhere to run, and nothing he could use as a weapon.

But instead of devouring him, the beast stopped.

And swung its huge head toward the book. Its vast shadow passed over Luc. It huffed out a breath that crystallized in the air, a million tiny prisms, before falling.

Suddenly, Luc realized: the *book*. The Library of the Dead flashed into his mind. All its books held the *souls* of the dead. And if Rhys's book held his soul within its pages . . .

He had to try.

Luc ran. As he did, the monster's blind gaze returned to him, and Luc felt the silence of its roar, as deafening as any sound—the air compressed around him, as if a giant palm were crushing him from all sides. He couldn't breathe. His vision went black. He reached out blindly and felt glass and more glass, shards cutting his palms and fingers.

And then his hand closed around the book.

He cocked his arm and threw as hard as he could. That silent roar hit him from all sides again, drove him to his stomach. He felt the icy explosion of the monster's breath—and then a weight like an airplane soaring an inch from his head, keeping him flattened.

He was dead. Or dying.

But all at once, the weight released. The roar ended. Luc sat up, sucking in air, as the monster's tail passed over him.

Luc saw the book land.

The beast lunged, tearing into the pages. It had worked.

There would be only seconds before the beast was done. Luc had to get away fast.

He heard a sigh behind him, a string of words, Rhys's soft voice—*time shadows forgotten when I last*—*Mira*—and then he heard nothing at all.

Miranda was gone.

He knew she must have made for the Crossroad. Where else could she go? The monster, sated, ignored him as he stumbled through the maze of glass. Luc was bleeding. He took off his sweatshirt as he jogged and used it to stanch the cuts in his palms and between his fingers. He couldn't even feel the pain.

He was too focused on one thing: revenge.

Within minutes, he caught sight of Miranda's long black hair as she weaved among the glass peaks. The sun was gone now. The glass glowed blue and purple against the twilight sky, and Luc thought of Corinthe's eyes, and the way she'd clung to him, desperately, as she died. All of it, everything, was for Corinthe.

He moved faster, going as quickly as he could while stepping lightly, closing the distance between himself and Miranda. She was holding the glowing flame, blue and round, like a baby in her arms. She moved carefully, as if she was afraid of dropping it. She wasn't expecting to be pursued; she obviously thought Luc was dead.

When he attacked, he shoved her with all his weight from behind. She fell forward so hard that the flame skidded across the ground, stopping several feet away. Luc saw it begin to melt the ice around it. How much time did he have before it melted right through this world?

Miranda was strong, much stronger than he was, and she easily shook him off.

They both jumped to their feet, facing each other like wrestling opponents.

"Corinthe trusted you," he said. At the mention of her name, Luc heard a snapping sound, much like the first cracks of thin ice beginning to break.

"You stupid boy," Miranda said, watching the crack spread. "You said her name aloud."

"What does her name have to do with this?" he asked. As if to agitate her, he continued: "Corinthe . . . CORINTHE!"

The fissure grew larger, and a low rumble sounded. Miranda looked around wildly and Luc lunged for her. She sidestepped, but he kicked out at the last minute and hit the back of her leg. She went down but pushed herself nimbly to her feet almost instantly; she flew at him and wound her fingers around his neck. "Stop. Saying. Her. Name."

She squeezed her elegant hands harder around his throat and he couldn't breathe. He couldn't think.

"The glass here is special. It's strong because it absorbs

the anger of the universe—but when it hears something beautiful, it breaks." At the last word she tightened her grip. Luc felt his throat collapsing. *Corinthe,* he longed to say.

"But my anger, my bitterness—it makes it whole again. See?" She shoved his face down to watch as the glass cracks healed themselves. "Your love is not stronger than my resentment. You won't win this war. Not against me."

"He can't, Miranda. But I can."

Miranda released Luc and spun around. Even as Luc doubled over, gasping for breath, he couldn't believe it: Tess. Tess was alive and had come back, this time to save him.

"You can't stop me," Miranda said.

Tess shook her head. She looked almost sad. "I told you I wouldn't let you continue with your plan."

Miranda laughed. The sound was hollow. "You helped me escape."

"Because I owed you a debt. But I owe you nothing now." Her voice got softer. "And if you continue on this path, we are enemies. Please, Mira, stop this need for revenge and accept the Tribunal's offer."

It was as if they had forgotten Luc's existence. He inched warily toward the flame. He didn't care what happened to either of them. They could kill each other, as far as he was concerned. Tess had saved his life—but he knew it was only because she had a more important enemy in Miranda.

If the flame was powerful enough for Miranda to want it, maybe he could use it to make the tunnels move backward. *If* he could figure out how it worked.

Regardless, he would take it with him.

Miranda launched herself at Tess and the two of them fell to the ground in a tangle of arms and legs.

Luc reached down, grabbed the orb, and ran.

The landscape cleared up and soon he found himself running along the pristine surface of delicate glass. Somewhere was the exit to the Crossroad. Everything looked the same now. He stopped and turned in a complete circle, and lost his sense of direction. Which way had he been running?

The orb grew hotter in his hand, and he pulled the sleeve of his jacket down so he could hold it. Still, the heat permeated the fabric and soon became almost unbearable. He had to move, but in which direction?

Far to the right, a wisp of color caught his eye. As he ran toward it, the air filled with color, creating a wall of sorts. He'd seen pictures of the aurora borealis, and imagined that they must look like this up close.

So beautiful.

So much like the Crossroad.

It had to be the exit.

He looked over his shoulder and saw Miranda racing across the distance, with Tess right behind her.

She couldn't get the flame.

She would not win.

Luc plunged into the colors that came alive around

him. They swirled and coiled around his arms and legs until he was weightless, then became a swirling mass with winds so strong they howled.

Luc fought to hold on to the orb, despite its incredible, searing heat, but he was tossed into a ferocious river of color and was swept through the Crossroad on a writhing, snakelike current. He felt the flame slip from his hands, burning away through the Crossroad, beyond his control.

And then it was gone.

13

When Jasmine woke again, she hung in a delicious place between dreams and wakefulness for several long minutes. The rich scent of a forest filled her nose and there was something else just under the surface. Something familiar that made her veins feel filled with electricity. With immense hunger.

Blood.

She sat up quickly, clutching the blanket to her chin. For a second, she didn't know where she was and panic raced through her.

Then the sound of rain brought it all back: the attack. The chase. How Ford had brought her here, to this concealed room, his home. She was safe. She relaxed, letting her dream—or nightmare?—ebb.

The storm still raged outside, and she could hear the

waves smashing into the concrete tower. She could smell the mustiness of wet stone, the remnants of long-gone diesel and machine oil. Weirdly, it was kind of pleasant.

Ford was gone. She had a vague recollection of watching him spin water from his fingertips—surely, she'd been dreaming.

She shook off the blanket and stood, still in her jeans and sweater from the day before. Sleeping on the narrow mattress on the rock-hard floor had made her ache everywhere. She tried to stretch out the worst of the pains.

Then her stomach seized up. An awful idea occurred to her.

What if Ford hadn't left—what if time had shifted again, slid away from her, while she was asleep?

She felt her way down the dark hallway to the door. When she pushed it open, she saw nothing but gray-flecked waves and stormy skies. A fine mist blew against her face, causing her wavy hair to stick to her skin. It was raining, but was it *still* raining from last night? Or was this the beginning of the storm?

Was she stuck in Monday again?

She pulled the door shut hard. It helped ease her frustration. She needed to find proof—a person, a newspaper, *something*. She went to retrieve her bag from the room. Her temples started to pound, and she braced for the blinding light. Instead, the dull thudding of a regular old headache pulsed in her head.

Her backpack lay in the far corner, where she must have dumped it the night before. She was glad; she'd almost been afraid she would find it gone. When she reached out to grab it, she saw there was something pinned to the front.

A note, scribbled on a scrap of blank paper.

Jasmine, I have to say goodbye before things get more complicated.

Jasmine had to read the words three times before she could accept them. She sat down hard. She felt like all the air had been pushed out of her lungs.

He had left her. Ditched her, just like that. After everything. After all she had told him — after she'd trusted him. She crumpled his note and threw it as hard as she could. It bounced off the wall and landed next to the cold camp stove.

Screw him.

Hot tears burned the back of her eyes and she scrubbed them away. Who cared if she was alone now? It wasn't like she had people taking care of her up to this point. Except for Luc, she'd been pretty much on her own. Ford could go jump off the bridge for all she cared.

She shouldered her messenger bag and rifled around the small space, looking for anything useful — money, credit cards, anything. If he wasn't coming back, he wouldn't miss it. But there was only the tea and some batteries, a half-full bottle of whiskey, and a crumpled ten-dollar bill.

She grabbed the money, shoved the door open, and

stepped out into the gray, wet day. At the last second she remembered that the door had no handle and wedged a small piece of wood into the doorframe to stop it from closing completely. In case she needed to come back for whatever reason.

In case she needed to hide from the Executors. Just thinking the word made her shiver.

Jasmine pulled her jacket tighter and ducked her head. She glanced around as she walked, half expecting the Executors to jump out at her. Would they find her again? They had twice—technically, three times—already.

The chain-link gate felt icy cold under her fingers as she pushed a wide-enough gap to squeeze through. The rain muted all the other sounds that had been hammering in her head. Now the patter of drops hitting the ground muffled the cars honking and the people shouting and the huge machines clearing the earthquake wreckage.

A biting, salty aroma blew off the bay, and it was all she could smell.

She could almost pretend she was normal. Just a regular girl, heading home from school.

There was no one around to notice as she passed the fort. There was only one car in the parking lot, probably a sanitation worker, and she made it all the way to the entrance without seeing a soul. There was a bus stop just across the street, and Jasmine had to stand alone for only a couple of minutes before the bus pulled up.

She used the last of her coins and made the connection that would take her to Richmond. Before too long, she found herself in a familiar neighborhood. The street looked clearer than when she had left, and she easily ran to the steps of her building. Up two flights of stairs to the apartment door.

"Luc?" Her voice echoed in the empty apartment.

She knew immediately he wasn't there. The apartment felt vacant and cold. Pancakes sat in sticky dried puddles of syrup on the plates. She couldn't bring herself to clean them up. Anxiety felt like lead in her stomach. How many days had it been since Luc fobbed her off on Aunt Hillary? It was hard to tell. Was time skipping for Luc, too? Luc wasn't one to disappear like this, without a word to Jasmine. Something must have happened. She knew he would never have left her if he'd known how much danger she was really in. He'd thought the Executors were after *him*.

It struck Jasmine that Luc had known more than he let on—he said he might know *who* they were, but had he known *what* they were? *Executors?* Hadn't he basically said so?

The door to Luc's room was open. He was probably the only teenage guy who actually kept his room neat and clean. His books were stacked on his desk next to a secondhand laptop he'd found on Craigslist. His bed was neatly made, and there were no clothes on the floor. The only thing hanging on his wall was a Giants poster.

It all looked like he was coming right back. So where was he?

Jas went back out to the kitchen and picked up the phone. There was a dial tone this time, and she had to push Luc's number three times to get it right in her excitement.

"The number you have dialed is temporarily unavailable. Please try again later."

Jas hung up and dialed again. The same message came across the line. What the hell did that mean?

Maybe a tower was down because of the earthquake. Still, the feeling of unease didn't go away.

So what now?

Before she could make a decision, she froze. Someone was coming to the door. A girl—the sweet smell of flowery shampoo gave her away.

Was the Executor back already?

Jasmine grabbed a large kitchen knife off the counter. She was damned well not giving up without a fight. She tiptoed to the door and looked through the peephole.

Immediately, she felt like an idiot. It was only Karen, Luc's girlfriend. Or ex-girlfriend. Karen was chewing on her bottom lip, which was frosted with pink. She raised a hand, hesitated, then knocked. "Luc?" she called out.

Jasmine tossed the knife onto a side table and yanked the door open—maybe a little too forcefully. Karen's eyes went wide and she stepped back. "God, you scared me. Is Luc home?" Karen looked past Jasmine into the apartment.

Jas knew it was stupid, but she couldn't help feeling embarrassed. They hardly ever had people over. Luc had never had Karen over as far as she knew. Drunk father aside, he hated the idea that she might pity him—or worse, laugh at him.

Jasmine grabbed her backpack and slipped into the hallway, closing the door behind her and sealing off Karen's view of the apartment. "Luc's super sick. Really bad stomach bug."

Karen stared at the closed door for a few seconds, as if she was considering trying to burst through it. "He isn't answering any of my calls. I mean . . . I guess I don't blame him. But with the earthquake and everything . . ." Karen hugged herself. She was wearing a stupid pink sweatshirt with the word JUICY written across it, and she'd cheated on Luc. Still, she looked like she hadn't slept in days, and Jas couldn't help but feel bad for her. "I just wanted to make sure he was okay."

Jas said nothing. Karen chewed on her bottom lip again. She looked out of place with a backdrop of peeling paint and bad lighting in the hallway.

"You must think I'm a total bitch, right?" Karen asked.

Jasmine did, kind of—she'd always thought Karen was a bitch. But she forced herself to say "No."

Karen looked relieved. "I never meant to hurt him, seriously. He's a great guy. I—I loved him, I think." She looked away.

"Why are you telling me this?" Jasmine asked. Karen had always mostly ignored her, even though she was dating Jas's older brother.

Karen half laughed. "I don't know," she said. "It feels good to tell *someone*."

Jasmine knew the feeling. She thought of how much she had revealed to Ford and suddenly felt sick.

"Hey, are you okay?" Karen touched Jasmine's arm quickly and then withdrew, like she was afraid Jas might bite her.

Jasmine thought about what would happen if she told the truth. *No, thanks for asking, I'm not okay. People are trying to kill me, Luc's gone, and there's an entire weekend missing from my memory. I think it all has to do with someone named Miranda, but the only person who could help me left me when I was sleeping and now I'm all alone.*

Karen would probably call the psych ward.

"I'm okay," she said instead.

Karen didn't look convinced. "You want a ride to school or something?" She cracked a small smile. "It's better than busing it."

Jasmine felt a jolt go through her. *Crap.* She hadn't even thought about school, about real life. It was Tuesday. So school had reopened.

While she hesitated, trying to think of an excuse, Karen nudged her. "Come on," she said. "The passenger seat has a butt warmer. You'll love it."

"Okay," Jas heard herself say. She would be safe at school, at least. The Executors couldn't exactly come and knife her in the halls.

"Do you want to change or anything?" Karen asked carefully.

Jasmine instinctively smoothed down the T-shirt she'd had on for what felt like days. There was dust from the rotunda down her front, dirt streaked her arms, and though her jeans were *meant* to look worn, she doubted the designer had had this much real wear in mind. Next to Karen in her crisp white capris, expensive zip-up, and strappy sandals, she felt like a bum.

But being here, at the apartment, was giving her a bad feeling. A sliver of dread slipped up her spine. It was the same watched feeling she had in the rotunda, when the Executors were nearby.

"I'm cool. We should go so we're not late." Jasmine's excuse for hurrying Karen sounded lame even to her, but Karen said nothing.

They pushed out the front door. Jasmine scanned the street quickly, looking for the familiar shock of dyed red hair, or the boy in the dark hooded sweatshirt. Nothing—just a mom pushing a stroller protected with a plastic tarp and several people hurrying along the street, holding umbrellas. Still, the chirp of an alarm was piercing her head. Her senses were in hyperdrive.

Every tiny sound was amplified.

Every wisp of a scent filled her lungs.

Karen's car smelled like leather and vanilla, and the seats were the softest Jas had ever sat in. Karen pushed a button and the car purred to life. It seemed to take Karen forever to pick a song on her iPod, and Jasmine drummed her fingers impatiently on the seat.

"That's a good one," Jasmine blurted out. She glanced

outside the car, sure the people who had been after her would be standing right there, ready to attack again. Once again, the street was clear, but her feeling of unease remained.

The beat of a hip-hop song thumped from the speakers. Karen finally put the car in drive and smoothly pulled away from the curb.

Jasmine exhaled and sat back. It seemed like a million years ago that she'd last been to school. So much had happened since then.

Weird how a whole life could change so quickly.

Her uneasy feeling grew fainter the farther they got from her apartment. Normally, Jas hated going to school. But today it actually felt nice—to pretend she was normal, to pretend she might run into Luc in the halls and do their usual fist bump between classes.

Her throat tightened. Where was he?

"You're really lucky, you know," Karen said, out of nowhere.

"Lucky?" It was the last word Jas would have used.

"You have Luc," Karen said offhandedly, almost as if she'd been reading Jas's thoughts. She looked over her shoulder and merged into the line of cars heading into the student parking lot. "You're lucky to have someone who cares about you like that. I'm an only child. I always wanted a brother." Karen looked so lost that Jas again felt a pull of pity for her. Jas had lumped her in with all the rest of the entitled, spoiled rich kids, but there was a chance she'd been wrong.

She'd been wrong about so many things.

What had Ford said? *The universe is big, and complicated.*

Jasmine reached for the door handle. "Thanks for the ride. I really appreciate it."

"Wait," Karen said, reaching out to stop her. She bit her lip again. "Look, can you humor me for a second?"

"What do you mean?" Jas asked.

Karen smiled shyly. That was another thing Jas would never have suspected: that someone like Karen could get nervous. Instead of responding, Karen reached into her purse and pulled out a small white jar. She opened it and tipped a little of the jar's contents on her fingertip, then dabbed it under Jasmine's eyes. It smelled like peppermint.

"You sort of look like an insomniac. This will help. It's a godsend after an all-nighter, let me tell you." Karen put the jar away and pulled out a tube of mascara. She brushed some mascara across Jasmine's lashes, then sat back with a smile. "Much better."

Jasmine was unexpectedly moved. "I'll tell Luc you're sorry, okay? Maybe it will help," she blurted out, then climbed out of the car, before Karen was forced to thank her.

As soon as Jas started down the hallway, she knew it had been a big mistake to come to school. The sounds, the smells, the emotions were all overwhelming. Leather sneakers squealed on linoleum. The smell of old beef and industrial cleaner made her stomach turn.

Voices echoed off the walls; it was the first day of

school after the earthquake and everyone was giddy, shouting, comparing stories. Jasmine covered her ears and caught someone staring at her like she was a freak. She dropped her hands, but each sound was like a Ping-Pong ball getting rocketed across her brain.

She started for the cafeteria, thinking she needed water, then thought better of it when she saw Alicia, her best friend since first grade, sitting with a group of their Drama friends. At the beginning of the school year, Jas would have been sitting next to them, drinking hot chocolate they'd coaxed out of the ancient cafeteria machine and swapping stories from the weekend.

But Alicia had pretty much ditched Jas when she started hanging out with T.J. They'd all ditched her. Jas knew it was probably her fault. Alicia didn't even drink, as far as Jas knew. And Jas had started coming to school stoned and drunk and whatever else.

No more.

A locker slammed and the noise startled her. She jumped and let out an unconscious yelp, and two freshmen giggled. Trisha, a junior, smirked. Then first bell rang.

It drove straight through her head, like a spike between her ears. Jasmine doubled over, not caring what she looked like, clamping her hands over her ears. By the time the ringing stopped, Alicia and Trisha were full-on whispering and shooting her dirty looks. They probably thought she was high.

She hurried back down the hall, toward the one place where she could get away from everything for a little while.

MRS. COLE

GUIDANCE COUNSELOR

Jas knocked on the door and waited. Mrs. Cole had been trying to corner her for months, but Jas hadn't felt like talking about her life to anyone, much less a school counselor. Now, she'd do just about anything to get away from the crowds in the halls, from the dizzying amount of sounds and smells.

She'd even deal with Mrs. Cole.

"Jasmine?" Mrs. Cole's eyes practically popped out of her head. "What a surprise. Come in." Mrs. Cole shut the door behind them and ushered Jas to a chair in one corner. Instantly, the chaotic noise from the hallway muted and the tension in Jasmine's body began to dissipate. The office smelled like chamomile tea, and Mrs. Cole looked like she could be a mother on any of those '90s shows on late-night reruns. She wore her blond hair pulled back in a low ponytail, and loved sweaters with scenes on them and pencil skirts. Her glasses hung on a beaded chain around her neck.

Maybe Mrs. Cole would let her stay there for the rest of the day.

"Please have a seat. I must say, I didn't think I'd ever see you in here."

Jasmine sank into a chair gratefully. There were a dozen potted plants around the room, and framed prints of several of Van Gogh's most famous work. Jas stared at *Starry Night.* A memory danced just out of reach. Where had she seen a sky like that recently?

Mrs. Cole sat down in a rolling chair across from Jasmine's. "Tell me how you've been, Jasmine. I've been worried about you. We all have."

Jasmine looked away. She knew Mrs. Cole was talking about her grades. They'd plummeted earlier this year. Another post-T.J. effect. She picked at a piece of stuffing coming out of a hole in the armchair. "Things have been . . . weird."

"Weird, how?"

"I can't really explain it," Jasmine said. She wished she could. She wanted to tell so badly.

"How about if we start with right now and work backward?" When Mrs. Cole slipped her glasses on, she looked like an overinquisitive bird. "How do you feel right this minute?"

That was easy. "Confused. Alone. Scared."

Mrs. Cole latched onto the last one. "Let's talk about why you feel scared." Jasmine didn't answer. If Jas said there were strange people called Executors trying to kill her, Mrs. Cole would think she was taking drugs again.

"Is it the boy you're with?" Mrs. Cole asked softly.

"T.J.?" Jasmine shook her head. "I broke it off with him Friday night."

"And now you're scared," Mrs. Cole repeated. She sighed and leaned forward. "Is he threatening you, Jasmine? Did he hurt you? There's no excuse for violence. We can get the police involved. You don't have to be scared anymore." Mrs. Cole laid her hand on Jasmine's arm and squeezed.

Jasmine quickly withdrew her arm from Mrs. Cole's grasp. "T.J. didn't do anything. I mean, he was pissed, yeah. But I haven't heard from him since Friday." Jasmine was distracted by the memory of something else, something *right there on the edge of her memory*. Why couldn't she reach it? Why?

The woman . . . the beach . . . the ring glittering in the woman's hand . . .

And something else. Something afterward.

A forest. No, a garden.

"What are you scared of, then?" Mrs. Cole asked. Her voice sounded far away.

Jasmine answered automatically, without thinking. "I drive people away."

The words were out of her mouth before she could stop them, and suddenly she knew it was true. Why had she never seen it before? Her friends. Her family. And now Ford, who was barely more than a stranger. No one wanted to be around her anymore.

What was wrong with her? She ducked her head so Mrs. Cole wouldn't notice her eyes filling with tears.

Mrs. Cole leaned forward and took both of Jasmine's hands in hers, then waited patiently until Jasmine looked up. "Jasmine, you're young, and you've been through a lot in your life. It isn't fair, but you're strong, and you can overcome it. You just need to learn to trust yourself. You're a beautiful and special girl. You need to believe in yourself."

Something glittered just behind Mrs. Cole's eyes. It

wasn't pity. It was more like a personal understanding, something they had in common.

"Thank you," Jasmine said. "I—I feel better now." She did feel better after talking to Mrs. Cole, but the thought of going back out there, into the halls, into a classroom, made her head start to throb again.

Mrs. Cole stared at her for another long moment. Then she sat back and rolled her chair over to her desk. "I'll write you a pass. How does that sound? You can go sit in the gardens till next period." Mrs. Cole scratched her pen across a neat pad of passes and handed the pass to Jasmine, along with a key card.

Mission High had an amazing atrium in the center of the building where seniors could go and study on their free periods. The flora was gorgeous and lush and exotic. The school even had a gardener who took care of it all.

"But I'm not a senior," Jasmine said.

Mrs. Cole smiled. "Seniors and special passes only."

"Thank you." It was just what she needed—a place to hide out, to blend in, to think. Jasmine took the pass and started out the door.

"Jasmine, please don't be a stranger. I think we can make some good progress if you come and see me regularly." Mrs. Cole's voice trailed her out into the hallway.

The halls were empty now. Her sneakers squeaked loudly on the colorful tile. She could hear teachers droning on behind closed doors, the murmur of whispered voices, markers squeaking across whiteboards. She had never been in the atrium, and as she swiped the card across the reader, she felt a little like she had when Ford had guided her beyond the chain-link fence at the Golden Gate Bridge—like she was doing something illegal.

The air inside the atrium was thick with the sweet, musky smell of the flowers. Jasmine inhaled deeply and a strange urge came alive inside her. She felt part of nature, like she could actually tune in to the gentle hum of life all around her.

In the center of the room, a great weeping willow grew taller than any she'd ever seen. Its branches arched gracefully before letting down fine wisps of leaves like a beautiful waterfall. There were crescent-shaped stone benches around its base. Jasmine sat down gratefully and closed her eyes.

A low buzzing filled the air, like the drone of hundreds of bumblebees. She opened her eyes, surprised, but saw nothing. Even though the atrium was enclosed, the tips of the willow brushed her cheek, almost as if it were caressing her, dancing on some inexplicable wind.

An image sprang into her mind, of thousands of trees just like this one.

And humming—humming like the humming in her head.

A forest. No, a garden.

The vision felt so real, so achingly familiar. Something unleashed inside Jasmine's chest, made its way up into her throat. She began humming along with the noise in her head. The melody was a part of her, one she knew intimately already.

The willow branches swayed over her head.

It was magical and beautiful and wrong.

171

The shrill ring of a school bell snapped Jasmine from her trance. Outside the glass-enclosed atrium, the hallways filled with kids pushing and laughing and talking. The door clicked and several senior girls entered, chattering about an upcoming dance.

Jasmine stood up quickly as the girls settled at a table. She didn't want to answer questions about why she was there and how she'd gotten a pass, so she quickly made her way into the hallway. After being in the atrium, the overhead lights were so bright she had to squint to see. The air was heavy with the smells of sweat and body spray and *people*.

She needed air.

The soft humming had turned into a high-pitched whine that made her want to shove her fingers into her ears and scream. She practically threw herself out the front doors, into the parking lot.

The whine in her head stopped.

The silence was deafening.

Jasmine stood, blinking, inhaling the smell of gasoline and grass and openness. The sky was now a perfect blue and the sun was warm on her skin. She remembered now—there had been a forest, and she had been part of it, *connected* to it. There had been trees that spoke to her in an ancient language, and life that ran through her veins like sunshine.

A new urge came to life, fueled by fatigue and desperation. She'd been hiding and running away from the truth for days.

It was time to stop running.

It was time to stop hiding, too. She wouldn't go back to school—not while Luc was missing, not while there were people after her and a mysterious woman named Miranda controlling them all. She was reenergized, remotivated. She jogged across the soccer fields and cut toward the bus stop, enjoying the slice of air in her lungs.

No matter what Ford said, he had answers; she'd make him tell her what was going on, even if she had to follow him to the ends of the earth. He must be planning to return to his hideout at some point—he'd left his camp stove and bag. And when he did, she would be right there waiting for him.

Jasmine made the bus connections on autopilot and made her way toward Fort Point. There were several more cars in the parking lot now and people milled around snapping pictures, obviously relieved the rain had finally stopped. She had to wait fifteen minutes before there was a break in the continuous flow of people and she could slip through the gate.

As soon as she came to the corner of the brick building, she froze. Somewhere nearby was an Executor. She could feel it in the sudden electric jolt that went up her spine.

She took a deep breath. No more running. What she needed was a plan.

The waiting was the hardest part. She knew that the Executor could run very fast. If she didn't time it just right, if she didn't have the element of surprise on her side, she'd never make it. At the same time, she needed the Executor to see her, to follow her inside.

Patience was not something Jas was good at, but she forced herself to stay still.

Her entire body was tuned in to the Executor and she sensed it was the girl. Hopefully, that would make it easier to overpower her. When the opening came, Jasmine sprang from her spot behind the corner of the building before she could talk herself out of the craziness.

Her sneakers pounded on the pavement as she raced across the lot between the fort and the huge cement bridge footer. She could feel the Executor's eyes on her. Where was the other one, the boy? Jas knew he must be nearby. She ran as fast as she could. The girl was gaining on her—Jas could smell her and hear the rapid pace of her footsteps.

The door was still ten feet away.

Just as she felt the brush of the Executor's hand on her back, Jas stopped and spun wildly to the right, something she'd seen Luc do on the soccer field. The Executor grunted and stumbled. Somehow Jasmine managed to stay upright, and she sprinted to the door.

She yanked the door open and ducked inside, making sure not to dislodge the piece of wood she'd jammed in the doorway earlier. A faint glow came from the room where she and Ford had slept. She didn't have time to wonder about it. She thumped her bag to the ground and grabbed a pipe the length of her arm from the scrap heap in the corner, then backed into the shadows.

Pressed against the cold stone, concealed in darkness, she waited, holding her breath.

She heard the door open and close. The Executor was following her. Good. Jas adjusted her grip on the pipe.

The Executor came forward slowly, shoes squeaking on the floor.

As soon as the girl stepped into the light, Jasmine swung. As the Executor whirled around to face her, Jas brought the pipe down onto the hand clutching the knife. There was a sickening crunch and the girl screeched and sank to her knees. Jas lifted the pipe and held it over her shoulder, ready to strike again. She didn't need to. The girl was holding her broken hand, moaning.

Jasmine kicked the knife away, then knelt beside the girl.

"What do you want? Why are you following me?"

The girl's eyes were filled with pain as she looked at Jasmine. "It's not my fault," she said, almost sullenly. "I'm just following orders."

"Whose orders?" Jasmine said. The pipe felt heavier than before.

"It's your fate," the girl said hurriedly. "You can't escape it. You were supposed to die."

Before Jas could respond, an explosion of pain in her head sent her sprawling to the ground. Stars danced in her vision. Something pummeled her stomach and launched her across the room, where she slammed into the wall, sending all the air out of her lungs. For a second she was suspended in darkness.

Then her vision cleared. She saw the boy, the other Executor, backlit by the lantern, holding a knife. He crossed the room quickly. Jasmine tried to stand but found she couldn't make the command work its way from her brain to her legs. Her lungs were buckling ineffectually.

I'm so sorry, Luc. The thought fluttered in her mind and then disappeared, like a kite on the breeze.

She was cutting in and out of consciousness, and she saw everything in choppy images. The boy was above her. His knife was raised. The girl said something, but Jas couldn't make sense of the words. There was a throbbing pain in her head.

The knife gleamed in the lamplight.

"I'm sorry," the boy said. A look of pain passed over his face. "But this is the way it must be."

He tensed like an animal prepared to spring. Then he jerked violently and his hand went slack. The knife clattered to the ground. His eyes went wide and he opened his mouth in a silent scream.

Blinding light filled the room, and Jas shielded her eyes.

Lightning. Lightning came out of nowhere. It ran through the boy's whole body; his limbs jerked as if he were doing some sick dance.

There was a dull thud when he collapsed. The light disappeared.

Behind him, with sparks still dancing from his fingertips, was Ford.

14

Miranda watched Luc disappear with the flame into the Crossroad. She was filled with strength born of fury. The eternal flame belonged to her. She *needed* it.

"How could you?" she spat, lunging at Tess. She was too angry to be careful. Tess sidestepped her easily, then twisted Miranda's arm behind her back, holding her still. Miranda grunted in pain. She hated bodies and their frailty; she would have given anything to return to her natural formlessness. But her time in Vita had weakened her.

"Stop," Tess said. "Stop. It's over."

"I'll never stop," Miranda hissed, yanking herself free.

They were evenly matched; Tess, too, was weak. The fight could go on forever while her flame was getting farther away. Miranda reached into the folds of her gown and withdrew the locket that had led Corinthe to her death. The high-pitched notes of the music would shatter this world in seconds, and Tess would be destroyed with it.

Miranda was too full of rage to grieve. Tess had made her choice.

"I'll destroy this world and you along with it. I'll destroy *everything* in the universe if I have to."

Before Tess could stop her, Miranda pushed the tiny spring and the tinny music began to play. The melody was beautiful, and in response the glass around them started to crack, thousands of tiny fissures spidering outward. An enormous sound, like a giant mirror falling onto a sidewalk, filled the air. The whole world seemed to vibrate.

A roar erupted around them. The creature that had tried to kill Luc earlier sounded furious. And close. Miranda dove into the entrance to the Crossroad as the entire world gave a great shudder and shattered, exploding into millions of razor-sharp pieces.

Tess dove into the Crossroad right behind her and grabbed her ankle. Pain unlike any she had ever felt before radiated through Miranda. She kicked out at Tess but couldn't catch her breath.

The glass shards permeated the Crossroad exit and pierced her skin in a million different places. Tess was not immune, either, and Miranda heard her screams of pain before a blinding light appeared and Tess was gone.

When the fiery inferno became too much for her to bear, Miranda threw back her head and screamed. She longed to burst free from herself, to streak across the universe in one last defiant blaze of fire, but that took energy she didn't have.

As if mocking her wish, a tiny light streaked across the blackness. Then another. Soon, a shower of sparks lit up the vast unknown around her, a meteor shower of epic proportions. It reminded her of Rhys, of the beauty they had once created together.

Miranda watched, transfixed, paralyzed by its beauty, by the memories it evoked.

But then the direction changed. The sparks began heading toward her as if thrown by thousands of unseen hands. She could do nothing to protect herself. They pierced her body over and over, like tiny spears, and she felt a scream rip through her.

"Rhys!"

She could only cry out for him, his name, his memory, the only thing holding her together.

One last flash of bright light blinded her, and then she found herself lying facedown on a red-sand beach. Sand lodged under her nails as she fought to rise. A crippling stab of agony shot through her middle, and she gasped. What was happening to her? Even her birth — fiery, forged from a collision of two stars — had not been so painful.

"This is your own fault, Miranda." Tess stood over her, panting, blocking out the glare from the two suns overhead.

Miranda had never wanted to return to this desolate

red world that had been Rhys's eternal prison. Of course the Unseen Ones would send her there to die, too.

"What's happening to me?" Already her throat grew dry. This world would suck the life from her, especially in her weakened state. Rhys would have a potion to cure her. Her next thought sent a new kind of pain through her.

Rhys was dead.

They were connected, born from the same stars, and she felt it the moment he ceased to exist. Half the fiery life inside her had been extinguished. It had made her weaker and yet fueled her desire for revenge.

She tried to picture before, but all she could see was what he had become: a shadow of his former glorious self. *Rhys*. The Unseen Ones had taken everything from him—her Rhys, who had once turned back time to save her life.

They had crippled him, exiled him, taken his power.

Miranda wanted revenge.

"You destroyed Aetern. And you destroyed something else, something much closer to your own heart." Tess knelt down and pushed the hair from Miranda's eyes in an almost motherly gesture. "A part of your heart, actually."

Miranda struggled away from Tess's touch. It took all her effort to push to her feet, where she stood, weaving unsteadily. "What are you talking about?"

"You killed Rhys. He was your Other. Now you're dying," Tess said simply.

Miranda tried to laugh. The effort sent fresh spasms

of pain through her body. "Rhys died because he tried to use the tunnels again."

Tess shook her head. "His soul was in the book that Luc fed to the guardian of the flame. When you destroyed Aetern, you destroyed everything in it. *Everything*, Miranda."

"No." Miranda's entire body shook. Despite the heat, she was cold. So cold. Rhys's soul was supposed to live on in the Library of the Dead. But now it was gone forever. It couldn't end this way, not after everything she had done.

"It's over, Mira," Tess said softly. There was true regret in her eyes.

"It will never be over," Miranda gasped. A new shaft of pain nearly split her in half and she went down to her knees. She dug her fingertips into the sand, trying to find any sign of life in herself, something she could use to regain control. But there was nothing—no energy, no life, no hope in this arid world where her one true love had died.

She lay on the sand gasping for air, but none would enter her lungs. Hot tears ran down her face, and the dry sand devoured them as soon as they fell. She felt as if she were being pulled completely inside out.

She had always pictured her death as a glorious explosion of a sun in some faraway galaxy, fast and furious and brilliant. Not like this. Not lying on a dead beach writhing like an animal at the feet of someone she had trusted. Someone she had created.

Miranda could only watch as Tess leaned closer and

pressed her lips to her forehead. They felt warm against her cold skin. "I'm sorry," Tess said. "Goodbye, my friend."

The heat of the world made Miranda's eyes sting, and as her gaze grew watery, Tess's image wavered, and then was gone.

Miranda was left to face her last few moments completely alone.

15

"What—what happened?" Jas's brain still felt fuzzy, as if it were wrapped in a blanket. She staggered to her feet. Ford tried to help her, but she pushed him away. He'd killed someone. He'd just *killed* someone. The boy, the Executor, was lying slack, his eyes open and unseeing. Jas thought she might throw up. "What did you do?"

"Jasmine—" Ford started to reach for her.

Jasmine took two stumbling steps backward. "Stay away from me."

Then, suddenly, she felt the sharp bite of a blade against her throat.

"Don't move," the redheaded Executor said. She was holding the knife in her uninjured hand. The blade trembled slightly, and Jas could feel its vibration against her jaw. She was afraid to swallow. Afraid to breathe, even. The Executor had an arm wrapped around Jasmine's chest, keeping her immobilized. "You," she snarled, addressing Ford, "stay here. Don't follow us, or the girl dies."

"She'll die anyway," Ford said, hands raised, his eyes fixed on Jasmine's. She was sure he was trying to communicate something to her, but she couldn't tell what.

"Yes," the Executor spat. "But if you try to make trouble, I'll make sure she dies in pain."

Ford nodded, just barely.

The Executor tightened her hold and dragged Jasmine toward the door. A blast of cool air washed over them when the girl kicked the door open.

Jasmine stumbled as the Executor pulled her across the parking lot, and the knife nicked her skin. She felt a trickle of blood run down her neck and fought back a wave of panic.

"Where are we going?" Jas asked. The girl could have killed her in the room, or in the hallway, or even in the parking lot, so why hadn't she?

The girl didn't answer. "Just keep moving," she said. She pulled Jasmine toward a doorway hidden in the deep shadows of the old barracks building. As they got closer, Jasmine's skin began to tingle, like tiny electric shocks were hitting her all over.

There was something off about the door. It almost seemed to *shimmer.* Or was it a trick of the mist curling around it?

"Go," the Executor said, pushing her toward the door.

Just then, Ford dashed around the corner. Jasmine felt a surge of hope.

"Ford!" she screamed, and felt the blade pierce the flesh under her chin. She elbowed the Executor in the stomach and felt the girl's grip release slightly.

"No!" Ford's shout echoed through the fog, but Jasmine barely heard him.

The Executor grabbed Jasmine's shirt, and Jasmine was yanked off her feet. They were crossing through the door, *right through it,* and then the world Jasmine knew fell away in a rush of wind.

16

A gust of wind buffeted Jasmine's body backward, but the Executor kept her on her feet. Barely. The air came alive with undulating fibers of color, winding and twisting past her, over her, *under* her. It was as if the whole world had broken apart into a rainbow.

For a split second she forgot about the Executor still gripping her, and thought only about Ford—what would happen to Ford?—forgot even about the blade of a knife at her throat. Her blood was filled with tingling warmth. She was flying. She felt alive, at one with something greater than anything she knew.

Just as quickly, the terror came rushing back. The world didn't just evaporate. People didn't step through doorways into other worlds. It was the stuff of movies, of science fiction. Wind howled around them, and Jasmine felt the Executor's grip loosen. Earlier, she had just

wanted to escape. Now she was terrified that the Executor would let go and leave her in this nothing place, with
its shifting colors and its formlessness.

Then the Executor's grip tightened and she wrenched
Jasmine sideways. It felt as though they were falling into
a bottomless abyss, even though Jas counted only two
seconds in her head.

When they hit solid ground, the jolt knocked Jas flat
and the Executor temporarily released her hold. Jas had
lost her breath. She gasped soundlessly, found her lungs
shuttered as a window, useless. Above her was a rose-
colored sunset, a sky littered with stars. A sun, a sky, and
damp grass beneath her: Jas knew this was her chance
to escape.

In the time it took the girl to stand, Jasmine was already sprinting. Her breath came back, finally, along
with the hammering of her heart against her ribs. There
was a path that led off into a grove of trees, and Jasmine
followed it blindly, not daring to look back. She had no
idea where she was, but she knew instinctively she was
not home. Not in her world. The air was too sweet and all
the wrong texture—like a spoonful of honey. The bird-
song was different, and the light was wrong, too. It was
entirely possible that she was running straight into danger. But the Executor would kill her if she didn't escape.

Jasmine pushed through the dense foliage, smacking
aside huge leaves and flowers the size of dinner plates.
Plants she had never seen grew up over her head, interwoven like long fingers, with leaves as wide as her body
and large fragrant flowers drooping down like giant bells.

The girl was gaining on her. Jas's heartbeat felt like a dance track remixed all wrong—too crazy, arrhythmic. Jas was fast, but the girl was faster. Hurling herself into a place of thick growth, ignoring the scratches of branches and thorns, Jasmine crouched behind a heavy wall of green, willing her racing heart to slow down, willing herself to breathe silently.

After only twenty seconds, the Executor darted past, moving so quickly she was practically a blur, her long hair streaming behind her. As soon as her footsteps faded, Jasmine counted to twenty, then emerged carefully back onto the pathway and ran back the way she had come. There had to be a way out of this place.

The path split forty feet ahead. Jasmine didn't remember reaching a fork—maybe she hadn't been paying attention—and went left. After another minute, Jas spotted the shimmering of a river that wound its way across the horizon and reflected all the colors of the sunset sky above them. She knew she had not passed a stream, but a sense of déjà vu swelled up, so swift and fierce that she stumbled. Why did this place suddenly seem so familiar? It tickled the back of her mind, a familiarity in the soft purplish glow, as if she were entering a childhood bedroom.

She took a hesitant step forward, and then another. Some force seemed to be guiding her along, one that she couldn't resist.

She knew this place. She knew she knew this place. For the first time she noticed that the world around her—the very air—seemed to be vibrating, pulsing to a rhythm that called out to her, made her own heartbeat slow in response.

She heard something then—a disturbance on the wind, a footstep. She had to move. There was a narrow dirt path on her right, half as wide as the one she'd been traveling, winding up toward some distant high point where she could just see a gleam of white. She started running again. Her legs felt strangely numb, sluggish, as though there were weights attached to her ankles. She longed to return to the river, to lie down, to rest.

Then the Executor slammed into her from behind. They both fell to the ground. Jas got a mouthful of grass. She tried to roll the Executor off, but couldn't. The Executor grabbed both of Jas's elbows and hauled Jas to her feet.

"Leave me alone!" Jasmine cried. She knew it was hopeless. But maybe someone would hear her and come to her aid. The Executor was gripping her so tightly she left tiny half-moon fingernail marks in Jasmine's skin. "What is this place?" Jasmine asked. "How did we even get here?"

"You've just traveled the Crossroad—here, to Pyralis," the Executor said, pushing forward. Jasmine wondered why the Executor didn't just finish her off already.

"Why am I here?"

"Because you took life from the Great Gardens, and now you must pay for it in blood."

Jasmine dragged her feet, stumbled, leaned back,

forced the girl to slow down. "I've never been here before," she argued. "How could I take anything?" It was a
lie. She knew she had been here before—could feel it in
the humming of her blood. But she had never, ever hurt
anyone. She was sure of it.

"Stop whining," the Executor said, for a moment
sounding just like a harried mom leading her toddler
around a grocery store. "We've wasted enough time already."

"So you're just going to kill me, then?" Jasmine's fear
felt out of place, like it might somehow contaminate this
world, which was so beautiful, so peaceful and still.

"I've told you," the girl said. "I have no choice."

Jasmine thought she sounded a little sad. Or maybe
she just imagined it.

They stopped in front of a huge iron gate. Beyond it,
Jas could see a vast garden with an explosion of colors,
many of which Jas had no name for: petals that looked
like the tie-dyed shirts she used to love as a kid.

In front of the gate were seven enormous stone
statues—they all had a woman's body, but each face was
completely blank except for a crescent where the mouth
should be. Jas had the sensation that the statues knew
she was there, that they were watching, and as the Executor propelled Jas to the gates, she half expected them
to come alive and attack her.

"She has returned," the Executor said in a loud voice.
"Open the gate."

The gate squeaked open and the Executor dragged
Jasmine into the garden.

The perfume that filled Jas's lungs hit her almost like a drug, like taking that first pull of really strong weed and feeling the world get warm and fuzzy at the edges. She was suddenly filled with a fierce longing — not to escape but to stay, to be left here, alone and in peace.

It terrified her, the connection to this world.

"Please," Jasmine said in a low voice, giving in to the fear that welled up inside her. "Please. If you let me go, I can pay you. My family will pay you." Another lie: her family had no money. Her dad was in the hospital. But she was desperate, babbling now.

"That's not how it works. You took from the Garden. Now you must give back." The Executor grabbed Jasmine's hands before she had time to react, then bound her wrists together behind her back with thick green vines. "The nectar from the Flower of Life flows in your veins. It was never meant for you. Your brother crossed a line."

"What do you know about my brother?"

"Only that he has created chaos across the universe. The Unseen Ones are not happy. He should be careful, or he'll be next."

"Next?" Jas asked, but she already knew. They would pursue Luc, too.

The girl was crazy. It was the only explanation. She was certifiably, one hundred percent insane. Maybe all of this was some kind of weird acid trip. Maybe the girl had drugged her.

The girl yanked on Jasmine's bound wrists, verifying the knots would hold. A stab of pain radiated from Jasmine's shoulders. When the girl returned to face her,

Jas could see that her features were too perfect, like a porcelain doll's, and her eyes were the color of the sky swirling with storm clouds. Pale light shone against her skin, making it appear lavender.

Jasmine couldn't tear her gaze away from the knife. Why was a knife so much worse than a gun? At least with a gun she would feel it less. She felt sick. Her knees were liquid, and she didn't know how much longer she could stand.

"Please." Jasmine choked on the plea. There was a time only recently when she hadn't thought she cared about whether she lived or died. But faced with death, Jasmine realized that she very much did care.

She definitely, definitely did not want to die.

And then she felt a break in her mind, a sudden release, like the parting of a dark curtain. And she remembered a beautiful purple sky littered with stars, millions and millions of them. She could hear the gurgling of a stream nearby, saw thousands of tiny orbs bobbing in the current as they swept by. Luc stood over her, his face creased with fear. The ground under her trembled. She had never seen Luc so scared before. She wanted to reach out, to reassure him that she was okay, but she was so weak.

So tired.

Instead she lay on the ground, staring up at the stars, and felt life flowing slowly from her body. But Luc appeared—and brought something thick and sweet to her lips. She had swum through a river and waded past marbles carried by the current. . . .

Jasmine snapped out of the memory with a muffled cry. Her pulse thumped loudly in her ears. Was that a memory or a hallucination? For a moment, it had felt like she really was dying in that twilight world.

"You can feel it inside, can't you?" the girl said. It wasn't really a question. "The way you've changed. The way you sense things now." Jasmine didn't say anything. She was rigid with fear. The Executor was right. "No wonder you were able to escape us for so long. It's all because of the flower's nectar. A flower you were never supposed to have."

"You've made a mistake," Jasmine said weakly, although she wasn't sure of that anymore. With her hands bound behind her back, she felt like a prisoner in a movie about pirates, about to walk the plank.

"The Unseen Ones don't make mistakes," the girl said with a small frown, as if Jasmine should know better. "Besides, it's not my decision. Only from your blood can the flower regrow." She took a step forward and raised the knife. Jasmine wanted to keep her eyes open—she wanted to be brave—but at the last second, she couldn't.

"Let her go," a voice said, "or I'll kill you right here, right now."

Jasmine's eyes flew open.

Ford. He'd followed her.

He had one arm wrapped around the Executor's throat, the blade of a knife pressed under her chin. His other arm kept her immobilized, pinned, her own knife hanging uselessly at her side. Ford pressed the blade harder against her neck. All he'd have to do was angle it differently and he'd sever a vein. "Drop the knife. Now."

"It's her fate," the girl protested, but she dropped the knife. "You know I only do what I'm tasked with."

Jasmine began frantically working her wrists together, hoping to loosen her binds. The rope chafed her wrists, left her skin feeling raw and exposed.

"Why were you sent after Jasmine?" Ford demanded. He loosened his grip on the Executor, but not by much. "I know you read from the marbles. So what did you see about Jasmine?"

The girl made a sound in her throat. "It . . . showed us death. She must be killed in the Gardens. We were told that she had taken something that had to be returned."

Jas's wrists ached. Her head was pounding. She knew that Ford was trying to help, but she hated the way that they were talking in codes and puzzles, about reading marbles and something Jas had supposedly stolen. She wanted a straight answer—she wanted to understand.

"What marble?" she said. "What are you talking about?"

They ignored her.

"Told by who?" Ford asked.

The girl hesitated. "The Unseen Ones," she said quickly, when Ford moved as if to tighten his grip again. "The marble came directly from them."

Jasmine suddenly remembered the marble she had found in the apartment. "I have a marble," she blurted out.

Silence. Sudden, shocked silence. Both the Executor and Ford stared at her.

"There's something inside it. An image of the rotunda. Is that what you're talking about? I can show you, if you want." It was too quiet. The Executor had gone white. Jas licked her lips, which were very dry. "You'll have to untie me."

"You can see what's in the marbles?" Ford asked. It felt almost as if he wanted her to deny it.

Jasmine hesitated. She didn't like the way he was looking at her. Something had changed. "It was just . . . quick. Like an impression I had. It might have been a trick of the light."

"Only Executors can read the marbles," the girl whispered.

"They sent you to kill one of their own?" Ford turned on the girl. In his shock, he had released her. But she made no move to go for the knife. She was as still as one of the statues outside the garden.

"I . . . I don't know." For the first time, the girl looked uncertain. Then she squared her shoulders. She shook her head slightly. "But it doesn't matter. It must be done, no matter what she is."

One of their own?

Did they mean her?

"I'm not like her," Jasmine said, feeling the desperation again beating through her body like a force. "I don't know what she is or where I am or why I'm even here. I didn't take some flower from this garden, I swear. I'm not your enemy." She said the words to the girl but looked right at Ford.

Ford looked at her with an expression she couldn't

identify. Then he whirled around to face the Executor, raising his knife so it was level with her heart.

"Go," he said. "Tell them they can't have her."

"I won't stop trying," the girl said. "You know I can't. Even if you kill me, there will be others. You're a fool if you think you can stop fate. You can't save her." Her eyes flashed, turning a sudden, startling purple.

"Watch me."

They stared at each other for a moment longer. Then the Executor raised her hands, very slowly, a gesture of defeat. She took a step backward. Then another.

"Smart girl," Ford said. He turned toward Jasmine and his expression softened. "Are you all right?" He touched her face briefly, and Jasmine could have cried; his fingers smelled like smoke and metal. He stepped behind her and sawed at the restraints around her wrists. "Did she hurt you?"

It happened in an instant. Ford was bent over the ropes that bound her; Jasmine was immobilized, rigid, unable even to scream. The Executor rocketed across the clearing, her teeth bared like an animal's. She snatched up her knife from the dirt and leapt.

Then someone was shouting—Ford? Jasmine?—and pain tore through Jasmine's body and the Executor was falling, falling, like a bird out of the sky, and then Jasmine felt the blade of the knife right below her breastbone.

17

Smoke swirled and billowed through the Crossroad. It was almost impossible to see, and as hot as a furnace. The fire had spread quickly; already, it seemed to be everywhere at once. Parts of the Crossroad writhed as if in pain, and a horrific wailing filled the air.

Luc stumbled through the darkness and the smoke. He had to get back to the tunnels, to figure out how to turn back time and stop all this. He felt a moment of seizing dread—was this what Miranda had wanted all along, to destroy everything?—but forced himself to stay calm. If the fire spread from the Crossroad into the worlds they connected, it would be catastrophic.

Last time he had made it into the tunnels of time by accident. He had punctured the Crossroad, peeled it apart like skin. He shivered, remembering the way the Crossroad had sweated thick black liquid, almost like blood.

But he had no choice. The noise of the fire was tremendous. The Crossroad screaming, withering. Dying.

And if the Crossroad failed, he'd never make it home.

He drove his fingers into the Crossroad's colored membrane, the way he had before. This time, however, the Crossroad seemed to resist his attempts. Each time he broke through enough to see the darkness on the other side, the walls would mend themselves, effectively shutting him out. Thick currents of colored wind buffeted him backward, pushing him like a giant hand; each time, he had to fight his way back to a place he might attempt to break through, until exhaustion made his arms almost numb.

The smoke had gotten so thick, his lungs burned whenever he took a breath. Even his thoughts felt smoky—he was having trouble holding on to strategies, ideas. But he knew if he didn't get into the tunnels soon, he would die. Then no one would be able to stop the destruction.

Suddenly, through the thick layers of memory, an image surfaced: a game against Ridgemont, tied 1–1 and down to a penalty kick. His kick. *How bad do you want it?* Luc heard his coach laying it all out on the line. This *was* it.

Luc gritted his teeth and drove a foot straight at the wall. It was like kicking into soft dirt; there was a scattering of particles, a breach, but as soon as he withdrew his foot, the hole closed. *How bad do you want it?* He was coughing, tearing up, but he didn't stop. He charged headfirst, using momentum, using his weight. He tore at the soft membrane, which felt like human flesh and made him want to throw up. But the hole widened, slowly, by increments. His vision turned blurry, then went totally dark. His fingers were numb.

Black air compressed him from all sides. Now he couldn't breathe. He couldn't find his lungs to take a breath. He couldn't feel his legs to move them. He felt disjointed, like when traveling through the Crossroad. But this was different. There was no rapid falling. He couldn't tell if he was moving at all, or stuck in a place between the Crossroad and the tunnels, a nothing place where he, too, was nothing. His eyes might be open, but he couldn't see anything, and he might be upright, or upside down—there was no way to tell. He wanted to scream, but he had no mouth to scream with.

The only thing keeping him connected to himself was the ache within his chest. An ache that grew sharper, like a runner's stitch. *Corinthe.* He clung to her name; it cut through the fog in his brain. Luc pictured her crazy purple eyes, the way her lips turned up at the corners when she tried to fight back a smile, or the crease right between her eyes when she was trying to work something out in her head.

A huge shudder ran through the dark and Luc felt it echo through his body, like standing too close to a bass speaker at a nightclub. Bits of light flickered through the inky air—he could *see* again—dancing like the fireflies he'd seen in Pyralis, except they weren't fireflies. They were sparks dancing along the sinewy wires of the tunnels of time. They moved closer—or was he moving at last?—and tingling spread through his arms and legs. He could feel his body. He *had* a body.

Luc reached up and grabbed hold of a writhing wire. A jolt of sizzling electricity went through him, growing fiery and white-hot, until Luc feared he would burst. Still, he pulled. His muscles screamed.

At last, he was in. The last of the suctioning darkness released him, and he emerged headfirst into the tunnels as though surfacing from quicksand, able to breathe at last. There was the barest trace of smoke. He couldn't be sure whether it was from the spread of the fire or from the wires writhing like snakes all around him, letting off showers of sparks.

He raked a hand through his hair. He had to fix what he had done, he knew that. Had to go back in time. But there were billions—trillions—of wires. When he reached to grab hold of one of them, it disappeared, vanished under a tight coil of dozens of other wires, like an animal burrowing back in the ground.

Was each of these wires a moment, a second, a reality? Could he follow one of these wires back to a time when Corinthe was alive?

Or maybe all of these wires together—knotted so tightly, interwoven like threads—made up this present, this reality, where Corinthe was dead and Luc had screwed up and Jas was in danger. He felt a sudden surge of anger. He wanted to shatter the present, blast it away.

He reached up and several wires parted and skittered away from him, submerging themselves beneath the seething mass of other wires. But he managed to grab hold of a blue wire as fat as his thumb. It was like grabbing hold of an electric fence. His teeth buzzed with electricity. His mind was full of a sizzling heat.

Destroy.

He gritted his teeth and pulled. There was a shriek, and flames and sparks spit. The wire split apart in his hands. Air whooshed past him with the force of a train. The blast knocked him backward, and before Luc could scream, or do anything, he was sucked into that murky black nothing between this place and the Crossroad.

Then he was falling. The wind whipped his hair into his face and there were voices shrieking all around him and he knew he was tumbling through the Crossroad, out of control, panicked. Corinthe had always told him he mustn't panic in the Crossroad — that was how people got lost. Corinthe. The wind grew louder, screaming in his ears and blocking out even the memory of her name. The sound tore through his head like shards of glass. Piercing straight through his skull. Was that the wind or his own voice now?

Stop. Please just stop.

Everything went still. The force of the quiet hit Luc like something solid. He lost his breath and sat up, gasping, blinking colored spots out of his vision.

Trees and a large expanse of grass. People laughing somewhere nearby and a rhythmic thwacking sound, like someone was playing tennis. To his right was a small pond. A family of ducks skated happily across it.

He stood up, dazed. This was Mountain Lake Park, not far from his apartment.

Somehow, he'd made it back home.

It was a sunny day, and birds were singing in the trees. He could hear no bulldozers, no sirens wailing, no rescue teams shouting to each other. None of the usual after-earthquake sounds. As he exited the park on Tenth Avenue, he saw no damaged buildings or piles of debris. Parents pushed strollers; joggers kept pace with their dogs; the whole city looked like it had been coated in new paint.

The streetlights worked and businesses were open.

It was as if the earthquake had never happened. Or as if it hadn't happened *yet*.

Luc stopped so quickly that a jogger strapped with weights and water bottles bumped into him.

"Sorry," Luc mumbled automatically. He barely registered the man's dirty look.

For the first time in days, hope sprang to life inside him. What if it had worked? What if fixing the wires in the tunnel had actually moved time backward?

He started running as fast as he could, toward home. He cut across Lake Street, not even bothering with the crosswalk. Only when a tomato-red BMW slammed on its brakes, and the driver leaned out his window and called Luc an asshole, did he slow down. Jesus. If he got flattened by some dick in a sports car on his way back to the apartment, after all he had been through . . .

He waited impatiently for the light to change on Nineteenth, bouncing up and down on his toes, feeling like he did just before a big soccer game, like there were insects running through his veins. Left on California, and his heart hitched. Almost home.

Inside his apartment building, he took the stairs two at a time, then paused for just a second to catch his breath. His heart was hammering so hard in his throat, he could barely swallow.

"Hello?" he called as he stepped into the crappy little foyer and swung the door closed behind him. "Is anyone—?"

The words died on his lips. All the air seemed to go out of the room at once, taking Luc's ability to think with it.

Sitting on the living room couch, in low-rise jeans and one of Luc's old black concert T-shirts, was Corinthe.

He was afraid to move, as if any motion, the slightest vibration, might make her disappear. It felt like someone had pushed the mute button on his world, and cocooned him in this moment. He wanted to stand and stare at her forever.

But she had already seen him. She smiled at him and stood—moving, as always, fluidly, like water poured from a cup. She walked over to where his feet had become rooted to the dingy carpet. She laid her hand on his cheek. It was so warm. So real. She smelled real, too: like lilies and something else, something he couldn't describe. The smell of a sunset. "I was worried about you," she said, her purple eyes deepening.

Something broke in his chest.

Corinthe was here. She was real.

Emotion clogged his throat and tears burned the back of his eyes. He reached up and took her face between his hands. His hands shook as he brushed a thumb along her jaw. He moved his fingers through her wild, tangled hair, then pulled her close, into his chest. They fit together perfectly. He could feel her heartbeat reverberating in his chest: an echo of his.

"I missed you," he whispered into the top of her head. It was all he could do not to cry.

"I missed you, too," she said, and then pulled away, giving him a crooked smile. "Is everything okay?"

"It is now," he said. When he finally moved his lips against hers, felt her respond to his touch, it was as if everything that had happened, everything that had gone wrong, was driven back by the soft pressure of her lips.

He had done it.

Everything was fixed.

"I'm so glad you're back," he said, between kisses.

"Back?" She gave a half laugh. "You're the one who left. Where were you this morning, anyway?"

He wondered—where *had* he been this morning? In this life Luc could've woken up to get bagels next door, or taken a run through the Presidio. Not that it mattered now. There was so much he needed to say, so much to do and explain. It was strange—he felt as if Corinthe might vanish from in front of him at any second. But they had all the time in the world now. He took her hand and led her down the short hall. Jasmine's door was closed. He wondered where she was—he felt a great swelling of love for her, too. She and Corinthe would be close. They were both wild, in a way. Stubborn, too. They followed their own hearts.

His room was neat, as though someone had straightened it for him. Perfect, like everything else. He sat down on the bed and pulled Corinthe into his lap, wrapping his arms around her waist to hold her tight. He already knew the contours of her body from the night they spent together in the Land of the Two Suns.

They'd had such little time together, a few stolen moments and then it was gone. It all seemed hopeless, but now here she was, in his arms again. All the pain and uncertainty had been worth it. Corinthe was alive. She was here.

"Are you sure you're okay?" Corinthe said gently. "You seem . . . different."

"I told you. I just missed you." He swallowed the thickness in his throat. Did she know what he had done? Would she ever know? Did it matter?

She pulled away and stared into his eyes. "I'm not going anywhere, Luc." A spasm of pain crossed her face. He wondered at it briefly—why pain?—but dismissed the concern. He would be nothing but happy. He tried to kiss her again, but she evaded him.

"I talked to your dad earlier. He's feeling better. They want him to stay another week to be sure he can handle everything. I told him not to worry about you. I told him to stay as long as he needed. Of course he'll come for the service."

"Okay," Luc said cautiously, trying not to betray how little he understood. Was his dad still in the hospital? But that didn't make sense. Corinthe had been dead—he was afraid to even think the word when she was here, warm, vibrant—when his dad decided to go cold turkey. Had he rewound even further than he thought? But what kind of past was this, where Corinthe knew him, loved him already?

"The florist called when you weren't here," she said. He stared at her dumbly. She took a quick breath, stood up, and began pacing. "Look, I know it must be awful to talk about this stuff—to *think* about this stuff. The everydayness of it. So I went ahead and ordered lilacs and white calla lilies. And jasmine, of course. Lots of jasmine. I hope that's okay. They needed an answer and I didn't know where you were."

There was an idea flickering in the back of Luc's mind, like a warning signal blinking far off in the distance. Lilacs and white calla lilies. Funeral flowers. *And jasmine, of course.*

He cleared his throat. "What—what are you talking about?"

"Do you think the jasmine is too much?" Corinthe bit her lip. There were tears in her eyes. "I thought . . . I know I didn't know her that well, but I thought . . . well, that's what she would have wanted."

"Who?" Luc asked. The word seemed to take a long time to go from his brain to his mouth.

She stared at him. "Your sister. What do you mean, *who*?"

The look in her eyes felt like a punch to the gut. His chest tightened and breathing became difficult.

Impossible. He had turned back time. That had to mean Jas was okay, too. That meant she had never met Miranda, never been poisoned by the Blood Nymphs, never come close to dying in the Great Gardens of Pyralis. A knife of fear slid down Luc's spine. Was she in the hospital again? Had he gone back so far that she OD'd again? And had he failed to save her this time?

"Jas!" Luc shouted as he ran for her room. He threw the door open and it slammed against the wall. "Jas?"

She wasn't there.

Her room was too neat. The bed was made and there were no clothes piled on the chair or scattered across the floor. Jasmine always had incense burning or music blasting from her speakers. But there was nothing but empty silence.

"Luc, I'm worried about you," Corinthe said from behind him.

He turned slowly and saw the tears glistening in her grief-filled eyes.

"Where have you been? I thought you went after him," Corinthe said. "When you were so late coming back, I thought something happened to you, too."

It was like Corinthe was talking through a thick fog. Everything slowed down and it took enormous effort to hear her over the roaring that had started in his head.

"You thought I went after T.J.?" Luc's jaw was numb. The blood in his veins felt like cooled metal, thick and cold.

"T.J. Who's T.J.?" Corinthe frowned and shook her head. "I meant Ford."

"I don't know who you're talking about." Things were getting more and more muddled. He couldn't feel his fingers now. He stumbled to the window, wrenched it open. He needed air. Where was his sister?

Corinthe was looking at him as if he was crazy. "Ford. The Radical that Jasmine disappeared with. Don't pretend you aren't angry enough to kill him. You told me—"

Only a few words penetrated the fog in his brain. Someone had Jasmine. "Where is she? Where did he take her?" The panic inside him turned to desperation. He couldn't get enough air into his lungs. He was drowning above water.

Corinthe crossed her arms. Even from several feet away, he could see that she was shivering.

"Maybe—maybe you should call that grief counselor." She dropped her eyes. "The one the hospital recommended. I think I still have her card."

He crossed the room and grabbed her shoulders. She cried out. For a moment, she looked frightened of him.

"Tell me the truth," he said. He knew he was gripping her too tightly, but he couldn't make his fingers unclench. *Where's Jasmine?*

"She's gone," Corinthe said. She put a hand on his chest and eased him back. She was breathing hard. They both were, as though they'd been running. "You know that, Luc. You were the one who found her body near the rotunda."

Luc turned away, now certain he was about to be sick. Bile rose in his throat. He finally understood. He hadn't gone back in time—he'd gone *forward*. He'd leapt into a future where Corinthe was back and Jasmine was dead.

He rushed to the bathroom and slammed the door. He gripped at the counter, allowing the anger to build up inside him.

He took Jasmine's ring out, its little circle cutouts glinting dimly in the overhead bathroom light. She used to fidget with it when she talked, twisting it around her finger. . . .

How could he live in a reality where Jasmine was gone?

But how could he leave Corinthe behind, knowing he might never see her again? Finding her alive, touching her again, brought him joy unlike any he'd ever known.

He could not—he *would* not—trade one for the other.

This was not their fate.

This was not his fate.

"Luc?" Corinthe was hammering on the door. "Luc, please let me in."

He straightened up and put the ring back in his pocket. His eyes were rimmed with red. He sloshed some water into his hand and drank it, then slugged back the dregs of a mini bottle of mouthwash, not bothering to spit.

He wasn't done. He would fix this, too.

He took a deep breath. His stomach no longer felt like it was trying to digest a dictionary. He could do this. He swung the bathroom door open.

Corinthe swiped at her eyes quickly. "Luc, please talk to me," she said in a quiet voice that broke him. He wanted to stay. He wanted to hold her again and tell her it would be all right. "I'm scared."

Luc took her face in both hands. He had to duck a little so they were eye to eye—but just a little. They fit together perfectly. "I can't explain this to you," he said, his voice hitching. "But this isn't how it's supposed to be."

Corinthe wrapped her hands around his wrists. He could tell she was fighting the urge to cry again. "The counselor said . . . she said you might be in denial."

"This isn't about denial." He kissed her nose once, lightly. "Trust me. This is about acceptance." He took her hands in his, twining their fingers together.

"I—I don't understand," she whispered, searching his face, as if she could read the answer to a puzzle there.

He didn't reply. Instead, he kissed her: a desperate kiss, a fierce promise that he would find her again.

They walked down the hall, hand in hand. She had obviously given up arguing with him. Now she was silent. He could feel her body trembling. She seemed so different from the fierce Corinthe he had first met, the girl with the wild eyes and the secret smile and the knife clasped so easily in her hand.

Out of the corner of his eye, he saw the butcher block on the counter.

In one fluid movement, he grabbed the large serrated knife and wrapped it in a tea towel. He tucked it in his coat pocket, thinking only of revenge.

"I love you," he said to Corinthe. "More than anything in the world." More than almost anything, he amended silently. He wouldn't sacrifice Jasmine's life so that Corinthe could stay.

He knew that he could find a way to get them both back. He had to.

He stopped at the door. His chest ached. His throat ached. It was like the pain of taking a deep breath in the cold, a sudden slicing in his lungs. If he failed, this might be the last time he ever saw Corinthe. "I need you to wait for me. Will you do that?"

She had started crying again. "Luc, please. Whatever you're going through . . . whatever's going on . . . you can tell me. Stay here. We'll get through it together." Her eyes were a soft violet, the exact shade of the sky in Pyralis. He wondered whether she still thought of her old home. She had given all of that up for him. Now he was leaving her. He had a moment of doubt—but the thought of Jasmine dead, gone, was unbearable. Impossible.

"This isn't the end," he said. "I'll come back. I promise."

She wrapped her arms around his neck. "I'm not going anywhere," she said. Her lips brushed his neck. They were so soft and warm. She smelled like the best kind of summer day. "But come back soon, okay?"

Luc counted to three. He inhaled her, memorized the way she felt in his arms. His eyes were suddenly blurry with tears, and he knew if he didn't go now, he'd never be able to walk away. He pulled away, wiping his eyes quickly with his forearm.

"I promise," he said. He didn't look at her again. Just

turned and took the steps at a jog. After a minute he heard the door click behind him. It took all the strength he had not to turn and go back to her, start pounding on the door, tell her he loved her and wanted her to stay.

With each step he felt sicker and sicker. And then angrier and angrier.

What kind of universe did he live in, where choices were impossible, where people didn't get to be happy, where loved ones died?

He moved quickly, head down, as if depending on momentum to take him away from Corinthe. Each time his heels hit the pavement, he imagined the street cracking, fissuring under his weight. He wished he could destroy everything, the whole house-of-cards universe and its crazy rules.

He caught himself sympathizing, momentarily, with Miranda, and then immediately felt guilty. Even though he was tired, he started jogging, just to get some relief from the tension in his body and his head. He'd always liked to run. The ragged sound of his breathing drowned out the thunderous noise in his head, the thought of Corinthe's eyes and the softness of her touch.

Luc headed back to Mountain Lake Park, figuring that since the Crossroad had spit him out there, he'd be able to find a way back in. He nearly stumbled on a group of kids from his high school lying on the grass, the remains of a picnic spread out on a patchwork of beach towels and blankets. Even from ten feet away, he could smell the cheap, sugary wine.

Luc ducked into the treeline, not wanting to be seen. He hurried along the edge.

"I just can't believe it," a familiar voice said. "Just last week I gave her a ride to school. And now Jasmine is gone." Karen swirled the red wine around in her clear plastic cup.

"It's not like you knew her or anything," Lily said.

Luc clenched his fists. God, she was such a bitch.

Karen's shoulders stiffened. "She was Luc's *sister*, Lily. Can you imagine what he's going through right now?"

"You weren't too worried about him at your party," Lily said.

Luc watched Karen pour the rest of her wine over Lily's plate of pasta. The rest of the group oohed, laughing as if Karen had done something hilarious. She got up to leave, and a small affection for her tugged at Luc's chest. Karen wasn't a bad person. She had made a couple of bad choices, but so had Luc.

Maybe when this was over and he'd set things right, he would tell her he wasn't angry—that he didn't blame her. Mike got up and followed Karen, pulling her toward him into a hug. There was nothing else to see.

Luc turned away quickly, grateful he still had his sweatshirt. He tugged the hood over his head and felt for the knife in his front pocket. He headed the long way around to the banks of the pond where he had been deposited by the Crossroad. But there were no irregularities here. Nothing that even seemed vaguely out of place. Was it possible that the entrance had been sealed somehow already? The only other Crossroad he knew of was the angel on Market Square, but that was all the way across the city. At this time, when all the people downtown were getting out of work, it would take at least forty-five minutes to get there. Forty-five minutes in a world where Jas, his little sister, who used to make him have tea parties with her stuffed bears, was dead.

Then a memory tickled the back of his mind. He had brought Jasmine back through the Crossroad at the rotunda, the one at the bottom of the lagoon.

Was it still there?

Up the hill, two people—a boy and a girl, maybe a little older than him, both of them wearing white shorts and white T-shirts and scuffed Chucks—whacked a ball back and forth on a tennis court. Both of them were awful. Both of them were laughing. Luc watched as the girl leaned across the net and kissed the boy when she went to retrieve a ball. Near the pond, a group of kids was playing tag barefoot. A boy knelt by the water and sent a scattering of crumbs toward the feeding ducks.

Luc felt a sudden tightness in his chest. Wrong. This time, this place was wrong. He knew it. How come no one else could feel it? When he went back to the tunnels of time, what would happen to this future world? Would the boy and girl ever get their round of tennis? Would the ducks get fed?

He turned away from them. Not his problem. Still, the guilt weighed on him. He started running again. Down West Pacific, then down Lyon toward the Bay. He didn't stop running, even when he reached the Palace of Fine Arts. It was a beautiful day, and the paths were crowded with families and tourists. He dodged past them, pulling off his heavy sweatshirt as he ran. He tied it around his waist as sweat trickled from his back.

He slowed, breathing hard, and followed the curved, column-lined pathway to the lagoon. He hoped there were no cops around. He had no idea whether it was legal to swim here, and here he was, about to dive into the water. Fortunately, there weren't too many people by the lagoon. Luc ducked behind a group of shrubs that extended partway into the water so no one would see him and shout. The water was freezing and rapidly filled his socks and shoes. Mud squelched under his feet.

When he was knee-deep in the water, he took a deep breath and submerged.

His clothes were heavy and his shoes waterlogged. Every stroke was difficult. He kept his eyes open, even though the water was a murky green and he could barely see a few feet ahead of him. He scanned until fire burned in his lungs. Finally, he surfaced, taking another deep breath of air. Dimly, he heard shouting—someone must have spotted him—but he didn't care, just went under again, kicking with iron-heavy legs down toward the bottom.

The water grew warmer. That wasn't right. He kicked deeper, feeling the ache in his shoulders and lungs. And then the water wasn't water anymore but air, thick and colored. He could breathe. A current rose up from beneath him and pushed him toward the lights like a giant watery hand. His body reacted instinctively and he inhaled, even as his mind rebelled against the unnatural feeling of sucking in water.

When he emerged, he was in the Crossroad.

He didn't hesitate. He took the knife from his sweatshirt, letting the towel he had wrapped it in fall away. He began to saw at the membrane separating the Crossroad from the tunnel. Anger fueled his movements until he was thrusting the knife in again and again, opening up long gashes in the wall that would heal over itself almost immediately.

But he wanted to destroy it—to shred it to pieces. Sweat poured off his face and his arm ached, but he didn't stop. Luc stabbed furiously, dragging the knife down until he had opened up a hole big enough to climb through.

No more mistakes.

He'd fix everything this time, or rip the tunnel apart trying.

18

She was dead. She was in heaven.

Then she remembered that (1) she didn't believe in heaven, and (2) dead people didn't think about being dead. Jasmine sat up, groaning a little. Her body was tingling and her head hurt, but other than that she was okay. Unscathed.

How was that possible? Her fingers instinctively flew to her chest. She fumbled, feeling for a cut, a bruise, some indication that she'd been stabbed. Nothing. But she remembered the Executor descending on her like some giant bird of prey; she remembered the feel of the knife and the darkness. . . .

The *darkness*.

Suddenly, Jasmine understood. *Time*. Time had jumped at just the right moment. For once, it had saved her. Spared her.

She stood up, feeling dizzy. Ford and the Executor were gone.

What if it never ended? What if she kept jumping all over time for the rest of her life?

She pushed to her feet, trying to get her bearings. The beauty of this twilight world was seductive; the sweet smells and vibrant colors were a part of her. She knew now that the nectar of this world flowed through her veins.

But this wasn't her home. San Francisco was her home. *I swam through this,* she remembered. This was how she would get home. She surveyed the landscape and paused on the river, watching as marbles passed in its swift current. They looked so familiar, like the one she had. She pulled hers from her pocket and held it up in the light. Was that an image swirling inside? Or was it only her imagination?

Why did the marble seem to vibrate, as if it were alive suddenly?

Apprehension crawled along the back of her neck and Jasmine turned. No one was there that she could see.

She shoved the marble back into her pocket, not confident in her ability to hold on to it and swim, and dove into the river. She thought of summer trips to Lake Tahoe. Of splash fights with Luc, and sunbathing on rocks for an entire afternoon.

The river in Pyralis felt crisp; she swam into its depths until she couldn't tell which direction was up. She was almost out of breath, but she wasn't scared. *Andromeda, Apus, Aquarius, Aquila.* She listed constellations in her head, as she'd learned to do from Luc, as she always did when she needed to focus. *Aries, Auriga, Boötes.*

Her dark hair pooled around her and brilliant colors danced at the edge of her vision. She was swirling— caught up in a current and flying across the universe. Her heart squeezed.

She broke through the surface of the water and inhaled a deep, sweet breath.

The rotunda stood before her.

Jasmine jogged around the building, thinking that in the past three days she'd done more running than in the rest of her life combined. When she saw Luc again— she pushed away a tiny voice that corrected, *if* she saw him again—he'd make fun of her for turning into a jock. She tried to swallow back the lump in her throat. She would give anything—*anything*—to rewind, to go back to how things were: sitting on the fire escape counting stars while Luc busted her for smoking clove cigarettes and put her in a headlock, as if she were still five.

But then she would never have met Ford.

She paused, trying to get her bearings. The museum grounds were overgrown; the sign that normally marked the entrance to the park was missing. Even the hiking trails weren't where they were supposed to be.

What the hell was going on?

She finally made it to the street and started toward the bus stop. Cars rumbled past—first some old, junky VW Beetle, then a dust-blue Cadillac, then a car as big and boxy as a boat. Then another old VW Beetle.

Jasmine stopped. The world seemed to go still for several seconds as fear crawled down her spine.

All the cars were older. No. Not just older. Old. Classic. Like in that picture of their mom as a young girl, sitting on the hood of *her* mother's lemon-yellow Mercury sedan.

Her breathing sped up. She'd been skipping around in time—there was no longer any denying it. But only by a few days at a time. Could she have jumped even further—could she have gone back decades instead of days? Hot tears burned her eyes, and she didn't try to stop them. What the hell would she do now?

Luc didn't exist. Her father was probably only a small child—wherever he even was—and Ford? She had no idea how to find him again.

A young woman wearing flared jeans and platform shoes as high as wedding cakes strolled down the street holding hands with a guy dressed almost entirely in tie-dye. They shot Jasmine a troubled look. She suddenly realized how out of place she was, in her deep purple band T-shirt, tight jeans, and sneakers. She fought a growing sense of panic. What if time didn't shift again?

What if she was stuck here, forever? She'd probably get chucked in a mental institution. Or worse, she'd be forced to start wearing tie-dye.

She sat down on the curb and tucked her head between her knees, fighting a surge of nausea. *Andromeda, Apus, Aquarius, Aquila.*

Jasmine didn't hear the car until a quick horn burst jerked her out of her thoughts. When she looked up, a long yellow car had stopped next to her. A young girl who looked around Jasmine's age leaned out the window.

"Are you okay?" the girl asked, reaching for the radio to turn it down. The girl's stick-straight dark hair hung from under a large white sunhat that seemed way too big for her face.

"I . . . I'm not really sure," Jasmine answered honestly.

"Climb in, I'll give you a ride." The girl smiled. She had a nice smile. Trustworthy. Jasmine felt a rush of relief. She figured that back in the day, people didn't have to worry about ax murderers. And something about this girl made her feel safe right away. She knew one thing: she didn't want to be alone right now. "I'm Ingrid," the girl said as Jasmine slid into the car. She was grateful that Ingrid didn't comment on her outfit.

"Ingrid. That was my grandmother's name," Jasmine said. "I'm Jasmine." The vinyl seat felt hard under her legs and there were little cracks in the upholstery. She automatically reached for the seatbelt and was shocked that there wasn't one.

Fortunately, Ingrid didn't notice. She was pulling out onto Presidio. They looped around the bus terminal to head back toward the Marina. "Jasmine, like the flower. That's a pretty name," she said.

Up close, Jas could see that Ingrid's skin was blotchy and her eyes pink, as if she'd been crying. There was a handkerchief balled up next to her. An actual handkerchief. "So . . . where to?" Ingrid asked.

Jasmine hesitated. "I . . . I'm not sure, actually."

Ingrid nodded. "You hitching?"

Jasmine assumed she meant hitchhiking. "Kind of."

"Cool." Ingrid gave her a faint smile. Even then, the small line between her eyebrows—a worry line—never disappeared. "I always wanted to hitchhike around. Where'd you start out?"

Jasmine turned her face to the window as they wound alongside the bay. "A long, long ways away."

"Well, Haight-Ashbury's pretty cool, if you're looking for a place to crash," Ingrid said.

Jasmine couldn't stop herself from grimacing. She knew Haight-Ashbury as a pilgrimage site for old hippies who wore sandals with socks and multicolored fanny packs, or for young, dumb rich kids who wanted to buy pipes and filters from a head shop for their overpriced weed and didn't know where to look.

"I don't know," Jasmine said. "I have to think. I'm a little lost right now."

The girl half smiled. "Aren't we all?"

Jasmine glanced at Ingrid. She had on a white embroidered peasant top and a long colorful skirt. It looked like an outfit out of Thrift Town, Jas's favorite thrift store. It was actually pretty awesome.

They were getting closer to the city and as they passed the Palace of Fine Arts, Jasmine saw workmen all around the area. It looked like they were building the columns that flanked the pathways to the rotunda. Jasmine took a deep breath.

"Look, this is gonna sound weird," she said, "But . . . what year is it?"

Ingrid squinted at her. "Are you high or something?"

"What? *No.* I swear. It's just . . ." Jasmine fumbled for an excuse. "It's hard to explain. . . ."

"I'm not judging you," Ingrid said. She laughed hollowly. "My mom would say I don't get to judge anyone. People in glass houses, right? And God, it's not like I haven't tripped before. It's 1975."

Two men sat on the corner, shirtless, drumming on bongos, bobbing their heads. Several people stood around them, swaying to a beat Jas couldn't make out from a distance. One woman had on a maxi dress. The man next to her had on striped bell-bottoms and a dark leather jacket. His hair had to be standing out from his head at least a foot.

Behind them, plastered across the brick building, were dozens of posters.

The War Is Over!

Goose bumps lifted on Jas's arms. She'd always been fascinated by the 1970s. But it was different to be here, in the middle of it. She didn't belong here.

"Want to talk about it?" Ingrid asked gently.

Jasmine picked at her jeans, which were fraying at the knee. "I'm . . . not sure you'd understand," she said. Her throat was thick. *What now, what now?* She found herself wishing that time would shift again, and she would be thrown back into her own time, her own familiar streets.

"Try me." Something in Ingrid's voice made Jas look up. They were stopped at a light. With one hand, Ingrid smoothed her shirt down over her belly. Jasmine saw her stomach was tight and round. Like an upside-down bowl.

She was pregnant.

"It should be a good thing, right?" Ingrid said. She didn't wait for Jasmine to respond. "But my parents still don't know. They'd be so angry. And the father . . ." Ingrid's voice broke and her fingers tightened momentarily on the wheel. "The father can't handle it. Or doesn't want to. I don't know."

"I'm sorry," Jasmine said, forgetting, for a moment, about her own problems. Ingrid had to be, what, sixteen? seventeen? And she was all alone. And pregnant. "Isn't there anyone who could help?"

Ingrid didn't say anything right away. Then, without warning, she was crying. She pulled the car over and leaned forward, resting her head against the steering wheel. Jasmine didn't know what to do. She struggled to think of words of comfort but came up empty. Instead, she reached her hand out and very lightly touched Ingrid's hair.

Ingrid sat up. She pulled up her shirt and used its hem to wipe her eyes. Jasmine could see the high swell of her stomach. Ingrid smiled, even as she hiccupped.

"I'm sorry," she said. "I'm sorry. I picked you up because I wanted to help, and now . . ." She gestured helplessly, sniffling. "I'm just so tired, you know? And so scared."

Something passed between them, an unspoken understanding. Jasmine had the strangest sensation that she knew Ingrid, had met her somewhere before. But she knew it must be her imagination. "I do know," Jasmine said.

"He's not a bad guy," Ingrid said. She repeated it, as if she wanted to convince herself. "He's *not* a bad guy. And I'm sure he loves me. It's just . . . have you ever thought about what's out there? Like beyond what we know?" Her words spilled out over each other. "Would you think I was crazy if I told you that he's just . . . different?"

"How do you mean, different?" Jasmine asked carefully. She certainly wasn't going to accuse anyone else of being crazy. Not after the events of the past few days.

Ingrid had finally calmed down. Now she sat staring out the window, a muscle ticking in her jaw. "He has . . . a calling. Like a higher law he has to obey."

"Like a priest or something?" Jasmine asked.

"Kind of." Ingrid bit her bottom lip. "More like . . . he has to make sure everything happens the way it should." Her eyes flicked to Jasmine's, then quickly flicked away. "Like . . . fate. Like if fate needed help sometimes . . . Oh God, this is insane. I'm sorry, I don't know why I'm even telling you this."

Jasmine felt a chill spread through her body. An idea was tickling the edge of her consciousness. She needed to know for sure. Jasmine grabbed Ingrid's hand and squeezed. "It's okay. I believe you."

Ingrid looked up at her. Her eyes got bright. "You do?"

"Absolutely."

Ingrid took a deep breath. She searched Jasmine's face, as though looking for signs that Jas was making fun of her. "He told me things, you know," she said in a rush. "There are roads that connect our world with hundreds of others. *Thousands* of others. And he's special in a way that allows him to travel those roads. It sounds impossible, right? Aliens or something, but it's not like that. That's why—that's why he can't stay here with me." Ingrid laid her hand on her belly. "With us."

It felt like all the air had been sucked out of the car. Jas was certain now. The baby's father was an Executor. Ingrid must have mistaken the look on Jasmine's face. Her cheeks turned pink and she looked away quickly.

"Anyway, thanks for listening. I—I probably sound like a crazy person to you. I don't know why I just spilled my guts like that. I guess it felt good to tell someone." Ingrid started the car engine over and pulled back into the street. They drove in silence for several minutes. Jasmine wanted to ask more questions, but she could tell that Ingrid already regretted saying as much as she had.

While waiting at a light on the corner of Scott and Chestnut, Ingrid coughed and spoke for the first time in ten minutes. She pointed across the street to a huge neon coffee cup. DAPHNE'S DINER blinked in bright pink above it.

"That diner is my favorite place to go and escape for a few hours," she said, speaking politely now, as if she were a tour guide. "They have amazing milk shakes, and they let me sit for hours with a book and just read when it's not busy. If the baby is a girl, I'm going to name her Daphne."

Jasmine suddenly felt as though she were falling. It all made sense: the feeling of familiarity, the blue eyes, even the raven hair. The lemon-yellow Mercury.

"Is your last name Simmons?" Jasmine whispered. The pounding of her heart was so loud, she barely heard Ingrid answer. Ingrid was looking at her almost fearfully now.

"Who are you?" Ingrid said, her eyes narrowing a little. "Do I . . . do I know you?"

Jasmine closed her eyes. The world turned a somersault. Ingrid was her grandmother.

Which meant her grandfather had been an Executor.

Which meant she was an Executor, too. A part of her was, at least.

They sent you to kill one of your own?

Ford's words came back to her and she felt sick.

"Stop the car," Jasmine said. This was too much.

Ingrid pulled over to the side of the road and shifted the car into park. "Is everything okay?"

"No, it's not." Jasmine fumbled for the door handle and almost fell out of the car in her hurry to exit. She had no idea where she was, but she had to get out, get some air, get away.

Ingrid honked, but Jas ignored her. She couldn't bear to even look at her grandmother again. She turned and started to run back the way they'd come.

19

Luc stood on the bank of the river that flowed through Pyralis and looked around.

After pulling the wires apart again, he'd crawled from the tunnels exhausted, his only thoughts of Corinthe. Instead of taking him back to San Francisco, though, the Crossroad had opened here.

Pyralis. He had made it, barely. His fingers smelled like smoke. There were angry blisters on his hands. He was moving automatically, through the pain, no longer caring what happened to the rest of the world—the rest of the worlds.

In the tunnels, he'd moved as though possessed. Hacking with his knife. Tearing at the wires until the tunnels were filled with sparks. Until the tunnels were screaming.

"Bring her back!" he'd shouted in response, as though

time would hear, as though it would obey him. "Bring them both back!"

Then: an explosion. He'd felt a great weight hit him, as though a giant fist had punched him out of the tunnels, into the Crossroad. He'd nearly drowned there, suffocated by the swirling winds. But he'd managed to get the archer from around his neck. *Corinthe.* He focused on the feel of her lips on his. *Corinthe.*

And now he was here. In Pyralis. At the center of all known worlds.

He was almost afraid at what he would find.

Corinthe had died here.

It was hard to catch his breath, and panic gripped his stomach like an iron fist. Would he have to make a choice again? Now that he knew the cost of picking the Flower of Life, would he be able to let Corinthe do it?

If he didn't, would Jasmine die?

He staggered away from the river. He didn't see Jas anywhere, and didn't know whether that was a good or bad thing. He plunged down a white-pebbled path that wound through lush flowering plants and disappeared into a thick grove of trees.

He heard whispers on the wind. He stopped and turned, wrapping his fingers around his knife. No one.

"Hello?" he called out. Faint whispers again. Or was that the wind? He couldn't be sure.

He turned around and started forward once more. He hadn't gone five feet when two girls emerged from the trees. They were maybe nine or ten years old, wearing long white dresses and walking barefoot over the rocks. They were so lost in conversation they didn't see him until they were close enough to reach out and touch.

The dark-haired girl gasped. A hand flew to cover her mouth and her light-colored eyes went wide. "You can't be here." She took a step away from him. "You're not supposed to be here. *No one* is supposed to be here."

The other girl, the one with long blond hair, looked up.

Luc's breath whooshed from his lungs as he looked into familiar gray eyes.

"Corinthe?" he whispered.

She looked at him without curiosity. "How do you know my name?"

Luc stared. The eyes were the same but there was no feeling in them, no life. Like two of the marbles she told him she used to fetch from the river. Luc suddenly remembered Jasmine at that age — face always smeared with dirt, mouth wide from either laughing or crying, depending on her mood. Corinthe looked like she had never laughed, never cried.

This was Corinthe as a girl then, before she was sent to Humana. Despair opened in his chest. He had gone back. Too far back.

The dark-haired girl grabbed Corinthe's arm and tugged. "We're not meant to be curious. Come on."

Corinthe shrugged the girl's touch away. "I know, Alessandra. It's just a question."

"We're not meant to ask questions."

Corinthe frowned in annoyance, and for a second,

Luc caught a glimpse of the Corinthe he knew, the Corinthe who would someday be. But then it was gone. Corinthe continued staring at him blankly, as if he were a puzzle she couldn't quite complete and didn't have the energy for.

The other girl, Alessandra, looked terrified. She hesitated, looking from Corinthe to Luc and back to Corinthe, as though for guidance. Then she turned and bolted back the way the girls had come.

"Who are you?" Corinthe asked idly, as if she were asking *What's your favorite color?* "How did you get here? Only Fates are allowed in Pyralis."

Luc's throat was dry. "I'm Luc. I came through the Crossroad. I was . . . looking for someone."

At the mention of the Crossroad Corinthe's eyes changed again, and the wariness was gone. Again Luc saw a spark of the Corinthe he knew. She rose up on her toes and bounced slightly. "You've been through the Crossroad? What's it like? Was it dangerous? Were you scared? I've heard that if you don't know what you're doing, you can get sucked to the very edges of the universe where there's nothing but dry red desert."

"You've never been through the Crossroad?" Luc asked, though he knew the answer.

Her lips turned down. "We're not allowed. Our job is to sort the marbles and send them on to the Messengers. The Messengers travel between the worlds, carrying the marbles." She said it quickly, as if it was a line she had memorized and repeated often.

"To the Executors, right?" Luc prompted.

Corinthe's frown deepened and she took a step back, watching him carefully. "You know about the Executors, too?" Her gaze flicked toward the trees, and for a second, Luc thought Corinthe would run away.

"I've only heard of them," Luc said, trying to reassure her. His pulse was throbbing in his neck. Corinthe was safe here. Alive. She was home in Pyralis, a place she loved. Should he warn her about what would come? She had once told him that she'd been exiled from Pyralis because she'd been too curious, and lost a fate marble as a result. Should he tell her she must never, ever ask questions?

Then they would never meet. She would never, ever grow up and become Corinthe—wild and free and passionate and good. They would never fall in love.

"Oh. That's all right, then," Corinthe said.

Luc took a deep breath. "I've heard stories about the Flower of Life, too," he said carefully. "Have you seen it?"

Her face brightened. "It's in the Great Gardens. I love the Gardens. We're only allowed in the outer gardens, though." Her face darkened momentarily. "The inner garden isn't allowed. There are lots of things that aren't allowed."

"What happens if someone picks the flower?" he asked, though this, too, was a question whose answer he knew.

"Whoever picks the flower dies." Her tone was matter-of-fact, unemotional.

He was gripped by the irrational urge to make her see how wrong it was, to try to make her see before it was too late. "Doesn't that seem a little unfair to you?"

"Unfair?" Corinthe tilted her head to the side and looked at him curiously, as if she'd never heard the word before. "It's perfectly fair. The nectar of the flower gives life. But the blood of the receiver is what makes the flower grow again. That's what keeps the universe in balance, and balance is a gift from the Unseen Ones. Blood for blood and a life for a life."

Luc froze. Dread pooled in his stomach. *Blood for blood. A life for a life.* Corinthe had picked the flower, but she had not used it for herself. She had given the flower's nectar to Jasmine. Corinthe had died and Jasmine had lived. Would he have to choose between them in order to satisfy the Unseen Ones?

If he saved Corinthe, did that mean the Unseen Ones would keep sending Executors to try to kill Jasmine? Was it some kind of sick rebalancing act? Had the Executors been after Jasmine, not him, all along?

He knew immediately that it was true. He felt it. Jasmine would never be safe while Corinthe was alive.

Unless . . .

Unless he could find a way to go back to the beginning, before everything started, before Jasmine was taken, before Corinthe received her final task.

He felt a swinging sense of nausea. That meant going back to the tunnels.

Impulsively, Luc touched Corinthe's shoulder. "Whatever you do, don't stop asking questions."

Corinthe frowned, then nodded. Her eyes were now the color of a swirling thunderstorm.

He turned and started back toward the river. As he got closer to the end of the path, he could hear the roar of water rushing into the unknown. The sky was the same violet shade as ever; the water reflected thousands and thousands of stars.

Without hesitation, Luc dove into the river and swam toward the line where the stars met the edge of Pyralis. Soon the current grabbed him, propelled him along. He couldn't stop even if he wanted to. He knew he must be approaching the waterfall that bled out off the edge of Pyralis, and into the Crossroad. The roar of the water was thunderous. The spray got in his mouth and in his eyes. For a second, he was cold with terror and wanted to stop, to get out, to rest. But then the current pushed him over the edge of the waterfall, and he plummeted into the swirling mist below.

20

This time, when the spikes of pain and light came, driving through Jasmine's skull, it was almost a relief. She sat down heavily in front of the rotunda and waited. The ground beneath her trembled; she felt like she might get bucked off the surface of the earth. She took deep breaths, recited all the constellations through Dorado.

Finally, her head cleared. The blackness eating the edges of her vision dissipated. The sun was just breaking over the horizon, across the city. The rotunda was changed. Newer. It was the rotunda she recognized. A dozen feet away, a jogger was shouting to her—but she was too focused on his Nike sneakers, on his big digital watch and heart monitor, to make out what he was saying. With a rush of relief, she realized she was back. Or forward. Whatever. She could have cried out with joy.

Still, the ground kicked underneath her. She tried to stand up and stumbled. It was like trying to catch a wave; the pavement rolled and a loud *crack* split the air. Behind her, an enormous column split and toppled. Air whooshed past her and Jasmine felt the impact of the column against the earth from ten feet away. The air was filled with a low growl, and Jasmine instinctively went into a crouch and covered her head, as she'd learned to do during earthquakes as a young kid.

This was a bad one, one of the worst she'd ever experienced. The world turned to chaos, bucking like an angry bull, snapping trees in half and sending them crashing into cars. Across the street, windows popped and exploded along a row of well-maintained houses.

Jasmine heard screams erupting all around her. People ran in every direction; car tires screeched and horns blew, adding to the confusion. A longer, harder tremor shook the earth and more columns split and fell, bursting apart as they fell onto each other.

Somewhere a car alarm started to blare.

When at last the tremors settled, and no more aftershocks kicked up through the ground, Jasmine sat up. The rotunda was in ruins. It looked exactly as it had the day she met Ford.

Ford. She had to find Ford.

"Excuse me," Jasmine called out to the jogger who had been shouting at her before—probably warning her to take cover. He was unharmed, except for a scrape on his cheek. "What—what day is it?"

He was middle-aged, a little paunchy. He kind of reminded her of her dad, except for the jogging-gear part. "Are you hurt? Did you hit your head?" He came to her side, knelt next to her.

"I'm fine," Jasmine said, and stood up as if to prove it. "I promise. It's . . . it's Saturday, right?"

The jogger nodded, squinting. "Are you sure you're okay?"

Jasmine waved him off. "I promise. I guess I just got shaken up." She let out a laugh and walked quickly away from him, weaving through debris, before he could ask her any more questions.

So. Her intuition was correct. It was Saturday now, the day of the earthquake. That meant she had two days before she would meet Ford at the rotunda. Would he be there again? Would he recognize her this time? Would she make it two full days without time hopscotching around? Somehow, she doubted it.

Ingrid had confirmed what Jasmine had begun to suspect in Pyralis, that she *was* part Executor. Which meant Luc was, too. And now that she knew the truth, did that make her and Ford enemies? Wasn't that what he'd said the first time she confronted him? *We both know we're on different sides.* He had killed one Executor already, and had probably killed others before.

But she couldn't lose Ford. He was her only ally. No one else understood. She had to make sure that in two days she would meet Ford and know that he could help her.

She needed to leave herself a clue. But where? Fort Point? Should she leave herself a clue where they had spent the night together? But that wouldn't work, because how would she know to go there?

Another rumble shook the ground. Shit. She stood with her feet planted firmly apart and waited for it to pass. *Think, Jasmine. Where would you look?*

Then, in a flash, she understood. Here, at the rotunda. The note in the secret room.

Jas stumbled through the mess of concrete and branches. The air was filled with choking white dust and screaming sirens and panicked voices. She carefully picked her way to the hollow column that hid the secret stairway.

Dim light streamed down the steps. The shadows lengthened as she got near the bottom; it was so full of dust here, it was almost impossible to breathe. She slid her hand along the cool brick until a break in the wall indicated that the main room was right there. As she stepped into the room, she saw that part of the ceiling had collapsed. A bit of sunlight filtered through, casting a crazy array of shifting shadows.

Chills washed over her skin, and she rubbed her arms. The Executors had found her here twice. It wasn't a good idea to hang around. The girl had said more would come in her place until the task had been completed. Until Jasmine was dead.

A low rumble started under her feet and grew in intensity until the dishes in the cabinet on the wall fell and smashed into pieces. Jas darted to the doorway and braced her hands against the sides. Another large chunk of the ceiling fell and sent a blast of dust straight at her. She turned her face, felt the pressure of dust and plaster on her back.

She needed to do what she had to do and get out, before the whole frigging place caved in and she was buried alive. When the shaking subsided, she moved as quickly as she could into the small side room. In the nightstand, she found an envelope and a pen.

Find Ford. Ask him about Miranda.

It wasn't much. But it was enough.

She reached the top of the stairs just as a terrible noise began deep under the earth and seemed to claw its way to the surface. Everything shook, a harder aftershock than any of the previous ones. Jasmine hurtled through the doorway just as what remained of it collapsed behind her. Before she could react, a flash of light filled her vision and now-familiar agony ripped through her head. She stumbled and fell to her knees.

Why does this keep happening to me?

When her vision finally cleared, she saw that the sun was just now breaking over the horizon again. It was dawn once again, as if she were in a badly edited film. But the ground was still, and police tape crisscrossed the whole area like a giant yellow spiderweb. Teams of volunteers moved silently around the area, bagging and shifting debris.

"Jas!"

Jasmine turned, and her heart squeezed and then opened. Ford. He was here, really here, skirting the piles of rubble, his face twisted with concern. He was here and he knew her. Without intending to move, she crossed the distance between them and threw her arms around him. He pulled her close, holding her so tightly her feet lifted off the ground.

"I've gone crazy looking for you." He pulled back just enough to look into her eyes and cupped her face with his hands. "You're okay, right? I thought something had happened to you." When she nodded, he closed his eyes and rested his forehead against hers. He was breathing hard, as if he'd been running through the whole city. "I'm—I'm sorry for leaving. You were asleep and . . . I just freaked out. I got halfway across the city before I realized what an idiot I was being. But by the time I made it back to the bridge, you were gone."

Jasmine flipped back through her memories of the past few days. It must be Tuesday morning; the morning after Ford had vanished while she was asleep in his secret hideout. That meant the Executors hadn't tracked her to the shelter yet. Ford hadn't killed one of them. She hadn't yet been brought to Pyralis. She thought of the tip of the girl's knife breaking the skin on her chest and shivered.

She took a deep breath. "I'm sorry," she blurted out. Her voice hiccupped and she tried to take a breath. She didn't know exactly what she was apologizing for, but she knew she had gotten Ford mixed up with something very bad. And she was not like him. She didn't know *what* she was anymore. "I—I don't know what's happening to me. I don't know what's wrong with me. Or—I do know. There *is* Executor in my blood. My grandfather was an Executor. You've known that all along, haven't you?"

Ford nodded.

Jasmine swallowed. "That's why—that's why you said we were on different sides, isn't it?"

He made a sound, sort of a groan deep in his throat. His free hand rose and curled around the back of her neck. He pulled her closer, slow enough that she had time to stop him, but she didn't. "I don't care what I said," he whispered. His voice was low and hoarse and it sent butterflies dancing along her skin. His lips were so close to hers she could feel his breath skim across them. Suddenly, everything around them disappeared from her mind and it was only the two of them.

She slid her hand slowly up and stopped just over the frantic heartbeat in his chest. Heat radiated between them; the air felt charged. His thumb brushed her earlobe as he drew her even closer, and every cell in her body came alive, focusing on that one spot.

He closed the last breath of space between them and his lips brushed hers. It was like being struck by lightning. Jasmine wrapped both her arms around him, pulling him as close as possible.

Ford held her tightly and deepened the kiss, and a new hunger rose inside her. In her mind she could see millions of stars spinning out of control, suns exploding, comets with fiery tails hurtling through galaxies. She ached to be one of them, wild and free and out of control.

Ford finally pulled back with a gasp and rested his forehead on hers. His breathing was harsh and loud. When he opened his eyes, Jasmine swore she could see the same cosmic chaos swirling around in them.

"I won't leave you again, I promise. And I won't let anyone hurt you. As long as I'm able, I *will* keep you safe. Okay?" Ford kissed her again, softly this time.

A lingering warmth replaced the fire in her blood. Nothing in her life had ever felt this perfect before. She wanted to stay right there, in that moment, in Ford's arms.

"Remember how I told you last night about the time shifts?" Jasmine asked, and Ford nodded. "It's getting worse. More frequent. Bigger, too. I went back forty years. I met my grandmother. . . ." Ford's eyes widened. Jasmine rushed on, "I'm scared, Ford. I'm worried I'll get lost. Or stuck. Do you think this has to do with the Unseen Ones?" The Executor had said that the Unseen Ones managed everything in the universe. They *must* be responsible.

But Ford frowned. "That's not how it works. The Unseen Ones control the fates of all the creatures in the universe. But even they can't control the flow of time."

Jasmine wasn't convinced. What other explanation was there? Unless . . . unless it was some kind of weird effect because she'd used the Flower of Life, or whatever the Executor had called it. *You can feel it inside, can't you?* the girl had said. *The way you've changed.*

But Jasmine didn't want to believe it. Did that mean

she would keep bouncing through time forever, like some cosmic pinball?

"Do you know where to find them?" Jasmine asked. "The Unseen Ones," she prompted, when Ford looked at her blankly.

"I only know *of* them." He looked away, squinted. "The Unseen Ones are everywhere and nowhere."

"That sounds like a riddle," Jasmine said, getting impatient.

"Sorry." He reached out and touched her face again; then his expression hardened. "If I knew where to find the Unseen Ones—if I could get to them—I would. I swore after they destroyed an innocent life, that I would take revenge." Bitterness laced his words. He looked angry. Wild.

"Someone you knew?" asked Jasmine quietly. She knew the answer already, had seen it in the pain and loss in his eyes.

He didn't look at her. "A girl. A human girl who didn't deserve to die simply because *they* decided it. They sent an Executor. . . ."

Jasmine couldn't meet his eyes anymore. "I'm sorry."

"It wasn't anything you have to be sorry for. It was a long time ago."

She could tell from his tone of voice: He had loved the girl. She felt a brief flare of jealousy, and then immediately felt guilty, and then angry with herself. What kind of person was she, to be jealous of someone who was dead? Especially at the hands of someone just like her.

He had kissed her, saved her life, and yet there was a part of him that someone else had known. It made her feel . . . strangely alone. She had the sudden overwhelming urge to turn and run away as fast as she could. "I'm sorry," she said again, at a loss for what else to say.

"Jas." Ford breathed her name into her ear and she froze. He slid his hand up her neck to tangle in her hair and pulled her close. "It was a long time ago. Now, it's just you, I promise."

He pulled back just enough to press his lips against the frantic pulse in her neck. Then he moved higher, along her jaw, her chin. "I don't know what any of this means. But I know one thing: I won't let you go."

Finally, his lips were against hers again. They kissed until they were both breathless. This kiss was different from any of the other kisses she'd had, which were wet and sloppy and uncomfortable. Kissing him was like falling, or floating. It was *right*.

She couldn't be without him again. At any moment she might get pushed into another day or another year. He might stay lost to her in time forever.

"We need to figure out how to stop this," she said. "*All* of it."

"There might be someone who can help us." There was hesitation in Ford's eyes, and she could tell he didn't like what he was about to suggest. "Miranda might know."

The name gave her an uneasy feeling. She'd been so worried about dodging the Executors and rocketing back and forth through time she'd forgotten all about her original intuition that Miranda was at the heart of this whole mess. That Miranda might even know where Luc was. "Who is she?"

"Another Radical, like me," he said slowly. "She knows about the tunnels of time and hates the Unseen Ones even more than I do." He chewed on his lower lip, lost in thought. "Or she might not. Miranda has her own agenda. She's unpredictable, even for a Radical."

"We have to try," Jasmine said, even though there was a leaden weight in her stomach. "How do we find her?"

"Through the Crossroad." His eyes were like a summer storm, turbulent and wild.

The Crossroad. The Executor had brought her through the Crossroad—or *would* bring her through the Crossroad tonight, in some version of the future. Her stomach flipped at the thought of navigating the spinning vortex of color again. She had felt like she might drown.

But with Ford, it couldn't be that bad. At least, she hoped so. And she would be brave for him. "All right," she said. She felt as if the words were lodged in her throat, strangling her.

Ford laced his fingers through hers. Then he brought her hand to his lips, kissing each fingertip gently. "Remember what I promised you," he said. "I won't leave you again."

They had taken only a few steps when a now familiar voice filled the air.

"Ford," the girl Executor called out.

Ford stiffened and pulled Jasmine behind him.

"Don't come any closer." Ford's voice was low, and sparks danced along the edges of his fingers. "What the hell do you want?"

The girl, to Jasmine's surprise, held up her hands. "I'm not here to fight you. I've come with a message from the Unseen Ones. An offer of peace, if you will."

Jasmine could feel Ford's fury. The sparks grew brighter. "They convinced the Tribunal to lock me up in Kinesthesia. Why the hell would they offer me a deal?"

"They're prepared to grant you full immunity and your freedom," the girl said as she met Jasmine's gaze. "A pardon."

"The Unseen Ones don't negotiate."

"They want this matter resolved civilly—and quickly."

Jas took a step back, away from Ford, who had gone still.

"Give us the girl, and we'll give you your freedom."

Jasmine watched Ford with a sinking feeling. He hadn't moved. What if he took their offer? Freedom was a potent motivator, maybe even more so than revenge. She couldn't fight them all.

"One human for endless existence, Ford," the girl said. "You could burn as brightly as you want. Isn't that what you want the most?"

He stood unmoving, and his silence told Jasmine all she needed to know. She turned and ran for the street.

21

The suns' heat burned down on Miranda. Every inhale felt like fire burning her lungs. She squinted against the brightness.

Rhys had spent out his life in this barren world. Now she would die here. Would that have made her former lover happy? She thought of him, stuck in his dark world, all alone except for the Figments he helped. It was all because of her, because he risked it all to save her. They were born of the same chaos and should've spent eternity together.

He would say that the universe obeyed the heart, but she knew better.

The universe obeyed the Unseen Ones. Because of them, she had lost everything.

But she would have the last laugh. The fire that had started in the Crossroad had followed her into this world.

The eternal flame, she knew, would keep burning until everything was consumed. Already the fire licked away at the red sand, and spiraling stems of smoke curled upward, clouding the suns in a thick gray haze. The world melted around the flames, like a piece of paper fed into a fire, falling into the swirling darkness below. Into unknown parts of the universe.

How long would it take to destroy the entire Land of the Two Suns?

And after that . . . the rest of the universe?

For you, Rhys, she thought, glancing toward the cliffs where she knew he had lived.

A movement above caught her eyes, and for one fleeting moment, she thought it might be Rhys, that somehow he hadn't died. Her heart leapt inside her chest and she tried to call out to him, but the dryness of her throat prevented any sound from escaping.

The figure shifted and melted out of sight, but not before Miranda saw that it was simply a Figment who had been standing on the edge of the cliff. Had it been watching her?

She pushed herself slowly to her feet. The horizon dipped and dove crazily, and she staggered to the left, barely staying on her feet. She started toward the cliffs, one agonizing step at a time. At the base of the cliffs, she had to stop and rest her hand against the sharp rock so as not to fall. She looked up, following the lines of the rocks, and felt a moment of despair. It was too far. She was too weak. She collapsed to her knees, breathing hard.

I'm sorry, Rhys. It was fitting that she be alone. She deserved it.

She wished she could tell him that despite everything, she *did* still love him.

Miranda felt the smallest hint of wind. But no. The touch was too persistent to be natural. She opened her eyes and saw dark fingers wrapped around her wrist, tugging her gently forward. Two Figments were beckoning her forward. *Her* Figments — her shadows. She recognized them immediately because they were *her* shadows.

Their touch was insubstantial but strong, steady. Like a wind lifting her to her feet. They drove her forward, half carrying her into the dark crevice in the cliffs that would take her to Rhys's home. It was cooler inside the rocks. Miranda breathed a little easier, though she could not have stood on her own. She was so close to the end now.

At last they reached Rhys's home. Miranda saw the cage, empty, where Rhys had kept Mags, the crow that had served as his eyes. And the bed, also empty.

She would lie where he had lain. She would die there, pretending she was in his arms, until the fire consumed her.

The Figments edged closer to the bed, as if they could protect her from the oncoming flames. Miranda reached over and slid her hand across Rhys's pillow, as if they would be touching even in death.

Soon the flames were eating away at the rocks around her, bright orange and red fingers grabbing and turning substance to smoke, to nothingness. They were beautiful, the colors that blazed at the end of the world.

The cliff peeled away, shriveling into ribbons of flame, leaving a gaping hole directly in front of her. Smoke swirled and grew darker, growing so black that it appeared to be one solid mass moving down the cliffs. The fire hissed and sizzled.

And began to retreat.

That was when Miranda realized that the dark blanket rolling down the cliffs was not smoke but Figments. They were throwing themselves down the cliffs, at the fire. Thousands and thousands of them, a flood, a torrent.

Then Miranda understood.

The world would not fall apart under the flames. The Figments had sacrificed themselves to the fire.

Miranda gave in, at last, to the dark.

22

The fire had reached the tunnels now. Smoke stung Luc's eyes. If he didn't hurry, he'd suffocate before he could find a way out.

Every few seconds, the entire tunnel shuddered, as if inhaling a trembling breath.

Rhys had said once that the universe was alive.

What if time flowed like blood, pumped through the veins of the tunnels? Maybe the key was to turn it around, force it to *physically* flow backward. But how? He had done so much damage already, and though he had patched and reconnected the wires he had hacked through so carelessly in anger, he could feel the tunnels trying to expel him, to push him out.

Sparks leapt above him. They seemed to be going in every direction at once. How would he know which way was back and which was forward?

He scanned the tunnels again, examining every visible curve. Then something hard slammed into him from behind and he flew forward. He spun around and tried to back away, but she shoved her foot into his chest and he stumbled backward again.

"What the hell are you doing?" he gasped.

There was a cut along Tess's cheek and she looked wilder than he remembered. Out of control—like Miranda.

"Look what you've done!" she said. Her voice was a wild howl of grief. "You've ruined everything!"

Luc staggered, feeling the tender spot on his ribs where she had kicked him. "I'm trying to put everything back the way it should be."

Tess's eyes flashed. "Didn't Rhys tell you? Everything is connected, Luc. You can't change one thing without changing everything. And your stupidity has put the whole universe in danger. I should have stopped you sooner, but Miranda interfered. There's no one to help you now."

Tess picked him up and threw him against the wall of the tunnel. He dropped the kitchen knife. The wall immediately began pulling at him, sucking him through the thick blackness.

"No. *No!*" he shouted, tugging at the clinging membrane of the tunnel wall that stuck to him like tar. Tess slammed into him again, propelling them both through the wall and back into the Crossroad. Immediately, Luc smelled smoke, and remembered that the Crossroad was still burning. He could feel the extreme heat choking him. He watched in horror as the hole in the membrane closed in on itself, sealing off the tunnels once more.

Suddenly, he and Tess were no longer whirling through the Crossroad but falling, falling, for what seemed like forever. It hit him that they'd fallen into another world. And with the clanging of metal all around and sparks flying everywhere, he realized they'd ended up in a familiar place: Kinesthesia.

Luc had landed on top of Tess, and for a moment she simply disappeared, her body shuddering into nothingness as though in response to the impact. He gasped.

Just as quickly, Luc got up and began to run through the gridlike mechanical world, even as Tess began to reform herself: hair, legs, arms weaving together like a TV image coming slowly into focus.

He dodged the showers of white sparks erupting from enormous gears that grated together. He remembered what Corinthe had told him: how this was where the logic of the universe originated, the order and the time. A world laid out across a massive metal grid, hovering over an endless abyss. Only the steel grates beneath his feet kept him from plunging into the infinite nothingness below, and Luc could see gaps where the floor had already collapsed.

The fires from the Crossroad had reached this world as well. Horrified, Luc saw what Tess meant when she said he had endangered everything. Enormous gears grated and scraped with horrendous screeching sounds. Some of them stuttered and slipped before catching.

Corinthe had said Kinesthesia housed the heartbeat of the universe. If that was true, Luc knew the heart was on the verge of death.

Was that why the Crossroad had pushed him out here, to the center of everything in the universe? So he would witness what he had done?

Luc ducked behind a huge piston that pumped up and down with slow, rhythmic movements. His shirt stuck to his chest. Where was Tess? There was too much motion, too much sound. He couldn't see her. She could be anywhere. He knew he couldn't have left her behind. She was too fast.

The only way he knew out of this place was the door in the clock tower. Even from here, he could see it: the clock tower pointed to the sky like an accusatory finger. But the way he'd crossed the last time was blocked off. The narrow catwalk was made of rectangular metal grating: the two-by-six-foot sections soldered together formed a bridge that extended over the abyss, but it looked unstable.

He ventured out onto it. Still he didn't see Tess. But she must be nearby. He knew she was. He inched farther down the catwalk, hoping to make it across.

"Stay where you are!" Tess's voice rang out behind him.

He spun around. Tess had materialized, and she had her knife out now. She advanced on him purposefully. Luc backed up until he was balanced on the edge of the catwalk. White sparks spit below him. And beneath that: an endless fall.

Luc held out his hands. "Wait," he said. His throat was dry. He needed to stall until he could figure out an advantage. "Just wait. I thought we were on the same side."

Tess shook her head. "I'm on nobody's side," she said. "You're fighting the will of the Unseen Ones, but they will win. They always win. Fighting them will just bring destruction—for you, for me, for everyone."

"What about Rhys?" Luc said desperately. "He trusted you. Now you betray him by siding with the enemy?"

"Rhys is dead—as is Mira. None of the old alliances matter anymore. Survival matters, and we must maintain the balance." She lunged at him then, and he sidestepped, but not fast enough.

Luc slammed against the railing of the catwalk, and the narrow section of grating they stood upon shuddered. Luc barely kept his footing. The bridge would collapse and he needed to move forward to solid ground. He turned to run, but Tess grabbed his foot and yanked him backward. He stared down through the metal grate into the infinite abyss below Kinesthesia. Tess rolled Luc over and pinned him, lowering her knife to his neck.

The metal on the far end of the catwalk creaked and bent, causing the rectangular area to tilt suddenly. Tess's weight shifted and she fell backward. Her knife fell to the side and she scrambled for it, causing the catwalk to tilt even farther. Luc could see that the soldered portion that stitched the sections together would give soon. Sweat coated his face, matting his hair to his forehead.

If he could just kick it, would it be enough force to

break it? He crouched low on the precarious walkway, looking over into the void.

"It's beautiful, isn't it?" Tess asked, clutching her knife. "The Tribunal imprisoned a Radical here, in a lonely cell that hung just above the abyss. The Unseen Ones sentenced him, but he escaped to Humana. He had help. Somehow, someone brought him a key."

"Why should I care about some Radical?"

"Because your sister is with him right now." Tess took a step toward Luc and the walkway shifted with a groan. "And Ford is reckless. He has no alliances."

Ford.

The same name that Corinthe had mentioned in some future reality.

Ford had taken Jasmine.

A sick feeling grew in Luc's throat. That was why Jasmine wasn't in the future he'd found. Because this Ford Radical had killed her. Luc had to get back to San Francisco, had to warn Jasmine to stay away from him.

"Your sister's blood will spill in the Great Gardens." The gleam was back in Tess's eyes.

"So that's the plan?" he asked, shaking with rage. "The Unseen Ones decide that he kills Jasmine and you kill me?"

"No, *they* want to imprison you," she said. "*I* want to kill you."

"Why?" Blood was pounding in his ears. He eyed the weak soldered metal — so close to snapping. One chance. One chance was all he would get. "Why does it matter so much to you that I die?"

"Because I need you out of the way, and because I know you won't stop. You're obsessed with turning back time—for what?"

"For Corinthe," he said.

"Corinthe," she scoffed. "Everyone thinks that love solves everything, that love conquers all. What good has it done for you and Corinthe?" Tess almost sounded angry. "Or for Mira and Rhys? Or for your sister? It brings nothing but pain."

"What are you talking about?" Luc wheezed.

Tess took another step toward him and the walkway shifted. She clutched the knife in her hand even tighter.

"All of you have ended up the same. Even the Figments are gone. They sacrificed themselves to the fire. For what? For love?"

Shock echoed through his muddled head. Luc remembered the pairing, remembered how happy the Figures and Figments had been while dancing together. They were One, and now the Figments were gone?

Rhys had said that they all were lonely, that they sought out their Others, but it was more than that. What they were all looking for was simple. They were looking for love.

Just like he was.

Luc wound his fingers through the grating and kicked at the metal seam that held it in place. His sneakers made contact with the bent steel, and the bridge tore apart with a loud groan.

Tess tried desperately to find a handhold, anything to grab. Her eyes were full of panic. The knife fell from her hand, and she grasped at air as the walkway collapsed from under her. She was sent free-falling into the abyss.

Luc held on to the grate as it swung like a pendulum; then he climbed up to safety.

He continued to hear Tess's screams echo long after her body had disappeared below.

23

"Jasmine, wait!"

Ford's frantic voice thundered in her ears. She ran faster, her feet pounding on the pavement. A morning jogger swerved into her path and Jasmine had to jump off the curb to avoid running into her. Instead of following the sidewalk, she cut across the street and past a dump truck that sat idling near the intersection.

It was Tuesday. That meant that most of the earthquake damage had already been cleared. California was fast like that. But there were still several buildings with boarded-up windows where the glass had shattered. A thin fog hung over everything—maybe she could lose Ford. Jas could taste salt on her lips. She was running up Baker Street, and her heart felt like it would explode.

Just ahead, at the top of the hill, she saw a metro bus

pull up to the stop. If she could make it on, Ford wouldn't be able to catch her.

She needed time. Time to think, to try to figure out what the hell to do now. If she could just talk to Luc, get him to tell her what had happened Friday night and explain who Miranda was, then maybe she'd know who to trust.

The bus doors opened with a whoosh and Jasmine lunged inside, panting. She fumbled for a crumpled dollar bill in her back pocket. As she collapsed into the closest seat, she saw Ford crest the hill and stop. He scanned the road, then spotted the bus, but it was too late. It had started to pull away from the curb. Jas expected Ford to run after them, to make the bus stop, but he just stood there watching.

He looked devastated.

Jasmine tried to reconcile the boy standing there, the one who had kissed her so gently, with this one, the one who had considered taking her back to the Garden.

Would he do that? After everything he had said to her?

Tears burned her eyes. How well did she really know him? Was that the nature of a Radical—to burn bright, at any cost? And why had Ford been imprisoned in the first place?

The questions only confused her more. She wanted to trust him, desperately, but she didn't know what he'd be willing to trade for his freedom.

The bus swayed along Baker, halting at each stop,

and every time, Jasmine held her breath, expecting Ford to push his way on and drag her off. By the time she got to Jackson, where she could catch another bus straight home, her nerves were stretched tighter than violin strings. The feeling didn't ease up during the rest of the trip. It wasn't until she got off a block from their building that she relaxed slightly. There was no sign of Ford.

Nonetheless, she hurried along the street and up the stairs to their apartment. Nothing felt safe anymore. Every sound made her jump. She turned down the hall to their apartment, then stopped. Someone was waiting in front of the door. Jasmine forced air through her tight throat. Not someone, Karen.

Of course.

It was Tuesday.

Again.

Karen spun around when she heard Jasmine's sharp intake of breath. "Oh, hi," she said. "I was . . . I was just looking for Luc." She fidgeted with her purse. "I've been trying to call, but he won't answer. I wanted to see if he was okay."

Jasmine pushed past her. "He's fine. He's just sick. I'll tell him you stopped by, okay?" She shoved her key into the lock and opened the door. Karen craned her neck to peek inside and Jasmine blocked the opening with her body. Luc never brought Karen to their place.

"Do you need a ride or anything?" Karen asked. "To school, I mean."

"I'm not going today, but thanks," Jasmine said. She was too tired to try to be nice. "I'm kind of sick, too."

"Oh, okay." Karen looked disappointed, but Jas didn't have time to cheer her up. She smiled tightly, repeated her promise to tell Luc that Karen had stopped by, and closed and locked the door. Her gaze swept the room. Was anything different? Did it look like Luc had come back?

Her heart sank when she saw that everything was exactly as it had been. Even the worn afghan lay over their threadbare green couch, right where it was before.

Now what?

She started toward her room to get a change of clothes, then froze.

Something *was* different.

She tiptoed to the kitchen and grabbed the longest knife out of the block on the counter. She was tired of running. As she moved down the hallway, there was an aroma in the air, like a dryer sheet that got too hot. It was not *un*familiar, but she couldn't place it.

Not the Executors, but not like Ford, either.

God, was someone *else* after her now? Despair welled up inside her. She forced it back. She wouldn't give up.

She could hear drawers being opened and closed. That really pissed her off. Someone was going through her stuff. She eased the door open with a foot, knife raised, poised to attack.

The person inside spun around.

For a second, Jas thought she must be dreaming. "Luc?" she whispered.

"Jas!"

Luc's voice was like oxygen to an air-starved brain.

Jasmine let the knife fall to the ground. She launched herself at her brother. "Luc! Where the hell have you been?" Tears streamed down her face and she buried her face in his neck. He squeezed her so hard, she couldn't breathe for several long seconds. When he finally released her, she swiped her face with her shirtsleeve. She was laughing and crying at the same time. "I've been so goddamn worried," she said. Then she smacked him on the arm. "Where were you?"

He gripped her shoulders with both hands. "I should have been honest from the start, Jas. I'm so sorry. I thought I was protecting you." He shook his head. "Sit, okay? I need to tell you some things that are going to sound crazy."

I doubt it, she thought. But she just sat down and folded her legs underneath her. The despair she'd felt only a few minutes ago had all but dissipated. Luc was here. Luc would help.

He was pacing the small room, pivoting every few feet. "It started Friday night, when you went to the Marina. Do you remember that?"

She nodded and gripped the bedspread between her fingers. Finally, she was going to get answers. "I went to dump T.J.," she said. "I remember a black-haired woman. After that, it's all blank."

"Miranda," Luc said, his voice barely above a whisper.

Jasmine's heart gave a thump. Somehow, she had

expected this. "Miranda," she repeated. So Jas *had* met Miranda. And Miranda had done something to her—something so that Jas wouldn't remember. "Ford told me she might help us. . . ."

Luc's face went white. "Where is he?"

"Y-y-you know Ford?" Jasmine stuttered.

Luc just shook his head, his mouth a thin line. "Where *is* he?"

Jasmine had seen that look on Luc's face before. It was the look he got before he did something stupid—like trying to jump T.J. on a crowded street, or freaking out when a ref made a bad call. "I don't know," she said carefully. "I left him at the rotunda."

Luc knelt and took her hands. "You have to stay away from him, Jas. He's dangerous."

"I know," she said. It hurt to admit it out loud, like the words had punctured her lungs. Once again, she'd completely misjudged someone. Once again, she'd been an idiot. She took a breath. "You didn't say where you were all this time."

"I've been trying to make everything right." Luc stood up and raked a hand through his hair. "I wanted to save Corinthe."

The look in his eyes broke her heart. "Corinthe?"

"The girl I love," he said. "She . . ." He exhaled slowly. "She died. I promised her that I would find a way to turn back time so we could be together again."

Jasmine would have laughed if his words—*turn back time*—hadn't sent a shock of recognition through her. "It was you?" Jasmine asked. "*You're* the reason?"

Luc stared at her. "The reason for what?"

She stood up. She felt as if bees were swarming her insides. "I've been jumping all over the place. Back and forth to different days. Different *years*, even."

"Years?" Luc's voice broke. He passed a hand over his eyes. "Christ, Jas. I'm so sorry. I never meant to hurt you." He sat down heavily on the bed, as though suddenly exhausted. "This is all my fault."

Jas knew he didn't mean just the time-jumping thing.

"You saved me in Pyralis, didn't you?" she said gently. Luc looked up, surprised. "The Executor was right. You used the flower's nectar because I was dying."

"How do you—" he started to ask.

"I know a lot," she said. "I've been back to Pyralis, Luc. I've been to the Crossroad."

"Oh my God," Luc whispered.

Jasmine sat down next to him. The bed creaked. "Let's start from the beginning, okay? Tell me everything you know. And I'll tell you everything I know." Jasmine slipped her fingers through his just like when they were little kids. "Maybe together we can figure this out."

Luc took a ragged breath. "It started when I met a girl who tried to kill me. . . ."

The rest of the story tumbled out, and Jas asked questions, adding more to his story as bits and pieces of memory came back to her: snippets and fragments of images, like pieces of paper carried back on a wind.

"There were these . . . things. Creatures." She shivered, recalling the high-pitched whine, like the noise of a thousand mosquitoes. "I couldn't move."

Luc went pale again. "The Blood Nymphs."

"And you came and saved me. You took me to Pyralis. *That's* why it all looked so familiar. I'd been there before."

He nodded, but stayed silent.

"And now these Unseen Ones need my blood to make the flower grow again." Finally, Jas saw that the big picture was even more hopeless than she'd feared. The highest power in the universe—the forces that controlled everything—wanted her dead.

"It won't happen. I won't let it," Luc said, as if he had read her mind. "If we can all go back—if we can make it so none of this happened—I can save Corinthe. I can save you, too."

"Do you really think you can do it?" she asked. Luc had told her that the tunnels of time stretched infinitely in two directions, and were so strange and wild and confusing, he had nearly died there twice.

"I can do it," Luc said, with forced confidence. "I have to."

"It won't be that easy."

Jasmine jumped up, crying out, as Ford suddenly appeared at the window, on the fire escape. Before Luc could block his path, Ford had slipped inside. Luc shoved Jasmine behind him. She wished she hadn't dropped the knife.

"Get out," Luc growled.

Ford held up his hands. "I'm not here to hurt her." He met Jasmine's eyes, and her whole heart squeezed up. His eyes were so warm. So comforting. She wanted to believe him. "I promise."

"How did you find me?" she asked.

"Get out," Luc repeated. He took a step forward, as if he intended to shove Ford back out the window.

"You can't just go back into the tunnels," Ford said, speaking in a rush. Luc stopped. "Didn't you listen to anything Rhys said? Didn't you see what it did to him? He was a Radical. What chance do you think you have?"

"I know what you are," Luc said. "I know what you're planning to do. Why should I trust you?"

A spike of fear drove through Jas. Ford had killed an Executor, he'd have no trouble at all with a human.

"Luc!" she burst out. Both boys turned to face her. "I need to talk to Ford. Alone. Just for a minute." She tried to pretend the idea didn't terrify her.

"Luc," she said, laying her hand on his arm, "can I talk to Ford for a minute? Alone?"

"No way," Luc said. "I told you. He can't be trusted. I've seen what he can do, I've *seen* it—"

Ford was staring straight at Jasmine as if Luc weren't even in the room. The way he was looking at her made her whole body feel warm. "I promised to keep you safe and I will," he said.

She crossed her arms. It was like he could see straight *into* her—like he could read everything she was thinking. "What about . . . what about what the Executor said?" she croaked. "She said the Unseen Ones would pardon you in exchange for my life."

Ford laughed. "Do you think I care about their pardons?" He shook his head. His eyes blazed. "After everything they've done to me—after everything they've done to the people I love—you think that I'd play nice with the Unseen Ones?"

The intensity in his eyes drove straight into her heart. Her instincts hadn't been wrong, she saw that now. Ford had more reason than anyone to hate the Unseen Ones.

"Don't you trust me?" he asked softly.

Emotion clogged her throat and all she could do was nod. Tears blurred her vision, but she could see enough to walk to him. Jas wrapped her arms around his waist and held him tight. She felt his lips brush her ear.

"I don't like it," Luc said. Jas had almost forgotten he was in the room. He was still standing rigid, tight as a wire.

"Let me guess," Ford said, pulling away from Jasmine. "Tess told you I was bad news, right?" He raised an eyebrow. "Was that before or after she tried to kill you?"

"Before," Luc said grudgingly.

"I want to keep Jasmine safe, just like you do," Ford said.

"He saved my life," Jasmine put in. Now she saw how ridiculous it had been to distrust him. She'd be dead if it weren't for Ford. "He fought off the Executors."

Luc worked his jaw back and forth. He said nothing.

"How the hell did you find the tunnels, anyway?" Ford asked. His tone was admiring.

"Luck," Luc said gruffly. Then he sighed. "I had no idea how they worked. I didn't know what was happening to Jas, either. But I'm going to fix it. Jasmine won't be in danger anymore, and Corinthe . . ." Luc trailed off, but Jasmine heard the thick emotion in his voice.

"Corinthe," Ford repeated thoughtfully. "An Executor?" He pronounced the word carefully, as if testing it for the first time. Luc nodded, and Jasmine remained silent. Luc had too much to worry about without knowing that their grandfather was an Executor and that Jasmine herself had the ability to read the marbles.

"Do you think it's wise to mess with fate?" Ford said softly. "Don't you think you might end up right back where you are now?"

"I have to try," Luc said. His eyes were like hollows. "I love her, and I made her a promise right before she died. What would you do?"

Ford looked right at Jasmine. "I'd tear down the universe, if I had to."

For just a second, Jasmine saw a look of gratitude pass across Luc's face. There was a moment of silence; then Ford roused himself.

"I'll go with you," he said. "I might be able to help. And if the Unseen Ones happen to fall apart, so much the better."

"No," Luc said forcibly. "I won't put anyone else at risk. Besides, I need you to stay here with Jasmine. Keep her safe until I can make this all right again. If I fail, I'll need someone to make sure the Executors don't get to her."

Jasmine didn't miss the look that passed between Luc

and Ford. An unspoken agreement, or maybe a warning. Whatever it was, she didn't like it.

Icy panic slid down her back. She took Luc's arm. "Please don't go," she blurted out. "Please. I can take care of myself. We can leave San Francisco, go somewhere else. LA or Vegas or New York or . . . or . . . Maine, for all I care."

Luc shook his head sadly. "I have to save Corinthe, Jas."

Then Jasmine knew there was no point in trying to convince him.

"Just promise me you'll be careful," she said, her throat tight with emotion.

"I'll be fine," Luc said. "I promise."

She threw her arms around Luc's neck and fought back the tears. She couldn't help but feel it was the last time she would ever see her brother. Fear choked off any more words.

"I'll be back before you know it." Luc disentangled himself from Jas and turned to Ford. "You better not screw up," was all he said.

"I won't," Ford said, with the ghost of a smile.

Luc nodded. He gave Jas another quick squeeze, then pulled something out of his pocket. "Almost forgot . . . ," he said, holding the ring in his open palm. It was her ring. Jasmine took it from his palm and slipped it on her finger. It glinted in the light. She wanted to say something else but couldn't make her throat work. There was a boulder-sized weight in her chest.

"You have to trust him," Ford said softly, as soon as Luc was gone, as if he could read all Jasmine's fears on her face.

"I do," Jasmine said. "I'm just . . ."

"Scared," Ford finished for her. "I know."

Tears burned the back of her eyes, and she could only nod.

"We should go back to the Fort," Ford said, putting a hand on her back. "We'll be safer there."

"No," Jas said firmly. She wasn't going to hide. She'd done too much hiding—too much running. "This is my house. I'm staying here."

"Stubborn girl." Ford smiled. He kissed her forehead. "But brave, too. I admire that."

"Hardly," she said. She didn't feel brave. She felt tired and worn down and angry and anxious.

"You are," he insisted. "You're amazing." He slid his arms around her waist. Then his lips were on hers and he kissed her. Jasmine melted into his arms and kissed him back. She wound her hands around the back of his neck. They stood there for what felt like years, drowning in each other.

Ford was the first to pull away. He was breathing hard, his eyes closed. When he opened them, Jasmine forgot how to inhale. There was so much emotion shining from them, it took her breath away.

"You make me forget everything except right now, Jas," he said. His voice sounded raw and rough. "If anything happens . . . I want you to have this." Ford took his necklace off—on the thick chain was a heavy key. He gently slipped it over her head. "If your brother fails—if I screw up—if the Unseen Ones find me, they'll imprison me again."

Emotion lodged in her throat, cutting off her ability to speak. She didn't even want to know why he'd been there before, because it didn't matter. She trusted him and he trusted her.

Ford took her by the shoulders and kissed her again. There was no hesitation, only pure emotion when they came together. Tightness coiled in her stomach, almost painful, but it felt so good.

Nothing had ever felt more right in her life.

Ford slowed his kisses and trailed a slow path to her ear, as if he, too, were reluctant to stop.

"If they put me back in Kinesthesia, you and only you will hold the key to my freedom. Only you." He brushed his lips over hers again, softly. "I trust you with my life, Jasmine. Just like you're trusting me with yours."

Jasmine tucked the odd-shaped key under her shirt and wove her fingers through his.

Her stomach was heavy with dread. For the first time, she understood: If Luc succeeded in altering time, in turning back the clock, Ford would return to his prison in Kinesthesia. Even as her brother saved the girl he loved, Jasmine would lose Ford.

He wouldn't even know her.

They would never meet.

She had to believe that after everything was settled, she and Ford would be together again.

Ford slid his hand down her arm and tangled his fingers with hers.

She buried her face in his neck and inhaled deeply. "I promise that no matter where you are, I'll find you," she said.

24

The current sucked at Luc's clothes as he fought his way to the far end of the lagoon. The water was choppy, as if it were resisting him. He kept going, dumbly determined—beyond fear now, beyond exhaustion, beyond thought.

He had lied to Ford: he didn't know how to control the movement of the tunnels any more than he had days ago. He didn't know yet which wire was the one that would set everything right. Tess had said that he was putting everyone at risk. Maybe so. But there had to be a way to turn back time. Rhys had done it, so it could be done. Luc would do it, too.

Ahead in the water, a faint glow caught his eye: swirling colors, like an underwater tornado, one that lay sideways instead of reaching for the sky. He surfaced once more for air, then submerged again. He didn't even have to swim toward the colors: he let himself sink, let the weight of his sneakers and his sweatshirt weigh him down.

Then, once again, the water changed. It became lighter. He could breathe. At the same time, he lost control of his movements. The colors picked him up and spun him, and he found he was caught inside the spinning cycle of color.

The Crossroad was different this time.

Hostile.

The winds tore at his body, trying to rend him. Pain exploded in his arms and legs, and he couldn't get his bearings. Things were moving too fast. He remembered a story he'd once heard, about people who drowned because they couldn't tell which way was up.

The pressure on his lungs was so tight that he couldn't take a full breath. But somewhere in the swirling chaos, Luc felt something solid beneath his feet. He got down on his hands and knees and crawled along blindly until he found the membrane-like walls of the Crossroad.

He wished he hadn't lost the knife. He took the archer from around his neck and popped the tiny hinge. Luc drove the tiny arrow into the membrane and ripped downward.

It was a small opening, but he managed to push his hand through. He grabbed a piece of the membrane and ripped it open. The Crossroad shrieked around him and the winds picked up, gusts flying at him. He didn't stop until he was able to drag his whole body in.

His vision grew dark until there were only flickering

lights in the corners of his eyes. It was several minutes before he realized that the flickers of light weren't only in his imagination. They were real. Sizzling flashes of light zipped over his head.

Immediately, Luc felt his blood grow thicker in his veins. It took tremendous effort to push to his feet and even more to draw in a breath. Up and down the tunnel the lights raced.

He trudged along, not even sure which direction he was going in.

It felt like he was making his way through quicksand, and each passing minute his limbs grew stiffer, as if he were turning into a statue.

Miranda was right.

The tunnels would kill him.

He had to find a way to turn back time, but how long did he have until the tunnel claimed him as its own?

There were so many wires — millions of them — it was impossible to tell which was the right one. His throat tightened, and for a second he thought he would cry, or scream. How would he know what to do? How had Rhys known? Rhys, who was always talking about love and unity and the importance of finding your Other. What had he said the last time Luc saw him? *The path to righteousness goes straight through the heart.*

"What does it mean?" Luc found himself shouting. "What am I supposed to do?"

Above him, the wires shifted again. From within the thick ropes of steel and copper, a new wire was revealed:

thicker than his arm, different from the rest. Instead of bright white sparks along its length, there were red ones. Almost like blood flowing through a vein.

Another wire of the same thickness and weight was severed—buried under more layers of copper.

He had to try. This was it, his last effort.

If he failed, there would be no more. He had barely enough strength left to lift his arms over his head.

Luc reached up and grabbed an end of both wires with each hand. He tugged hard on the ends until he finally got them to meet, and a scarlet fire showered down on him. The tiny embers burned his skin, but he held on. The wire pulsed under his fingers like a heartbeat.

His shirt was soaked with sweat as he struggled to keep them together. A wind began to whip through the tunnel, and it buffeted his body, making it hard to hang on to the wires.

And the wires themselves writhed in his hands, as if trying to escape from his grasp.

The acrid smell of burning flesh filled his nose as the sparks rained down on him faster now. The air around him whooshed harder and he fought to stay on his feet.

Push through the pain, that was what Coach always said. If you want it bad enough, make it happen. Luc had no idea how, but he found the strength to hold the wires, despite the agony in his muscles.

A sudden current rippled out of the wires and pulsed through him. There was no pain, only a sense of weightlessness, of being outside his own body. It wasn't an electric shock, it was something more powerful. It centered in his chest, where his heart thumped with each heavy beat.

Awareness of the tunnel settled around him. The wires stilled, and he continued to hold one in each hand. He could feel the sparks running across his skin, *through* his body. It was as if he were somehow a part of the tunnel.

The path to righteousness goes straight through the heart.

Rhys's cryptic words echoed in Luc's head. He hadn't understood what it meant, had thought it was just another one of Rhys's riddles, but now it felt significant.

Not only significant, but the key. This was how Rhys had manipulated time, by giving up his own body to the force of the universe and letting the current flow through him—through his heart. Rhys had once given his own energy to alter the winds of time.

Luc closed his eyes and let go of the last bits of resistance. If he had to die to save the people he loved, he would gladly do it. In the darkness, the pulse of the tunnel grew louder, and soon his breathing and heartbeat synced to the same rhythm.

He became one with the tunnel. One with time. One with the universe.

Billions of stars shone behind his eyelids, and it was beautiful. It reminded him of Corinthe, of when they'd first met on the boat and gazed up at the stars together. In each world they had found themselves in, the stars had been the constant guiding force.

Luc focused on them now. His awareness expanded

and a new force moved through him. In the span between the beats of the universe's pulse, a whisper emerged. With each pause, it grew louder.

The stars started to swirl in his mind, and a name surfaced in the silence.

The universe was chanting.

The entire pulse of the universe focused on one thought.

Corinthe.

Her name became the rhythm that powered the heartbeat.

Corinthe. Corinthe. Corinthe.

Each time her name beat inside him, the force grew stronger, as if a speeding train raced inside his head. The wires in his hands grew hot and throbbed with life. He struggled to hold on even as he started to break apart from the inside out.

The wind in the tunnels increased, picked away tiny bits of him as it rushed by. He would be torn apart one cell at a time. His grip began to slip and the wind became even stronger, howling Corinthe's name all around him.

He couldn't hold on any longer.

The wires slid between his fingers. He couldn't fight anymore. He wasn't strong enough. He had failed.

The wind ripped him free from the wires and lifted him off his feet. As he tumbled through the tunnels, he held on to only one thought.

Corinthe.

25

Corinthe waited in silence just inside the doors of Mission High School. She leaned close to the windowpane and fogged it with her breath. With a finger, she wrote *No*. Then she wiped the condensation away with a fist.

It didn't matter that she hated deaths. It didn't matter that she liked the principal, Sylvia—as much as she liked any human, at least. The marble had shown her what she must do. She didn't have a choice.

Tick, tick, tick. Corinthe could hear Sylvia's heels clicking on the linoleum. She didn't turn around until Sylvia had rounded the corner.

"Oh, Corinthe. You startled me." Sylvia withdrew her hand from her purse. She seemed jumpy, as if she already knew something was going to happen. Humans were more perceptive than the Unseen Ones gave them credit for.

Corinthe stared at her silently, trying to remember how to smile. She so rarely had a reason to.

She'd been enrolled in school only a couple of days, but already the principal had taken an interest in her. Sylvia had been careful to emphasize the importance of one's appearance when they'd met for the first time yesterday to fill out her transfer paperwork—probably because Corinthe's hair was in a wild tangle down her back, and she was wearing ripped jeans she'd stolen from a thrift store. When Miranda disappeared for days at a time, Corinthe sometimes forgot to keep up appearances.

Sylvia told Corinthe that she'd been a principal for ten years, and that she could see potential. That she had a good eye for these things, and if Corinthe applied herself, she could become an outstanding student.

Corinthe hadn't bothered to argue. It wouldn't matter soon.

During Sylvia's "Welcome to Mission High, Keep Your Nose Clean" speech, Corinthe had simply gazed at her, almost without breathing. She couldn't let herself get attached—not to Sylvia. Not to anyone.

It would only lead to disappointment.

Corinthe shifted slightly in the doorway. "My foster mom was supposed to pick me up, but she never showed. Do you think . . . ?" Her voice trailed off and she raised her eyes expectantly. She hated lying. Back when she lived in Pyralis, she hadn't even known how to lie. But this, too, was the job of an Executor.

Sylvia shuffled her stack of folders from her left arm to her right so she could check her watch. Corinthe could see indecision in the principal's expressions. She probably had plans tonight, but Corinthe knew that Sylvia would never leave a student in the lurch.

She cared about her students too much. Corinthe felt a pulse of—what was it? Guilt?—feelings she had never known before coming here.

"Where do you live?"

Corinthe tilted her head slightly. "It won't be a long drive." She spoke in measured tones. She had to be careful not to give anything away.

"Come on, then," Sylvia said with a sigh.

They left through the main doors. Sylvia walked quickly down the sidewalk, and Corinthe followed a few steps behind, trying not to notice the way the principal's shoulders slumped with exhaustion. Not her business.

Sylvia turned left at the end of the block and continued toward the staff lot. "Here we are," she said cheerfully. She stopped next to a small black sedan parked under a flickering streetlamp and pulled out her keys. A quick mechanical chirp echoed in the thick spring air. She threw her things into the back and slid into the driver's seat. Corinthe quickly climbed into the passenger side.

The car growled to life and Sylvia maneuvered it onto the street. "So. Which way?" she asked.

Corinthe pointed. Sylvia eyed the girl, then turned,

zigzagging the car right onto Church, left onto Duboce, right onto Castro Street, each time in response to a silent gesture from Corinthe. The pendant hanging from her rearview mirror swayed back and forth with each turn. Corinthe glanced at it each time it swung her way. Something about it made her feel uneasy.

"It's St. Jude," Sylvia explained. "The patron saint of lost causes. Kind of a sad saint, when you think about it." She half laughed. "Still, everyone could use a miracle, don't you think?"

"Sure, I guess," Corinthe said neutrally. She didn't really believe in miracles—had not even known the word until coming to Humana. Fate was controlled by the Unseen Ones. Everything that happened was orchestrated and carried out exactly as planned. There were no last-minute reprieves. No changes in plan. No sudden moments of salvation.

And today, Sylvia would die.

26

At first, Luc thought that the silence meant he was dead.

But the ache in his muscles felt too real. There was a ringing in his ears. Then, gradually, sound began to reassert itself. Birds calling to each other. Someone laughing. Wind rippling through trees.

He slowly opened his eyes. He was staring up at a domed ceiling. He sat up with a groan, blinking. He was at the rotunda. Late-afternoon sun streamed in between the columns, speckling the ground with patterns of dark and light. When he carefully pushed to his feet, the sound of laughter filtered through the air.

Everything was perfect. The columns were standing, completely undamaged, and on the street, there was no sign that an earthquake had ever happened.

His heart stopped. Had it worked?

He fumbled in his pocket and pulled out his phone. Five-thirty.

There were several missed text messages from Karen.

> Reminder. Dinner at six. Don't be late again.
> Want to talk about my party tomorrow night.
> <3 K

He read the message: once, twice, three times.

If Karen's party was tomorrow, that meant it was Thursday night. Which meant it was the day he had first seen Corinthe.

He'd done it. He'd turned the clock back.

He was running before he realized it. Thursday. Thursday was the day of the accident—the day Corinthe caused the car to swerve, the day he extracted her from the wreckage. He had to stop her. He needed time to explain everything to Corinthe, to make her remember that they loved each other.

That they *would* love each other: it was their future and their fate.

As he ran toward the intersection of Pacific and Divisadero, darting around the people crowding the sidewalk, he tried to remember exactly when the accident had happened. His lungs burned as he forced his feet to go faster.

Would she be there? Would he be too late?

He rounded the corner of Divisadero Street just as a

dark sedan hurtled around the corner. He remembered that car. It was the same one. He caught a glimpse of blond hair in the passenger seat.

"Corinthe." His voice was lost in the sounds from the street.

He wasn't going to make it in time. The realization made his blood run cold. He tried to push through the crowd, but there were too many people hanging by the crosswalk—tourists with shopping bags and baby strollers.

Then someone ran into the street—he saw a blur of dark hair, the fast cycle of legs. He shouted. This was wrong. Different. The woman behind the wheel—face white, terrified—jerked the car to the left. Brakes screeched and the air smelled like burning rubber. The car jumped the curb and hit a streetlamp. Steam hissed from the engine.

Luc was at the passenger door in seconds.

He jerked it open and came face to face with Corinthe.

"What—what are you doing?" she stammered. Confusion clouded her face.

Luc felt a wave of relief. Corinthe was okay. The driver was okay, too. The dark-haired woman was gripping Corinthe's arm.

"Corinthe," she was saying. "Corinthe, are you all right?"

"You ruined it," Corinthe whispered to him. When he reached across her to unbuckle her seatbelt, she froze. "What are you *doing*?"

"Corinthe . . ." As soon as she was free, he pulled her out of the car and threw his arms around her. He had to hold her, to know that she was real and okay.

She stiffened and stepped back abruptly. "How do you know my name? Who—who *are* you?"

He took a deep breath and let it out to keep his voice steady. "I promised that I'd find a way to save you, and I did. I know you don't remember me yet, but you will. I love you, Corinthe. And you love me."

"What?" She shook her head. He saw a flicker of fear in her eyes. But when he leaned in, she didn't pull away again. She let him brush his lips against hers. Softly. Like one of the fireflies that carried the marbles to different worlds.

He wanted to keep kissing her forever.

"Have . . . we met before?" she whispered. Her expression had softened. Her eyes were wide with wonder.

Luc gently took her hand. "Yes," he said. "Yes, Corinthe. We've met." He brought a hand to her face. She didn't draw away. Her eyes continued searching his face, as though for an answer to a puzzle.

"This is our second chance," he said. "I'm not wasting a single second of it. I love you."

And even if she didn't know it yet, he could see a promise shining from her beautiful purplish-gray eyes: she would love him, too.

She already did.

Epilogue

Jasmine watched Luc and the girl, Corinthe.

She was beautiful, with wild blond hair spilling like a river down her back, and violet eyes. Jasmine could see why Luc had fallen in love with her.

Jasmine's heart beat painfully in her throat. Luc had his happy ending, but Ford was gone. The headache had come on fast in the apartment, but no matter how hard she tried to hold on, Ford was ripped from her side.

When the darkness ebbed, she had found herself clutching a marble instead.

The urge had been undeniable, irresistible—like cresting in a roller coaster and plunging down, down, down, stomach soaring, wind whipping. She had been drawn to this street corner as though by some inner magnet. She hurtled out in front of the dark sedan like a crazy person, her legs, feet, body obeying a more powerful command than she could resist.

And then she saw Luc run up to the mangled car. Even from a distance, Jasmine saw the relief on his face.

He had done it.

The marble felt smooth and cool between her fingers. When she held it up, the image swirled inside again: a couple kissing.

Corinthe and Luc.

In the street, she could see Luc kissing Corinthe, a life-sized reproduction of the image in the marble.

The marble cracked apart in Jasmine's hand, and a small firefly emerged from the orb. She held it up and it hovered there, darting around the palm of her hand, then circling her shoulders.

Jasmine reached up and wrapped her fingers around the key that hung from a chain around her neck. Luc's fate had been fulfilled, and *she'd* made a promise to Ford.

But there was something she had to do first.

She turned and began walking toward the rotunda.

First, Jasmine had to send the Messenger home.

Acknowledgments

It takes a village to publish a book, and this book was no exception. I have some really great editors who can weave my imperfect sentences into gold. PLL and especially Rhoda Belleza helped turn the chaos of *Chaos* into a compelling story that I hope my readers love as much as I do. Thank you for such an amazing opportunity.

Wendy Loggia at Random House is a wonder, and through her edits and questions, *Chaos* came alive. It was an amazing experience working with her and her team.

My super agent, Mandy Hubbard, not only handles the nitty-gritty stuff but is a master at hand-holding and taming writerly angst. Without her, I'd probably be rocking in the corner with a half-finished manuscript in my lap.

It goes without saying that I couldn't have done this without the support of my family. Their encouragement and love keep me going on this roller-coaster ride that is my dream. My hope is that my boys will see that anything is possible and will chase their own dreams one day. I love you guys!

Last but not least, a special thanks goes out to my readers. I still can't believe people are actually reading the words that I write. I'm humbled by you all and thank you all so much.

About the Author

Lanie Bross is the author of *Fates* and, as Lee Bross, *Tangled Webs*. She was born in a small town in Maine, where she spent the next eighteen years dreaming of bigger places. After exploring city life, she and her husband and two young sons ended up going right back to the wilds of Maine. They now live just one house down from where she grew up. Fate, perhaps? Lanie loves chasing her rambunctious kids, playing tug-of-war with her ninety-five-pound Lab, and writing for teens.

WHAT IF YOUR DESTINY
WAS TO KILL THE ONE YOU LOVE?

A FATES STORY

DESTINED

LANIE BROSS

In this exclusive ebook original short story, Corinthe attends a beachside party at a glamorous mansion on Point Reyes, where she must help fulfill a mysterious— and potentially deadly—destiny.